"Does it bother you?"

asked Lavender.

Wyatt blinked, puzzled. This lady was spooky. But he played it cool. "Does what bother me?"

"Being *caught* with me."

"Of course not," said Wyatt. "It's no one's business what I do on Sunday."

"It's Glover's business. The business of knowing everyone's business. The whole town thrives on it." Lavender dipped her chin, and her eyes shone provocatively. "I'm a particularly curious specimen. Have you noticed the way they look at me as though they're expecting my head to spin around or something?"

He'd probably looked at her that way himself. "Is it the screw-on type?"

"No. I have to do a little incantation and wiggle my nose."

Dear Reader,

When two people fall in love, the world is suddenly new and exciting, and it's that same excitement we bring to you in Silhouette Intimate Moments. These are stories with scope and grandeur. The characters lead lives we all dream of, and everything they do reflects the wonder of being in love.

Longer and more sensuous than most romances, Silhouette Intimate Moments novels take you away from everyday life and let you share the magic of love. Adventure, glamour, drama, even suspense—these are the passwords that let you into a world where love has a power beyond the ordinary, where the best authors in the field today create stories of love and commitment that will stay with you always.

In coming months, look for novels by your favorite authors: Barbara Faith, Marilyn Pappano, Emilie Richards, Paula Detmer Riggs and Nora Roberts, to name only a few. And whenever—and wherever—you buy books, look for all the Silhouette Intimate Moments, love stories with that extra something, books written especially for you by today's top authors.

Leslie J. Wainger
Senior Editor and Editorial Coordinator

KATHLEEN EAGLE

To Each His Own

SILHOUETTE·INTIMATE·MOMENTS®
Published by Silhouette Books New York

America's Publisher of Contemporary Romance

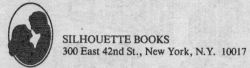

SILHOUETTE BOOKS
300 East 42nd St., New York, N.Y. 10017

TO EACH HIS OWN

Copyright © 1992 by Kathleen Eagle

ISBN: 0-373-07428-X

First Silhouette Books printing April 1992

Printed in the U.S.A.

Books by Kathleen Eagle

Silhouette Intimate Moments

For Old Times' Sake #148
More Than a Miracle #242
But That Was Yesterday #257
Paintbox Morning #284
Bad Moon Rising #412
To Each His Own #428

Silhouette Special Edition

Someday Soon #204
A Class Act #274
Georgia Nights #304
Something Worth Keeping #359
Carved in Stone #396
Candles in the Night #437
'Til There Was You #576

Silhouette Books

Silhouette Christmas Stories 1988
"The Twelfth Moon"
Silhouette Summer Sizzlers 1991
"Sentimental Journey"

KATHLEEN EAGLE

is a transplant from New England to Minnesota, where she and her husband, Clyde, make their home with two of their three children. She has considered writing to be her "best talent" since she was about nine years old, and English and history were her "best subjects." After fourteen years of teaching high school students about writing, she saw her own first novel in print in 1984. Since then, she's published many more novels with Silhouette Books and Harlequin Historicals that have become favorites for readers worldwide. She has received awards from Romance Writers of America, *Romantic Times* and *Affaire de Coeur.*

For two of my special friends:
Christine, who weaves,
and Ruth, who does wonders with seaweed.

To Each His Own was my parents' song.
I miss them.

Prologue

Lavender Holland had one small thing in common with her neighbors. Mail time was one of the highlights of her day. Midmorning, she listened for the mail carrier's car to slow down at her approach. As soon as she heard that four-cylinder engine idling out of tune, she set her shuttle aside and fished around beneath the loom for her clogs. The little car revved up and moved on just about the time Lavender opened the front door. She always waved. Sometimes Carrie Bieber waved back, but most of the time she seemed intent on getting back on the highway to keep her appointed rounds.

Lavender couldn't personally attest to the friendliness of the rural folk, for which her home state was famous, but she believed it was out there somewhere, for those who were able to conform to their way of thinking a little better than she was. The second thing the people of North Dakota were known for was their conservatism, and Lav-

ender Holland just naturally flew in the face of all that
was holy in that respect.

Her rural mailbox was a case in point. If you were going to have a decorative mailbox on Rural Route 2, it
could be attached to an old plow or shaped like a barn, or
maybe even stippled with rosemaling, the stylized floral
designs favored by those neighbors who were of Scandi-
navian descent. Lavender's less traditional mailbox had
been assaulted twice and bashed in once since she'd replaced her old standard with a super-size model. She had
customized the black box with silver stars and gold moons
in all the phases. Then somebody had shot the red flag off
and plugged a star with a .22. Last winter Donny Kuy-
pers had banged into it with the propane truck, and now
the mailbox post listed, as though backing away from
another attack.

Still hanging in there, the box was crammed every
Tuesday, Thursday and Saturday—delivery days on RR
2—with two Bismarck Tribunes, an occasional letter, and
clothing and fabric orders from all over the country. Last
night's frost had killed the daylilies planted around it, and
as Lavender tugged on one of the tightly wedged newspapers she thought about adding some hex signs to the
decor before her mailbox got as holey as most of the road
signs. Boy, that would get them talking.

Not that hers was the only wounded mailbox on the
route. This surely was gun-happy country. Always had
been, and Lavender guessed it always would be, which
was another fact that wasn't on her list of good reasons
for moving back to North Dakota. Ah, but the high, wide
and handsome blue sky was. She squinted into the late-
morning sun and watched a red-tailed hawk wheel overhead. Crisp buffalo grass crackled beneath the rubber
treads of her wooden-soled clogs as she headed across the

yard. She flipped through the stack of mail. A black cat skittered around the corner of the schoolhouse. The sparrow he was chasing landed on the crossbar of the swings.

"Give it up, Jasper," Lavender advised as she pushed the front door open. "We're vegetarians, remember? We took a pledge." She held the door open for Jasper. The cat pranced into the house ahead of her with his tail poised like a shepherd's crook. He knew darn well there were meat by-products in that dish of kibble next to the kitchen table. Otherwise he would have insisted upon sparrow-under-grass.

Lavender added three pieces of cordwood to the stove that heated the living space behind her weaving studio. She still thought of her renovated home as "the school-house." She had been a student at Coyote's Call Creek Rural School until she was expelled two days before the end of the sixth grade for chipping Buck Braun's front teeth with her lunch box. Buck, of course, had it coming for asking her if she'd gotten a bra yet. She'd had the lunch box in her hand, and those big gopher teeth had made an irresistible target when his hand came groping. The Brauns had been especially unfriendly after that, even though the Hollands had paid for Buck's caps, and the following year Lavender's mother, "that woman from out East," had driven her to school in town.

Twenty years later, Lavender had turned the white clapboard building into her place of business and her home. On the outside it still looked like a schoolhouse. She had refurbished the paint and removed the words "Rural School" from the Coyote's Call Creek sign, but the school bell still hung in the little belfry above the steeply pitched roof, and the swings and seesaw still stood in the yard, along with a woodshed and two outhouses. It was all hers now. No one could kick her out. She'd bought the building and paid the lease on a quarter section of county-owned school land.

On the inside, the building was warmer and more inviting than it had ever been when it served its original purpose. The contractor had warned that the remodeling would cost more than the building would be worth in this part of the country, but Lavender knew what she wanted. The building was big and old and full of memories. Her father had attended school there, and her grandfather had helped build it. The ceiling was high enough to permit the addition of a loft bedroom with indoor plumbing. She'd kept the tall, narrow windows with the eight-inch-square panes, the wood- and coal-burning stove, and the openness of the interior. She'd refinished the plank flooring herself. No walls had been added, but two sets of freestanding shelves separated her studio in the front from the living area. Everything she needed under one high roof.

It had once seemed like an isolated place where the grassy prairie took a dip toward the clutch of cottonwoods tucked in a bend in Coyote's Call Creek, but the gravel road had been paved. Bismarck was only fifty miles to the north. The town of Glover was sixteen miles south. Coyote's Call Creek emptied into the Missouri River to the west, and across the river was an Indian reservation. A ribbon of blacktop brought all those places as close as Lavender wanted them to be.

Close enough, too, was the abandoned farm where she'd grown up, three miles east. The access road was impassable now, but it was good to know that the home place was there. It was part of Lavender's fabric. In touch with her roots but unfettered by convention or close neighbors, she was free to stretch her wings.

She dropped the mail on her desk and took the newspapers to the dining table behind the studio divider. Mint tea simmered in the kettle. The stove timer buzzed, but she knew by the aroma that her bran-and-raisin muffins were done. While Jasper crunched his cat food, Lavender sampled a muffin and sifted through yesterday's news. Her Bismarck store was doing well, and the ad she'd placed looked good. Bismarck was not the best market for designer clothing, but she'd hired a manager who had an eye for original artwork, which they took on consignment. It was a good outlet for local artists and a place to test market her handwoven clothing. But most of her orders came through the mail.

For a chuckle she always turned to the "Find-a-Friend" column before she read her horoscope. She liked to try to imagine the person who placed each ad, maybe conjure up a match. She'd made a bad one for herself once, but the odds had been against her to begin with. She was a Scorpio who always went for Leos. Terrible combination. She was much better at picking a prospect for somebody else.

The things women looked for in men were pretty predictable. She wanted to write to these ladies and tell them to use a little imagination. This one was typical.

Interested in meeting a man with a sense of humor. Good dancer. Must like children. Must love cats. Age 25-60. Interested in a permanent relationship.

Try matching that up with the things these men were looking for in a woman.

Wish to meet slim, attractive lady, 20's to early 30's, who's looking for good times with a great guy. Must be warm, sensitive, willing to listen, ready to share a good laugh. And don't forget, slender. Recent photo must accompany response. Prefer petite proportions, but a good personality is important, too. As long as she's looking good. (Just kidding. But not about the photo.)

Poor man. A hostage to his hormones.

Wait a minute. Lavender snapped the paper, making it stand to attention. Here was a good one.

I'm tall and dark. Maybe even handsome, but too modest to admit it. Spend most of my spare time working out, which means I've got muscles to spare but nobody to appreciate them. Some people think I ought to get a life. Well, I'm sort of new in town, haven't met too many people. (Kind of shy, I guess.) I don't drink or smoke, don't cuss too much. Pretty smart, too. Went to college, got a good job. So I'd be interested in meeting a nice woman who can make weight without starving herself, somebody with plenty of grit and staying power. Somebody with a soft heart. I'm the serious type. I need somebody to make me smile.

The ad made Lavender smile. Definitely a Leo. She clipped it out and tossed it in a drawer full of clippings—human-interest stories, letters to advice columnists and editors, more ads, more hands reaching across the printed page. She kept the ones that touched her. More to the point, she refrained from throwing them away.

Chapter 1

She looked as out of place as he felt in this one-horse white man's town.

She was sitting alone at the table in the middle of the tiny tan faculty room, leafing through a magazine that was draped across her knees while the fork in her right hand hovered above a plastic refrigerator bowl. The other lounge—the one where smoking was permitted—was the place to be at the tail end of the noon hour, but Wyatt Archer didn't frequent either place. He hadn't joined the Glover High School faculty to earn a spot on the town's social register, but he *had* thought he'd met all the teachers. He hadn't met this woman. He would have remembered. He let one tennis shoe squeak against the linoleum as he paused in the doorway.

She looked up, tossed a wild mass of honey-toned hair back from one shoulder and offered a sensuous sloe-eyed smile. She was earthy. Her easy-fitting soft blue dress draped seductively in front, teasing the imagination without baring the curve of her breast. Her legs matched her dress—tights, he guessed—and her chunky, slip-on shoes seemed a little out of season. But then, what did he know about fashion? More to the point, what did he care? She looked touchable. She looked like a woman who would enjoy being touched.

He knew a come-on look when he saw one.

"Hi, Coach," she said brightly. "Lose your team?"

He glanced down at his gym shorts and his sweat-soaked T-shirt and tried to remember why he'd interrupted his workout as he propped one shoulder against the doorframe. "Haven't got a real team yet. Just some kids who've been watching too much 'Wrestlemania.' You subbing for somebody?"

"Lord, no. I'm just visiting." She offered a long, slender hand. "I'm Lavender Holland."

He'd heard the name more than once, and he realized too late that he'd fairly pounced on the opportunity to stride over and shake hands. Hers was warm and slight. "Wyatt Archer."

"I guessed."

Of course she'd guessed. In a town of eighteen hundred blondes, everybody saw him coming. Lots of polite greetings and furtive stares. The new wrestling coach was an Indian. He'd been hired to teach social studies because he'd coached two state-championship wrestling teams. No other qualifications were necessary, and the fact that he came from the other side of the river was pardonable in view of his accomplishments.

"I've heard a lot about you already," she continued. "Most notably that you're a slave driver."

"Now let me guess. The activities association sent you down here to see if I started practice early." She raised an eyebrow, and her blue eyes sparkled, inviting him to go on guessing. "We're doing some weight training over the noon hour, that's all. Practice starts Monday, just like it does for everybody else."

"When do they have lunch?"

"Who? The boys? Whenever it's on their schedule."

"No girls on your team?"

"Told you. I don't have a team yet. It's not a team until Monday." He propped one foot on the chair across from hers and braced his forearm across his knee as he assessed the look in her eyes. She was having fun with him, and he was, frankly, intrigued. "Did that Title IX outfit send you? Listen, the girls can try out if they want to. I had a girl on the team at Prairie Island. The local TV station did a story on her. She quit before the first meet."

"Did they do a story on that, too?"

"Nope. Guess that wasn't news." With both feet planted back on the floor, he searched the pockets of his shorts. The meager jingle didn't sound promising. "I came in looking for some pop," he explained, tipping his head toward the machine in the corner.

"Pop is terrible for you. You need to replace your fluids."

"Is that a fact?"

"Pop is just chemicals. I have some extra grapefruit juice here." She reached into a big denim bag that hung over the back of her chair and produced a pint bottle. "Actually, the Texas Grapefruit Growers sent me here. Today, Glover, North Dakota. Tomorrow, the world."

"Interesting strategy." He'd come up with twenty-three cents and a stray key, which he repocketed quickly. "I guess I don't have enough change anyway. Thanks." After he'd popped the cap and swallowed half the bottle's tart contents, he eyed her bowl. "You mind if I ask you what you're eating?"

"Salad."

"I've never seen a salad like that. It looks like—" He took a step closer, just to make sure. Sure enough. "—weeds."

"Seaweed. Sprouts. Seeds." She speared a forkful of the stuff and brought it close to her bow-shaped mouth. The teasing sparkle in her eyes made him want to taste what she tasted . . . like. She knew it, too. "Good stuff."

"For a hamster, maybe." He sat down, took another swig of grapefruit juice and set the bottle on the table. "I've run out of guesses."

"I'm giving demonstrations in Mrs. Breen's home-economics classes."

"What are you demonstrating?"

"Spinning." She dropped the fork into the bowl and slid both hands between her knees, palms together, making a valley of her skirt. "Oh, we're having a marvelous time. You should stop in next hour."

"Spinning what?"

"Yarn. We've been spinning all kinds of fabric—lamb's wool, llama, cat, dog. . . ."

Her eyes were full of promise, as if she'd brought toys or ice cream to school. "Where'd you find a llama?" he asked.

"At the zoo in Bismarck. They shed, you know, just like cats and dogs. Someday I think I'll make an Afghan afghan."

Okay, she'd earned half a smile. "You go around collecting dog hair?"

"People save it for me. Most people like the idea of finding clever uses for their castoffs. And it makes school demonstrations more fun."

Enchanted, he tilted his chair back, balancing on two legs the way he often told his students not to do. "What do you do besides spin dog hair?"

"I'm a weaver. I make handwoven clothing from my own original designs. Like this." She sat up straight and held her arms out, inviting him to admire the handwoven dress. The prettiest part was the way she filled it out, kind of delicately, he thought. Weed eaters had to be light-weights.

"Very nice." Dressmaker, he registered. Now he had a face to connect with the name and the cryptic comments he'd heard. Pretty strange bird, someone had said, but he always made it a point to let small-town gossip go in one ear and out the other unless it involved one of his boys. "Are you the one who lives in the schoolhouse out on the highway?"

She smiled. "That weird Holland woman. That's me."

"Yeah, I guess I've heard about you, too. I pictured somebody different, though."

"I *am* different." Her eyes widened, and she leaned closer. "Especially when there's a full moon. And Jupiter aligns with Mars. And the locoweed is in full bloom." With a laugh, she sat back in her chair, but she kept him fastened to her hook. "You're kind of different yourself, Coach."

"People around here seem accepting enough."

"You're the wrestling coach, and wrestling rules in this town. Ever since you accepted the position, fathers have been recounting your trophies and amateur titles to their sons around the dinner table in every household. Did you put all that in your résumé?"

"They didn't ask for a résumé." She quirked a pale eyebrow. "Those of us who are—" that knowing look of hers irritated him, but he wasn't going to let that show

"*—different* usually need a special ticket to get us in the door. Wrestling's my ticket. It always has been." *Okay, lady.* "What's yours?"

"I don't have one. That's why I live sixteen miles out of town. That way I can be as weird as I want to be."

He glanced at her salad. "They say you are what you eat."

"I can live with that."

Wyatt was just getting comfortable with the conversation when Carl Hausauer walked in with Marv Clark, who took a quick head count—just the two of them in the room—as he announced, "Hey, Wyatt, the janitor says he fixed that pulley on the Universal Gym."

Neither of his fellow teachers was too subtle about checking out the situation. Wyatt could almost hear the gears spinning in their heads. *Is he making a move? Is she buying it?* He nodded. "That's good. I've got some boys coming back after school."

"Well, hello, Lavender." Hausauer's acknowledgment sounded like an echo from a grade-B movie.

"Hello, Carl. Marv."

Marv nodded, and Carl followed up with, "Where you been keeping yourself lately?"

"That's a funny question, Carl," Lavender said. "You know where I live. Your sister stopped by the other day to pick up a new warp."

"I haven't seen Sherry since school started. You know, you get so busy. You two get introduced?" He waved a hand in Wyatt's direction.

"Yes, we took care of that." Lavender slapped a plastic lid on her salad bowl and stuffed everything into the denim bag. "I promised Mrs. Breen I'd be back at one. She took one of the boys home to clip his poodle." Suddenly in a hurry, she pushed her chair under the table.

"He swore up and down his mother said it was okay. Nice meeting you, Coach."

The three men watched the lady glide out the door.

"What do you wanna bet there'll be an irate mother and a bald dog in the office after school?" Wyatt offered.

"Coach?" Marv Clark had known Wyatt in college. They hadn't exactly been bosom buddies, but Marv had called him when the Glover position opened. He grinned now, as though the two of them had been sharing confidences all along. "Coming from her, that's downright personal. You two exchanging phone numbers?"

"We exchanged names."

"What's she doing here?"

Carl Hausauer had the inside track. "Oh, you know, teaching the home-ec classes how to make hippie clothes and eat dandelions."

"Seaweed," Wyatt supplied.

"The kind of stuff they eat in California. She used to live there, you know. La-La Land, where her kind of people sit around in hot tubs and do things most of us only read about." Carl picked up the empty juice bottle and bounced it in his hand. "That's one piece of action that's bound to be pretty easy to get, Wyatt. If you're ever desperate."

"Desperate?" Wyatt chuckled. Carl sounded like a man who'd tried and been turned down. "That's the best-looking woman I've seen in a long time. I take it she's not married."

"Are you kidding? Marriage is too normal for Lavender Holland."

"Hey, she was once," Marv put in. "Nobody around here ever saw the guy. Some California dude. She moved back here after he divorced her."

"He kept saying, 'Where's the main course?' And she kept putting seaweed on the table." Pleased with his wit, Carl used the bottle to pop a clunking free throw into the corner wastebasket.

"She looks healthy." Wyatt preferred a little glamour, but he respected a healthy look.

"And agile, huh? Inventive?" Carl was still eyeing the basket as he hitched up his beltless polyester pants. "Her mother was a hippie from back East."

Marv folded his arms across his chest. "Nah, I think she was a beatnik, Carl. Get it straight, now. The beatniks came before the hippies."

"Whatever. You want a little 'free love,' you go see Lavender. If you don't mind incense and scented oil, that is." Carl's eyebrows were jumpy. "They say she even does a little black magic."

Marv shook his head as he waved off Carl's comments. "How would you know, Hausauer? You've been out of circulation since you were a junior in high school."

"Yeah, well, Lavender was a freshman then, and that girl was hot. You could just tell by looking at her. And you know what old Buck Braun used to say about her, uh..." Carl held cupped hands in front of his chest and waggled his eyebrows.

Wyatt shoved his hands in his pockets and moved toward the door. Carl followed, still anxious to supply his insights, which didn't interest Wyatt. But an unfamiliar word did niggle at him some. "What was it your sister picked up from her?"

"Oh, my sister, Sherry. Something to do with that weaving. Sherry works for her."

Marv brought up the rear as they headed down the empty hallway. "Lavender's got quite a business with that clothing she makes. She's taught three or four women in town, helped them get their own looms, pays for whatever they can turn out." Classes were in session, and Marv lowered his voice against the threat of hallway echo. They'd reached a set of fire doors, and he stepped in front of the two men to claim the push bar, then paused and turned to Wyatt. "I don't know about any black magic, but she's created some jobs, and this town needs jobs."

"Hey, I'm not knocking her. Different strokes for different folks, right?" Carl tapped Wyatt's shoulder and grinned knowingly. "She likes you, Wyatt. I'd say put her name in your little black book."

"I don't need a black book. I've got a pretty decent memory." Wyatt checked his watch. "I've also got a world-history class in twenty minutes. See you guys later." Marv pushed the door open for him, and he headed for the gym to change his clothes.

Marv let the door swing shut. He scowled at Carl. "What'd you tell him all that stuff about Lavender Holland for? Weren't you laying it on a little thick?"

"He's bound to end up at her house sooner or later if he wants female company. There's a reason why the founding fathers put a river between Glover and the reservation." Carl hitched his pants up again. It seemed to help him make his most important points. "I don't care how many wrestling trophies he's won, he's still an Indian, isn't he? And she's still Lavender Holland."

John Tiger loved wrestling. When he was out there on the mat, it didn't matter that he was the Indian kid from across the river. The ref's signal gave him permission to bring his opponent to his knees, and it didn't matter who the guy was or where he lived or what his father did for a living. Out on the mat, John had an equal chance to prove he was as good as anybody else. He'd had no trouble making the team and it had nothing to do with the fact that the new coach was an Indian, too. He could tell right now, Archer wasn't the kind to play favorites. He was out to put together the best Class-B team in the state, and John had earned his spot on it.

Ally Nordstrom didn't make the cut, but he was elected unanimously by those who did to be the team's student manager. John was glad Ally would be with the team. Ally would never make it as a wrestler, but he was a great one for comic relief. Now he could do what he did best, which was to stand around telling jokes about the size of Hoss Sandland's shoes. He wasn't much for pumping iron, but he didn't mind counting reps while somebody else lifted.

"Way to go, Tiger," Ally crooned while John bench-pressed his third set. His arms were about to fall off, but Ally's face loomed directly overhead, and he was saying, "You can do it, big guy. That's eleven. One more."

Be sure you remember how much I can press, Nordstrom. Be sure you mention it to Teri.

The best thing about Ally was that he had a sister. Teri. John couldn't see much resemblance between sweet, soft-spoken Teri and that clown face grinning down at him, but then, nobody in the world resembled Teri. She was one of a kind. He'd do reps from now till Christmas if he thought Teri might be impressed.

Ally steadied the bar and helped him lower it back to the rack. "Look at Christian, working on those trapezoids," Ally said, nodding toward the boy who was working out on the Universal Gym. "He looks like a sparrow trying to do chin-ups on a twig."

John smiled as he mopped his chest with a towel. He'd have to catch his breath before he could laugh at any of Ally's wisecracks. Mark Christian had taken the spot Ally was trying for, which was the lightweight berth at ninety-eight pounds. Ally was right. Mark did look funny doing those pull-downs, but he was working. John didn't figure Ally really wanted Mark's spot. Too much work. Ally had tried out because almost everyone did. Wrestling was the passion of Glover. But Ally was the perfect manager.

Archer was pushing them hard to get ready for the first meet, and when they hit the showers everybody stood under the water and groaned. Everybody but Ally. He told jokes, trying to keep their spirits up. That was his job, and the guys liked the way he did it.

"Hey, Ally," Mark sang out. "Has anybody answered that ad you put in the paper yet?"

"You mean on the snag-a-date page?" Ally asked. "Nope. Maybe I should put it in again."

"We gotta do something to make him ease up a little." Mark closed his eyes and wiped the sluicing water from his face, sputtering effusively. "We can't all be big stars like he was."

"If we get an answer, we'd better check her out first," Donny Anderson suggested, bellowing above the six spattering showers. Steam rolled above the six heads—five blond or nearly so, one glistening raven.

"I should have asked for a picture."

"You don't really think he's going to go out with somebody who answers a newspaper ad, do you?" Kirby Streeter shouted.

"Why not? They say it's getting tougher to get dates nowadays, and the guy's an Indian." Ally amended quickly, "No offense, Tiger."

"Yeah, no offense." John Tiger turned his shower off and reached for the faded green towel he'd tossed over one of the wall hooks. Most of the time John preferred the quiet observer's role, but every once in a while an observation deserved to be voiced. "Tell you one thing. When Archer finds out, he's gonna be ticked off."

Ally laughed and launched into his rendition of one of his favorite reruns. "He's gonna say, 'Ally, you got some 'splainin' to do.'"

"Nordstrom!"

All heads turned toward the door to the locker room. Big Hoss Sandland, the team's heavyweight, was calling.

Ally grinned mischievously and nodded toward the door. "Come on. I think I just caught a whopper."

The showers ended abruptly with everyone grabbing for towels, tucking them around their waists or throwing one end over their shoulders and taking a swipe at their sodden hair. No one wanted to miss anything Ally might be up to. John had to hand it to the crazy little guy. He had guts. Ally was the first one to peer around the lockers and face up to Hoss. The rest of the boys followed, some risking a chuckle when they saw Hoss sitting on the bench, one stockinged foot and one booted one planted firmly on the floor in front of him. He had a tight grip on both knees.

"You put cold water in my boot, didn't you, Nordstrom? Didn't you?" The burly boy glared at Ally, who said nothing. Hoss snorted. A muscle twitched in his jaw as he stared Ally down and reached slowly for his other tall brown Western boot. Grinning, Ally watched. Hoss fit his fingers into the pull-on holes and slid his foot in. His eyes ballooned.

"Ahhh! Damn you, Nordstrom!"

Red-faced, Hoss puffed up his barrel chest and, amazingly, stomped his foot into the boot. Water ran over the top. Like a fairy-tale giant, he rose from the bench and started stalking. His boots squished with each step. Bystanders in briefs, towels, or naked and dripping wet, tried to stifle their chortles. Hoss looked mighty big and mighty angry.

Backpedaling toward the door, Ally turned to one of the boys. "You owe me five, Streeter."

"I didn't think he'd go for the second one."

"You're dead meat, Nordstrom," Hoss warned. Speed wasn't necessary. Hoss had a long stride and a hell of a reach.

"Aw, c'mon, Hoss, ol' buddy. What's a little water between—" Ally's toes scrabbled over the floor as Hoss brought them nose to nose "—frien-n-n... Whoa, Hoss!"

Teri Nordstrom was both excited and nervous about having her friends over to Lavender's for a party. She hadn't had a birthday party since she was six years old. Her parents had been divorced since then, and Marge, her mother, had never been much for kids' parties. Teri had stopped asking, even for her sixteenth. But Lavender seemed to think that a girl couldn't actually *become* sixteen without some kind of celebration, especially on Halloween.

Lavender was her employer and her friend. Teri had foregone cheerleading in order to work for Lavender after school. She had arranged her schedule so that she was finished with her classes by two-thirty. Then she drove out to Lavender's, and the two of them spent the rest of the afternoon working side by side at Lavender's looms and talking over anything that came to mind. Boys, for one thing, and birthdays, for another.

Everybody was excited about the party. The boys had pointed out that the timing was bad because their first meet was the next day, but what Coach Archer didn't know wouldn't hurt them. The girls had helped decorate

Lavender's house for the party. House parties were hard to come by in Glover, since nobody's parents ever left town. It was fun to go to Lavender's, partly because most of their parents liked to shake their heads and grumble about the idea. Teri knew exactly what kinds of things they'd said. She'd heard them all herself.

"Has that woman ever offered you anything like marijuana? I'm sure she must use it herself."

"If I find out there's been anything going on over there, you'll be in big trouble. And so will she."

"It seems pretty strange that a woman with no kids would want to throw a kids' party. Pret-ty strange."

But, like Teri's mother, her friends' parents had given in, especially since someone else was willing to do the chaperoning. Even if the someone else were Lavender Holland, it meant that the kids would have something to do besides drag the town's three-block Main Street. It meant there might be fewer Halloween pranks around town. It meant the sheriff would know what part of the county to patrol. And it meant that Marge Nordstrom could spend Teri's birthday with her new boyfriend instead of her daughter.

Lavender Holland was nobody's mother, and that suited all Teri's friends just fine. They knew she wouldn't serve any alcohol, but she would let them crank up the music, and she wouldn't make them feel as if they were making out on a microscope slide every time a few kisses were exchanged.

The only thing Teri was nervous about was this idea of being the hostess. She had no experience, and she knew her mother's idea of partying wasn't a particularly good example. As with everything lately, she was looking to Lavender for cues.

When Beth Hague brought the first carload of party-goers, Teri went to the door to meet them. They had all agreed not to wear costumes, because costumes weren't cool. Teri wished she'd had the gumption to wear something besides the usual T-shirt and jeans. Lavender, who was busy setting out the munchies, was wearing a long red skirt and a jangling array of bangles and beads. A flowered scarf tied around her forehead trapped the misty profusion of her long, kinky hair. Of course, Lavender didn't have to worry about being cool. She was too old. Besides, she was her own drummer.

Teri hoped to be like that someday, but it was hard to imagine having that kind of nerve. Lavender never worried about what people thought of her. Most of the kids liked her, but some of them could be pretty two-faced when it came to joking about some of Lavender's more unusual habits. Teri knew she didn't have to come to Lavender's defense. It was the kind of thing Lavender just shrugged off, knowing kids. And knowing Glover. Her doors were still open, and her schoolhouse held considerable appeal.

Nobody could pull off party decor with quite the flourish that Lavender managed, either. She had a creative flair that turned milk jugs into swooping bats and cotton thread into intricate cobwebs. If the kids weren't impressed with the way she had draped dark bed sheets for an Edgar Allan Poe effect, they had to appreciate the handmade owls perched in the tree branches that Teri had helped her plant in big cans salvaged from the school cafeteria. Strings of red Christmas bulbs provided the eerie lighting, and the shelving partitions cast long shadows over piles of floor pillows.

Standing on the step, hugging herself against the night's crisp chill, Teri greeted her friends as they piled out of

Beth's station wagon. They were all welcome, but she was waiting for one special guest, hoping, *praying,* really hard for him to show up. He'd said he would try to find a ride, and she hadn't pressed. Pressing him would drive him away. She'd told him it was her birthday, and she really wanted him to help her celebrate, but with John Tiger you never knew. He'd just moved to town last summer and was one of only two Indian kids in the school, so she understood. He was just a little shy.

He was also the most wonderful boy Teri had ever met.

And when Mark Christian pulled up and all four of his car doors swung open at once, John Tiger was also actually *there!*

Teri's mother would have killed her if she knew Teri had been seeing an Indian guy, but Teri didn't care. John was a senior, the best wrestler on the team, and he had the nicest smile. He'd come to Glover to live with his married sister, and his soft-spoken charm had won Teri over the first time she'd met him at the Brinker Burger Drive-In.

He flashed her that sweet smile as he closed the car door. Oh, he was such a babe! He wore a blue-and-gold letterman's jacket from his old school, unlike the rest of the boys, who sported Glover's orange-and-black.

"Hi, guys," Teri said, her overly bright tone a dead giveaway that the man of the hour had arrived. "Come on in. Lavender says we can put on our own tapes as long as we don't blow her speakers."

"All ri-i-i-ight. Put her folk music back on the shelf and play us some rock and roll," Ally crooned as he churned his arms like a locomotive, chugging up the steps.

Teri let the rest of the crew sidle past her as she stood beneath the porch light, waiting for John. He brought up the rear, and she took his hand discreetly, signaling with a little tug that he should follow her up the steps. He tugged back, and she stepped down. For a moment they simply shared two shining smiles.

"Happy birthday," he said finally.

"Thank you." She squeezed his hand. "Come on. The party's inside."

"Just a minute." His hand disappeared into his jacket pocket, emerging as a tight fist. He pressed something into her hand. "Don't open it till after this is over, okay? After everybody's gone."

"John, you didn't have to..." It was a tiny box wrapped in tissue paper. She could feel the tape across the bottom.

"I wanted to give you something, but I didn't know what you'd like."

Her heart fluttered wildly. "Whatever it is, I'm sure it's nice."

"Put it in your pocket for now, okay?" He glanced behind her, taking a moment to regain his *machismo*. "Is this a schoolhouse?"

"This is Lavender's house. Isn't it great?"

"It's different. I'll say that much." Secreting their clasped hands between them, he mounted the steps at her side. "I guess she doesn't have to worry about any neighbors complaining about the noise."

Except for the music, it wasn't a noisy party. Lavender provided plenty of food and activity, and no one was bored. They played Twister and danced the limbo. Lavender read palms and tarot cards and coaxed a blue bowling ball into revealing glimpses of the future. Even the boys ventured to the gypsy's table to have their fortunes read. It was Teri's night, and everyone was enjoying it. She knew she could ride the wave of popularity for some time after this, and she had Lavender to thank for it.

The little box was a warm spot in the pocket of Teri's jeans, and she was dying to open it. But John would have to leave first, and she wasn't dying for that. He was sticking close to her, maybe because he felt a little out of place, since he'd shied away from most social events. But she hoped it was a sign that he was beginning to think of her as his girl. She wanted to be.

They sat together on the end of a sofa and shared one slice of pizza between them. Neither was very hungry. "I'm glad you decided to come," she said.

"I wasn't going to. We've got a wrestling meet tomorrow, way the hell on the other side of the river somewhere."

"I know." It wasn't that far, really, but they would have to drive up to Bismarck to cross the river. Teri wished she could go, but they weren't taking a pep bus.

"Mark and your brother brought over a couple of beers, and I let them talk me into jumping in with them, you know, just to check things out."

"But you had a present for me." She smiled. He wasn't fooling her.

"I was gonna give it to you at school or something."

The word *beer* suddenly sank in, and her smile disappeared. "Don't get too close to Lavender. If she smells beer—"

"I'm not gonna cause any trouble, Teri. You want me to leave quietly?" His cocky smile said she wasn't fooling him, either.

She nudged his shoulder with her own. "No, of course not. Just don't get in line for a palm reading, okay?"

"I don't believe in stuff like that." He set the paper plate aside and took her hand. "Do you?"

"No, not really."

"You've got a nice palm." He traced the creases solemnly with his thumb, then lifted his chin and looked deeply into her eyes.

His lips were two inches from hers, and her mouth was dry. She swallowed and croaked, "So do you."

Her dumb brother had great timing.

"Guess what the future holds for me? 'A short trip and an unexpected cash windfall.'" Ally plopped beside her on the sofa and bit into his own slab of hot pizza. "Your friend Lavender might be gettin' off on some pretty weird stuff, but she sure knows how to make pizza. You don't even hardly miss the pepperoni."

Why did Ally always have to talk with his mouth full? "She uses a lot of herbs and spices."

"She forgot to spice up the punch." With a sly grin, Ally pulled the sealed top of a half-pint bottle of vodka from the knitted cuff of his school jacket. He pushed it back up his sleeve and went on eating.

Teri gasped. "Ally, you didn't, did you?"

"Not yet."

"Don't you dare try to slip anything into that punch."

Ally chuckled. Cheese slid over his chin, and he slurped it up, hooking it with his tongue.

"Don't spoil my birthday. Please."

"Let's lay off it now, Nordstrom." John's suggestion brought a look from Ally that said, *The Indian kid's gonna cross me over spiking the punch?* "Anybody finds out we even had a beer, we're on suspension for six weeks," John reminded him.

"Nobody's gonna find out," Ally promised. "It's a manager's job to keep the boys out of trouble."

"You're not spiking the punch tonight." It was no longer a mere suggestion. "It's Teri's party."

Ally shrugged. "Suit yourself. If you want it to break up early..."

"Lavender's going to send everybody home ear—" A flash of headlights in the window interrupted Teri's explanation. She frowned. "I'm not expecting anyone else. Everyone's here."

Ally tossed his plate on the table and peered out the window, using his cupped hands like horse blinders. "Uh-oh." He turned from the window. "It's Archer."

John rolled his eyes. "Great."

Somebody cut the music. "Hey, it's Coach Archer."

"Oh, geez. He is gonna be so—"

"Hey, we're not *doin'* anything."

"Yeah, but he said—"

Lavender answered the door. Even though they *weren't* doing anything, the whole bunch, girls included, fumbled around, checking to see if it looked as though they were.

Her greeting was warm and full of innocence. "Coach Archer, come in. We're having a birthday party for—"

"I heard." He stalked past her. In a few steps he had a clear view. Wrestlers. Girls. Food. Punch bowl.

Teri glanced at John, who looked neither scared nor embarrassed. She was both. She felt as though she'd been caught doing something terrible, even though she wasn't quite sure what it was.

Their backs were against the wall, and the only thing missing from the scene was a rifle in Coach Archer's hands. "Anybody who expects to wrestle tomorrow had better get his butt home now," he told the boys, who were bunching together as if a chilly breeze had just swept through the door.

"But, Coach, it's not even nine o'clock yet."

"What's this junk you're eating?" The coach took a plate out of Kirby Streeter's hands, sniffed the rich tomato sauce and tossed the plate back on the dining room table. Then he surveyed the room again. "Sandland's the only one on this so-called *team* who doesn't have to worry about making weight."

"It's just vegetarian stuff, Coach," Kirby whined. "Hardly any calories."

"Yeah, right. If you run alongside the bus tomorrow, you might just work it off." In the half-light, standing there with his hands on his hips and his eyes blazing, Archer looked like the Colossus of Rhodes. "We've got a two-hour drive ahead of us, and weigh-in is at nine. I thought I'd made my rules pretty clear. You don't party at night and go to a meet the next day."

Ally leaped to the rescue. "They're going home now, Coach. I'll tuck 'em all in personally."

It didn't bother Archer that the boy he was poking a finger at was half his size. The situation obviously called for massive doses of intimidation.

"I expect total commitment out of my student manager, Nordstrom. That's in school, out of school, nights, weekends. You look out for this team until the season's over, or you're out of a job. Got that?"

"Sure, Coach."

"Now get on outta here."

Massive intimidation produced scurrying on all sides.

It was exactly what Wyatt wanted. He had a point to make here, and it was for the woman's benefit, the kids', and, for that matter, the whole town's. He'd been hired to do a job. He was going to build a team and take it to State, and there was only one way to accomplish that. One straight and narrow path. When he said no parties before meets, he wasn't just jacking his jaws.

Lavender followed him to the punch bowl, while all around them there were shoes quietly being sorted out and jackets being snatched up. The kids had gotten the message. Only Lavender continued to try to explain. "I had already told them the party would be over at ten. And it *is* Friday night."

He could feel her watching him ladle a spoonful of fruit punch up to his nose, sniff, then sip. "Would you like a glass?" Lavender asked.

"No, thanks." The ladle clinked back into the bowl. "Just testing."

"I don't serve alcohol to kids, Mr. Archer."

"I'm not accusing anybody."

He picked up a bowl of guacamole and sampled it with a forefinger. "Just testing. You know, you can put two pounds on a kid the night before a meet just by letting them eat stuff like this." For good measure he tested again and allowed, "Not bad."

"I make whole-wheat pizza crust with—"

The kids were out quickly, mumbling their good-byes and thank-yous as they went. Wyatt turned to Teri, who was trying to be discreet about collecting scattered punch cups. "You're John's girlfriend, right? Teri?"

Wide-eyed, Teri stood up straight, clutching cups in both hands. "I . . . I don't know. We're friends, but—"

"I do know. I make it my business to know what every one of my boys has on his mind besides wrestling." He took a step closer. Teri backed up. He didn't want to scare her too badly, so he softened his tone. "You want John to stay on the team this year, Teri?"

"Wrestling means a lot to him. I know that."

"If it means a lot to him, and if he means anything to you, I suggest you stop having parties when he's got a meet the next day."

Lavender stepped between them. It was the first time he'd seen a hint of anger in her cool blue eyes, and it struck him that if he'd been about to grapple with her, her eyes alone would have given him pause. "Mr. Archer, it's Teri's sixteenth birthday."

"Sweet sixteen, huh?" He nodded, giving the news some thought. "That's a nice age. John Tiger's almost eighteen, and at the end of this year he's going to be looking for a wrestling scholarship to put himself through college. And if he doesn't get it..." He drew a deep breath and exhaled slowly. He thought about the options open to an Indian kid who lived with his married sister in a white town, and his voice grew softer still. "Sometimes eighteen is not such a nice age."

"I didn't mean to get anybody into trouble, Mr. Archer," Teri said timidly.

Wyatt cast a glance at Lavender. "I know you didn't. And I'm sorry I had to break up your birthday party."

"It's Halloween, Coach," Lavender reminded him. "Things could have been worse. They could be trick-or-treating for chocolate bars."

"They should have been home in bed." He considered the woman for a moment—the scarf, the bangles, the bare feet. She reminded him of a cactus flower, an unexpected bit of color in the unfamiliar landscape his travels had brought him to. The corner of his mouth twitched, threatening a smile. "You make that outfit?"

"Yes, I did." She gestured toward the table and her "crystal" ball. "Would you like me to give you a reading? See what fate has in store for your future?"

He stared at her until neither had any urge to smile. No games, he told himself. He had neither the time nor the patience for games. "My future's tied up with this team. My fate's what I make it, and so is theirs. I don't leave anything to chance. I do my homework and I make sure they do theirs."

His position clear, he gave a curt nod and turned on his heel. "Good night, ladies."

Chapter 2

"Talk about your tough nuts to crack." Lavender offered Teri a look of sympathy between removing the scarf and lifting four necklaces over her head. Teri was gathering up paper plates dotted with slivers of cold pizza and puddles of dip. "Does he have those boys on a starvation diet or what?"

"They have to be careful what they eat, I guess. They're usually pushing the upper limits of their weight class."

"Aren't we all? But everything I served here is good for mind, body and spirit." She flipped another light on and surveyed the litter. Nothing so threatening to the health as a greasy slab of sausage had touched her guests' lips. "And who does he think he's kidding? Not one of those boys would have been in bed before midnight on Halloween."

"You'd be surprised, Lavender. Even Ally jumps when Coach Archer blows his whistle."

Poor girl, Lavender thought. She was keeping such a stiff upper lip through it all. "Well, I'm really sorry he blew the whistle on us tonight. Kinda spoiled your birthday."

"Oh, no. He couldn't. Everything was perfect." Her face bright with feminine indomitability, Teri dug a small box from her pocket and tore off the wrapping paper. She gave a little squeal when she opened the lid, looked up, peeked again and then extended the box Lavender's way. "Look."

"Oooh, very pretty." Earrings. Two small gold hearts. Lavender raised an eyebrow. "John?" Teri nodded, her eyes singing a teenage *Gloria in Excelcis*. "He seems like a nice guy," Lavender said, taking the box in hand for a closer look at the gift that had saved Teri's evening.

"He *is*. Ally, that *brat*, was trying to spike the punch, but John stopped him."

"It's a good thing." Lavender had been keeping a discreet eye on Ally, who was notorious for his mischief, but she didn't want to take anything away from John's gallantry.

"I know. Boy, wouldn't it have been awful if Mr. Archer had caught them—caught *us!*"

Lavender pulled a tack and let her purple bed sheet fall to the floor. "I have a feeling Ally's not going to last the season."

"Not just Ally. These guys are working hard, but the coach never gives them one bit of credit. He just keeps pushing them harder." With maternal tenderness she added, "Especially John."

"Has John wrestled before?"

"Oh, yes, and I know he's really good. Even Ally says so. Indian schools usually play up basketball more, so John hasn't had a chance to really shine yet, but he will."

Teri found the pierced hole in her ear and smiled dreamily as she anchored one of her new earrings in place. "John's so strong. You wouldn't believe how incredibly strong he is."

"I believe, I believe." Lavender laughed and shook her head, remembering how much easier it had been to believe at sixteen.

"They're both Indians." Teri hastened to add, "You know, John and Mr. Archer."

"I noticed."

"You wouldn't think Mr. Archer would pick on John, but he does." Lavender questioned the possibility with a look. "I'm serious," Teri insisted. "John says at practice a lot of times he has to take Mr. Archer on because they're close in size. And Mr. Archer is still really good, even if he is pretty old."

Lavender remembered the first time she'd seen him, dressed in tennis shoes and gym shorts and looking for a can of pop. "Over the hill, is he?"

"Well, you know. I'm sure he's a lot older than you."

"That's old." She wouldn't be Teri's age again for the world, but she knew Teri would never believe that. The only consolation for the throes of adolescence was the conviction that everyone else's lights were dimming.

"You still act young," Teri assured her as, on hands and knees, she straightened up the pillows that had been scattered on the floor.

"Wonder why he's not married."

"See what I mean?" She tossed Lavender a sofa pillow. "He's been too busy torturing kids, probably. He's had some good wrestling teams, I guess. They hired him to help Glover make a comeback."

"Sports should be *fun*." Lavender put the pillow in its place, then kicked off her sandals and sat down, suddenly contemplative. "Men are strange. They bash heads with each other for fun. Afterward, they shake hands, rub their heads and say, 'Wasn't that a blast?'"

"I don't know. John acts like his whole life depends on his winning every match this year. *Every* match." Teri sat next to Lavender and put her bare heels up on the edge of the sofa seat. "He keeps to himself a lot. I know he likes me, but I have to kinda try to be where I think he might show up. If I have the car, sometimes we go for a drive, and we talk. He's more the quiet type around other people, but with me..." She hugged her knees and offered that dreamy-eyed smile. "He's funny and crazy and serious. You never know what to expect. It just takes a little while before he trusts people, you know?"

"Well, he took a chance and came to the party tonight. It's not easy to be different from everybody else. Especially in a town like this."

"We don't get very many—" Teri manipulated her toes while she groped for phrasing "—*new people* here, do we?" It was silly to beat around the bush. Lavender knew what she meant. She sighed and confessed, "I haven't said anything to my mom. About John, I mean."

"If she hasn't heard by now, there must be a hole in the grapevine somewhere."

"We're just *friends*. There's nothing wrong with that, is there?"

"What do you think?" Lavender asked.

"I think it's right. But I'm too chicken to try to convince my mom of that."

"Maybe she should meet John." Teri looked horrified. "Maybe Ally would introduce them," Lavender suggested. "That might take some of the pressure off."

"I don't know. I don't think John would feel comfortable about meeting someone who's so..."

"She's your mother." Lavender patted the girl's foot. "Don't assume, Teri. Give John a chance to tell you what he's comfortable with. And expect him to do the same for you." She gave the girl's big toe a parting "little piggie" tug. "And you tell him what you're comfortable with. That's important."

After the place was back in order and Teri was gone, Lavender was closing the drawer on the last of the silverware when the drawer next to it caught her eye. The clipping drawer. Dreams and wishes, questions and problems. People needing people. Lavender's old job had sucked her dry, she remembered, but she couldn't help tuning in to people's needs. She didn't have to be a social worker. All she had to do was get up in the morning and look at the paper, and there it was.

She was a personal-problem junkie, her ex-husband, Phil, had said. If someone wanted to talk, Lavender was there to listen. Well, she had cut back on her habit, starting with Phil, but she hadn't kicked it entirely. She listened to the women who worked for her. She listened to Teri and her friends. She listened to customers. The only difference was that these days she was listening as a friend, not a counselor.

Still, she had her collection of clippings.

She opened the drawer. The "Find-a-Friend" ad lay right on top. Funny. She could have sworn she'd tossed at least a hundred coupons and clippings in that drawer since she'd cut out the ad.

She was supposed to answer it. This was strange. *Weird,* in fact. She never answered these things; she just sort of tuned in to them. But she was *supposed* to answer this one. No doubt about it. Whenever she got this feeling, she didn't bother to question it. She simply did what the feeling called her to do. In this case, she had to write a letter.

* * *

Chest heaving from exertion, Wyatt dragged his arm across his sweat-slick forehead as he hovered over the boy on the mat. He was getting old. The kid had almost had him. If he hadn't been "Coach" and John hadn't been John, the boy might have accomplished a nice reversal.

"Get up, Tiger."

John's shoulders trembled almost imperceptibly, but Wyatt saw it, and he cast up a quick prayer that he hadn't reduced the kid to tears. If he had, he'd gone too far. He'd lost him. Stubbornly, the boy stayed where he was, refusing to look up, refusing to unglue his hands and knees from the spongy mat.

"Stand up and look at me, Tiger. Now's the time." Wyatt stepped back to give the boy a little space. John pushed himself to his feet, but he refused to lift his chin.

"You should have gone for the reversal," Wyatt asserted. "You had about a tenth of a second to make up your mind—a tenth of a second when you and I both knew you could have had me. You blew it when you looked up at me, like you were asking permission."

"Maybe I was."

"Then maybe you deserved to get your butt nailed to the floor."

Fists clenched at his sides, John struggled with the humiliation that clotted his throat and made his ears burn. His eyes were bright with anger, but he dared not look his coach in the eye. "You're stronger—"

"*You're* quicker. Quick as a rattlesnake when you want to be. You've gotta use that, John." Wyatt laid a conciliatory hand on the boy's shoulder. "*Use* it. That and anything else you've got going for you. Otherwise, they'll bury you."

"Nobody buried me Saturday." John stepped back, shrugging off Wyatt's hand. "I only lost two matches last year."

"Oh, yeah? How many can we count on this year?"

Feet shuffled. Dark stares glanced off each other briefly, like a stone skipping in still water. "Maybe none," the boy huffed.

"Maybe?" It was one of Wyatt's least favorite words. "*Maybe* none. If you doubt yourself, the man across the mat from you will see that doubt. And he'll use it against you. This team doesn't need doubters. Take ten laps while you're thinking that one over, John." He turned to the huddled mass of John's teammates, who were sweating, shifting, surely yearning to breathe free. "The rest of you, hit the showers."

Ally hung back while the rest of the boys disappeared. "Uh, Coach."

Wyatt turned, then scowled at the paper and the unsteady hand that offered it up to him. "This came for you today."

He took the purple stationery in hand as he watched John Tiger jog along the wall beneath the backboard. Then he gave the feminine handwriting a piece of attention. He blinked, refocused, signaled for the matching envelope still in Ally's hand and examined the postmark.

"What the hell is this?"

Ally swallowed. Never had he returned a meeker tone. "I think . . . I think it's a date, Coach."

He could have strangled every one of them. "Find-a-Friend," for God's sake. Did they think he was *that* pitiful? Or *unsica*, as his grandmother would have said. Ally's explanation sounded halfway sincere. They all knew he didn't frequent the bars, and there wasn't much else happening socially in Glover. Ally's Aunt Janine had met a nice guy this way, he'd said. The coach needed to loosen up a little. The rest of them, all but Tiger, had stood around looking well-meaning as hell. Tiger had kept right on jogging.

Wyatt hadn't had time to think about women lately, thanks to the shabby condition he'd found this bunch of nervy twerps in when he'd taken them on. He was getting around to thinking about them. Or *it*. Sooner or later. He knew how to get dates. Hell, he was thirty-six years old.

Meet me at Gladys's Kaffee and Kuchen at four on the ninth, Serious Type, and we'll see if I can make weight and make you smile. Look for a red flowered scarf.

He had to drive to Bismarck, but at least she'd picked a Sunday. He was usually free on Sundays. She'd given no name and no phone number, so it was show or no-show. He figured he was setting a good example for the boys. He'd spent much of his adult life actively acquiring social skills, and he'd learned that consideration was a respected trait. A responsible adult didn't leave people hanging in the lurch. Invitations were to be accepted cheerfully or declined with regret. You didn't hedge, hoping something better would come along. And if you accepted, you showed up.

Not that he'd been given a chance to decline, but that wasn't the lady's fault. He should have made Ally Nordstrom come along and apologize, but that might have made the woman even more uncomfortable. He would buy her a cup of coffee, shoot the breeze a little, maybe tell her he was sorry about the boys' little prank but pleased to meet her, and let her be the one to say she had to be going. No big deal.

He'd become a master at handling off-reservation protocol, and it was going to help get him a nice piece of the

American pie. A position with a university athletic department, a classy wife, a house with a nice lawn and two kids. He would acquire them in that order, and he knew he'd have to play the game along the way. Do the job, produce a winning team, stay out of small-town squabbles, make them forget to apply their racial prejudices— the ones they all claimed not to have—to him.

So here he was, watching the fence posts fly by as he tooled down the road to meet this mystery woman so the boys on his team would see how a responsible man handled a kid-made mess. He didn't have to admit to anyone that he was a little curious. He'd always wondered who in the world would ever answer those crazy ads.

Gladys's was a home-cooking café just off the interstate. The big yellow sign proclaimed Sunday's specials to be German potato soap and Indian tacos. The coffee and *kuchen* combo was advertised at a dollar and questionable cents. One of the numbers had blown away. Above the gas pumps, the price of diesel fuel was listed above regular gas, and there were six rigs parked in the huge lot.

Maybe he had a date with a lady trucker.

With its pine paneling, heavy woven-wood blinds and brown vinyl seating, the place was dark. If Wyatt could get this over quickly, he decided he would head for an orange-and-yellow McDonald's to find a little atmosphere. Just look for a woman with a red scarf around her neck, he reminded himself. The sooner you find her, the sooner you can...

The red scarf wasn't tied around her neck. It was wrapped around her head, just the way she'd worn it at the party. Her blue eyes were heavily lidded, heavily lashed, and her mouth was pouty. He wondered what kind of a tool it would take to rake through that wild hair. But she was pretty in an offbeat sort of way. Wyatt felt a little relieved—at least she was no stranger—and a lot stupid. But he'd always been great on defense.

"You looking to find a friend?" he drawled, treating her to his cockiest smile.

"You?" She managed to look shocked.

"Don't tell me you weren't expecting me." He laughed and slid into the booth across from her. "Come on. You and the kids cooked this up, right?"

"I didn't know you ran that ad."

"The boys on my team ran the ad. Actually, Ally masterminded it, so he said."

Lavender groaned and rolled her pretty eyes.

Wyatt was willing to play along with her as long as she gave him credit for seeing her game. "I should have known they'd set this up with *somebody*. There never was any ad, right?"

"Oh, there was an ad. A cute one. I have it at home." She put her hands on the table, palms down, and leaned forward a little. "And I had nothing to do with this. Really."

Bright teasers danced in her eyes. She was too offbeat to be so thoroughly attractive, and he didn't know quite how to take her. "You mean, you were expecting—"

"I didn't know what I was expecting. That's what made it fun."

He had a better word. "Risky."

"Risky can be fun." She tapped long, slender fingers on the table as though she were playing scales.

"So do you—" He watched her sip her water. Her upper lip was left glistening with the moisture, and suddenly he had no doubts about how he might take her. Or about how willing she might be. "—often meet guys this way?"

"Never. I just knew I was supposed to answer this ad, so I did."

"Supposed to?" He hiked an eyebrow. "Like fated to?"

"Not exactly. It was my inner voice telling me." She shook her head when he chuckled. "Don't laugh. You have one, too. We all do. Some people listen, others don't."

"I mustn't be listening."

"I'll bet you are. I'll bet you call it instinct. Sometimes you just know—" He wasn't buying, so she changed her terms. "Or you have a hunch. Do you like that better?"

He shrugged. His leather bombardier-style jacket squeaked against the vinyl seat. "I think it's pretty spooky. Somebody actually answers this crazy kid's ad, and it turns out to be . . ."

Her laughter reminded him of tinkling bells. "That weird Holland woman. The ad was irresistible."

"I never saw it. Did they make me sound like the Incredible Hulk, or some poor, homely slob who needed a woman to take pity on him?"

"I'll show it to you sometime." She took a menu from the rack that also held salt- and peppershakers and packets of sugar. "You might consider letting Ally be your publicist."

"I can't figure out why you answered." He eyed the other menu, pointedly leaving it in place. As always, he knew what he wanted. Just coffee. And a hint of what this woman was up to, so he would know how to proceed. "Some kind of Halloween inspiration?"

"As a matter of fact, it *was* that night. I didn't know it was you. I just knew it was calling me from my kitchen drawer." He waited for her to explain. "The ad. I'd cut it out. You see, it's just a matter of tuning in to—"

A waitress in a brown-and-white uniform appeared beside the booth, order pad and pencil poised.

Over the top of her menu, Lavender offered Wyatt an indulgent smile. "You were just planning on having coffee, I'll bet. But I have to say, I'm starved."

And he had to smile back. She was tuned in pretty well.

She glanced up at the waitress. "Do you use vegetable oil for deep-frying?"

"Yeah, we switched over a couple months ago."

"Very wise. I'll have the Indian taco. No meat. Can you serve it with beans instead of meat?"

"Separate out the beans?"

"You must have some beans that haven't been touched by meat yet," Lavender said patiently.

"Virgin beans," Wyatt supplied.

The waitress sighed and scrawled something on her pad. "Yeah, I guess so. Some people want meat with no beans."

"Perfect! I'll have their beans. And no sour cream, just salsa." She closed the menu, clearly satisfied with her choices. "And I'll have mint tea. And separate checks." She flashed Wyatt a reassuring smile, seemingly oblivious to the disgusted looks she was getting. "I understand they make good Indian tacos here."

"Without the hamburger, it's not an Indian taco."

"No vegetarians where you come from?"

"Not by choice." He offered the waitress a winning smile, which he figured would make up for any trouble caused by anyone at his table. "I'll have coffee." He added a friendly wink. "And a real Indian taco. Give the lady my beans, and give me her bill. I owe her."

"For what?" Lavender demanded.

"Grapefruit juice."

"We've got grapefruit juice," the waitress offered.

"Not this time, thanks." His smile was a polite dismissal.

Lavender sipped her water again and spoke of the subject closest to his heart. "The wrestling team is doing well."

"Two meets under our belts." He shrugged out of his jacket and shoved it toward the corner of the seat. "So far, so good. A lot of potential there, but they have to be willing to work."

"They're kids. They have to be allowed to do other things, too."

"Until the season's over, I decide what other things they can do. Partying the night before a meet is not one of them." The waitress served their drinks, and Wyatt stirred sugar into his. "I tell them how to eat, sleep, work out and study. Parents and girlfriends can fight over the couple of hours they have left over."

"How do you like teaching social studies?"

The question put a little wistfulness in his smile. "I've always been interested in history. It's like—"

"Hey, Wyatt!" Wyatt's smile melted into surprise as he glanced over his shoulder toward the door. Ruddy-cheeked from the cold, Carl Hausauer left his wife to deal with the waitress, who was doubling as the hostess. He shucked his jacket and wagged a finger at Wyatt as he approached their booth. "Caught you two at it again. What are you doing in Bismarck on a Sunday?"

Just what Wyatt needed. "I've been living in Montana, Carl. I forgot about the stores being closed on Sunday in this state."

"Crazy, isn't it?" Carl rearranged the thin strands of blond hair over the top of his shiny pate. "Of course, you have your own shop up here, don't you, Lavender?"

"Yes." She smiled. Wyatt wished she would take that scarf off. It made her look like some kind of a kook. "It's closed today."

"We're just up here visiting the wife's parents," Carl explained. "Stayed overnight last night." He waited, expecting the reciprocation that was expected when people from Glover ran into each other in Bismarck.

His wife peeked over a plastic philodendron. "Carl, we're sitting in the corner over there. Hi, Lavender."

"Oh, they've got us a table." Carl cupped his hand beside his mouth and confided, "Can't stand her mother's cooking. See you tomorrow, Wyatt."

As he watched Hausauer walk away, Wyatt wondered how quickly this chunk of gossip would get around.

"Does it bother you?"

He blinked, puzzling. This lady was spooky. But he played it cool. "Does what bother me?"

"Being 'caught' with me."

"Of course not." It did bother him that the waitress, who'd appeared with their food suddenly, might be hearing snatches of this, even though he didn't know her from Eve. He leaned back and let her set his meal in front of him, and when she was gone he added, "It's none of Hausauer's business what I do on Sunday."

"It's Glover's business. The business of knowing everyone's business. The whole town thrives on it." She dipped her chin, and her eyes shone provocatively. "I'm a particularly curious specimen. Have you noticed the way they look at me as though they're expecting my head to spin around or something?"

He'd probably looked at her that way himself. "Is it the screw-on type?"

"No. I have to do a little incantation and wiggle my nose." She laughed as she used her fork to prod at the mound of colorless shredded lettuce on her plate. "I make a much better salad than this. You'll have to stop over and let me try to change your mind about kelp and sprouts."

"That would take some doing."

"I also do a terrific therapeutic massage for those in need. I suspect you will be."

He didn't know which was bigger—the mouthful she'd said or the one she bit into. It didn't matter. She looked pretty damn cute with that fringe of lettuce tickling her lower lip, and it sounded like a hell of an invitation.

Two days later, Wyatt met Marge Nordstrom. He was about to lock up his classroom for the day and head down to the gym when she appeared in the doorway. Her jeans were tighter than her figure warranted, and she had the look of a woman who had made much of time.

"Mr. Archer?" She took his notice as an invitation to enter the room. "Hi."

"Hello."

"I'm Marge Nordstrom. Ally's mother."

"Oh, sure." He nodded, smiled and hoped this wouldn't take long. "Nice to meet you."

She took another step, launching a verbal barrage. "Mr. Archer, I just wanted you to know that I did not give my approval for that party out to Lavender Holland's place. I told Teri that was not the time, even if it was her birthday. But, oh no, Lavender said she could have that party at her place. And you know how they are when they get to be teenagers—well, you're a teacher—you just can't tell 'em nothing anymore, once they turn thirteen. I told them both it was *their* necks, and I wasn't in favor, especially not out to Lavender Holland's place."

What had Shakespeare said about the lady who protested too much? This one, standing there with her hand on her ample hip, was doing just that. "I've talked with the team about the incident, Mrs. Nordstrom. I think—"

"Marge." She raised her right hand as if to swear to something, and he noticed the nicotine stains on her fingers. "It's just plain Marge. Ally thinks the world of you, you know. He's been a handful, and I never know what he'll be up to next—his father and I are divorced—but I can tell already that you're a good influence. Boys will be boys, and it takes a man to keep them in line sometimes, but he loves being the team manager."

Wyatt slipped a set of tests into a leather portfolio. "He's working out just fine."

"Of course, Teri works for Lavender Holland, weekends and after school—it's hard for teenagers to find jobs, you know. So that's why Lavender had the party for her, but just between you and me, I'm not so sure that woman is such a good influence."

"Teri seems like a—"

"Her mother was a communist or some such thing. A radical, anyway, from back East, and Lavender has strange ways herself. I tell Teri, just do your job and don't get involved in any of Lavender's—" Wyatt gestured toward the door, and the woman followed, taking a breath to reveal what she clearly thought was a shocker. "She doesn't even eat meat."

"Your daughter?" Wyatt asked as he locked the door.

"Lavender Holland. You know, she's lived in California, where everybody's into things that we just don't—"

He made sure the door was secure before he pocketed his keys and turned to the woman. "The party is past history, Mrs.—Marge. I'm not holding it against Ally or Teri or anybody else. They tested me, and they found out that I mean what I say."

"That's the way you have to be with kids. Give 'em an inch and—" She was half a step behind as they headed down the hallway. "Did you smell anything funny when you went over there? Like drugs?"

"I'm not a police dog. They were drinking fruit punch and eating pizza."

"Whew." She gave a nervous little laugh. "I worry about that, you know? Drugs. You just can't tell where they might get into that stuff."

They rounded a corner together and ran into Ally. Marge brightened artificially. "Hi, honey."

The boy's face fell when he saw her. "What are you doing here, Mom?"

"Just visiting with your coach." She offered up a painted smile. "I wanted to touch base. You know, I've seen you around town, Mr. Archer, but everybody's so busy these days, I wanted to make sure you knew who I was and let you know you could call me anytime. You know, if there's a problem."

"That's good to know." Wyatt laid a hand on Ally's shoulder and kept walking. "We've gotta get some wrestling practice going here. Right, Ally?"

"Kirby wants to know if he can practice today, if I wrap his shoulder for him."

"Kirby's gonna let that shoulder rest. I've got some leg work for him to do." They'd reached the wing of the building that was all gym. Wyatt turned and stuck out his hand. "Nice meeting you, Marge. We've got a home meet coming up next week. Hope you're able to come out for it."

"Oh, I wouldn't miss it. You know, you don't look like most wrestling coaches."

The handshake was a mistake. Marge didn't want to let go, and Ally's face was turning red. Wyatt hated it when parents embarrassed their kids like this, with the kind of come-on look that Marge was giving him right in front of her son.

"Really? How do most of them look?" Wyatt asked as he withdrew his hand.

"You know, beefy, thick. Sort of Neanderthal. You look more—"

His breezy chuckle was usually good for putting everyone at ease. "Careful, Marge. If you say aboriginal, I'll have to take exception."

"I would never say that." She attempted a girlish smile. "Teri's always calling Ally a Neanderthal, so that's about as fancy as I can get."

"That's pretty fancy. Well, I'm neither. Coaching these kids is my way of deluding myself into thinking I'm still as young as I used to be." He glanced at Ally and read the pain in his face. "My right-hand man's giving me the high sign. Thanks for stopping in."

The gym offered them sanctuary. Ally glanced up apologetically as Wyatt steered him behind the doors. "She can't quit talking, can she?"

"She's a woman." He knew he would get clobbered in mixed company for that one, but this was the gym. Still, he felt obligated to amend with, "A mother. Wanted to see how her son was doing."

"Yeah, right."

"She seems like a nice lady, Ally."

The boy did a double take, and Wyatt gave him a reassuring shoulder punch.

Yeah, right. The woman was checking out the new coach, plain and simple. Wyatt made a mental note to give Lavender a call.

Chapter 3

With their looms and benches side by side in the work area at the front of the schoolhouse, Teri and Lavender had spent long hours becoming friends. Lavender was a good listener. Teri was a teenager in need of someone to talk to. Almost daily they practiced their craft, sliding their shuttles back and forth across colorful warps, making the wooden heddle bars click and then clack and then click again as they beat the weft threads into place and spoke of everything from political candidates and school policies to dry skin and menstrual pain.

"I thought I'd come over tomorrow and put in a few hours on the loom," Teri suggested on a typical Saturday afternoon. "Then maybe take next Saturday off."

"And follow the boys?" Lavender teased.

"There's a big meet up in Minot."

"You're welcome to take Saturday off anytime, honey, and work almost any Sunday but this one. I'm having company."

"Oh." Teri looked up from her work, expecting more, but she was too polite to ask.

Lavender ignored the unspoken question. "We can put a loom in your basement at home anytime you say. A sewing machine, too. You're as good as any seamstress I've got."

"I don't think that would work. Drake's got his stuff down there now." The girl's lip curled disgustedly. "You know. Drake Starky, my mother's latest."

The name was familiar. Summertime always brought a few new faces to town, but most of the summer labor was usually gone by now. "I haven't met him."

"You're not missing much. He's a big yawn. He's moved in lock, stock and stupid stuff like cases of spark plugs. I think he's going to open up a garage or something." Teri sighed as she passed the shuttle of soft yellow weft yarn through the warp. "Mom sure can pick 'em."

"Well, my mother used to say, 'To each his own.' It's one of the clichés I live by. Another one is 'Live and let live.'"

"But you don't have to live with . . . *that*."

"You're right." It wasn't fair to minimize Teri's problem with a cliché. Lavender knew when and how to sympathize. "You don't like him much, huh?"

"He acts like a jerk most of the time. Mom laughs at his stupid jokes and cooks what *he* likes all the time. It's sickening."

"So mostly it's the two of them together that bothers you," Lavender reflected.

"*He* bothers me."

Time to tread lightly, Lavender told herself before asking, "Bothers you how?"

Teri tossed her head as though her hair were in her way. "I just don't like having an oily sleazebag like that in my house." Squaring her slight shoulders, she gave Lavender her toughest look, which fell short of the woman-in-charge mark. But Lavender was satisfied that the girl knew what she was aiming for when she said, "Don't worry. If he ever got too close to *me,* I'd disable him."

"You'd tell someone," Lavender instructed. "Someone you could trust to help you."

"I'd tell you." Teri shook her head and shifted her bottom on the cushioned bench. "It's really not like that. I just wish she had a little bit better taste in guys, that's all."

"How does he get along with Ally?"

"Oh, they get along okay. Ally's into spark plugs, too. Drake has a big motorcycle, and he lets Ally ride it, so they're friends." Packing the weft with the beater bar, Teri tapped her fingers along the fabric she'd just made, admiring her own artistic accomplishment. Even as she did so, she spoke softly, as though owning up to something not quite normal. "I don't want a loom in the house because I'd rather spend the time here."

"I like having you here," Lavender assured her.

Brightening, the girl added, "Or with John."

"Big, bad John." Lavender smiled as she slid her shuttle along. "How's he doing with Mr. Archer?"

"He must be doing great. He just won two more matches, and you can really tell how hard he's been working out. His arms are like—" she cupped her hand over her own arm "—Mr. Muscle or something, and his chest is like, I can barely get my arms around it."

"Wow." Lavender's eyes widened approvingly.

"But he never eats."

"He must eat *something*."

"Well, something, yes, but I don't know what. Half the time he skips lunch to work out. So I sneak him something during fifth-period class."

"Like a candy bar?"

"Sometimes."

"Teenagers! In the richest country in the world, most of you are malnourished by choice." She slid her bench away from the loom and went to her desk, where she kept her snack jar.

"Are we still the richest country in the world?"

"I don't know. That was another of my mother's expressions." Lavender spun the lid off and stuck the quart jar under Teri's nose. "Here, try some of this. It's my latest concoction of dried fruits, grains and seeds, with a little—" Teri was chewing, concentrating on the taste. "You like it?"

Teri nodded, sending Lavender back to the desk to prepare a care package. "It's good," Teri said. "Your concoctions are always good. Just don't talk about what's in them, and nobody'll suspect you of being a nefarious nutrition supplier."

"Nefarious," Lavender echoed, dragging on the vowels. "Sounds like a good old *Word Wealth* word. Here's a supply for your purse." She poured some of the mixture into a plastic bag she'd pulled from the desk drawer. "Take it to fifth-period class."

"John really likes those white-chocolate candy bars. You know, the ones with almonds?"

"*Whom* did you say only cooks the foods her boyfriend likes?" With a laugh, Lavender tucked the bag into Teri's denim purse, which sat on top of her history book in the Boston rocker by the woodstove. "Welcome to the women's club, sweetie. We'll add some yogurt-coated almonds to the recipe. Deprivation leads to cravings. Doesn't Mr. Archer tell these boys to—"

Teri turned around quickly. "Don't tell Mr. Archer about this. They have a balanced diet they're supposed to go by, but John says he can't keep his weight down if he follows it exactly." With a wave of her hand, she warded off wrong conclusions. "Not that he has a weight problem. He's really—"

"Built like a Greek god. I know." Lavender returned to her bench, sliding her knees under the front of the loom as though she were settling down to play piano. "When you worry a lot about weight, for whatever reason, you have a problem. So what if he puts on a few pounds?"

"Then he has to compete in a heavier class, against bigger guys. You know, you want to be just under the limit."

"If you have to sneak him something to eat, that little recipe is better than candy. But just remember, this is John's problem. Not yours. He's the one who should talk to Mr. Archer."

"He'd do anything for Mr. Archer. He wants to be just like him." Teri shifted the heddle bars with the foot pedal, threw her shuttle again, trying hard to leave it at that. She couldn't. "But he won't tell him he gets the shakes sometimes when he skips meals."

"Oh, dear." Lavender shook her head and cast a glance at the rafters. "I don't want to be told this, Teri. Not if I have to keep it a secret."

"Well, it's not *that* bad. Just sometimes when a meet's coming up and . . ." She turned to her mentor to explain. "What you do is, John says, you weigh in when you get there, and then you go get a hot dog or something."

Lavender grimaced, mischief dancing in her eyes. "Miscellaneous animal parts. Greasy, grimy—"

"Don't say it!" Teri shrieked, and they dissolved into giggles.

"Ground pig lips. Yum, yum."

"Oh, yuck." Teri pumped her knees and stamped her feet, running in place as she whipped her hair from cheek to cheek. "I hate it, I hate it! We're having them for supper. Drake loves them."

"What does that tell you?" Teri groaned, and Lavender shifted the topic slightly. "Has your mom met John yet?"

"Ahhh, nooo," Teri admitted dramatically.

"Does she know?"

"She hasn't said anything. If she does, I'll just say, 'To each his own,' right?" The heddle bars clacked again. "Ally said she was flirting around with Mr. Archer after school one day, acting like some kind of a—" Teri sighed "—a silly woman who can't get it through her head that she's not sixteen anymore. *I'm* the one who's sixteen."

"A woman's allowed to think young once in a while." *Flirting with Mr. Archer, huh?* She couldn't resist fishing a little. "So, what happened to Drake?"

"He wasn't along. Out of sight, out of mind, which is easy to do with Drake." Teri shook her head as she reached for the beater. "I don't know. My mom's just…like that. She acts disgusting around men. At least, *I* think it's disgusting. I hope I never get like that."

"I like you the way you are. You're very centered." It was something her own mother had told her many times in many ways. She wasn't like everyone else, but she was fine. Lavender offered Teri a reflection of that well-remembered reassuring smile. And even though she realized that most teenage girls found themselves suddenly looking at their mothers through a critical haze, Lavender found it hard to figure fate putting Teri and Marge

Nordstrom in the same family. "I think as long as *you* like the way you are, you have nothing to worry about."

"Centered?" Teri considered the word—one of Lavender's favorites. She was beginning to understand what it meant. "Yes, I think I am. Centered." She thought about the feeling. She didn't always have it, but it was good when she did. Nothing could push her then. "At least, sometimes. Meditating helps. I can do it at home now. I can feel the light inside me, and I can move it up and down, from my stomach to my head, just like you said."

"It's a peaceful feeling, isn't it?"

"Really." But she could only claim so much peace for herself before she felt the nudge of budding female instincts. "Maybe meditation would help John. He'd probably think it was silly, but maybe if I could get him to—"

"You can't take care of him, honey."

"I'm not. He spends as much time with Ally as he does with me. But when we *are* together...alone..." There was that dreamy smile. "He's just so sweet."

As was young love, Lavender recalled. As for mature love, she'd wondered about that from time to time. It was the stuff that dreams were made of. For all the listening she'd done over the years and all the relationships she'd helped women put into perspective, the accepting, enduring, weathering-the-storms and growing-old-together kind of love had eluded her. That, too, would have to be sweet.

Wyatt had suggested they get together for coffee. Lavender had offered Sunday dinner at her place. He wasn't looking forward to a vegetarian meal, but he was ready to spend a little "quality time" with a good-looking woman.

He parked his fairly new Toyota next to her fairly old brown Buick station wagon in a space near the house that had obviously been graveled for parking in ancient times. It was reverting to prairie, but there were remnants of former improvements. He closed the car door and enjoyed one more chuckle over her mailbox, which stood down at the end of the driveway. Somebody with a gun rack in his pickup had taken potshots at her cosmos.

His boot heel skittered over a patch of gravel as he shoved his hands in the front pockets of his jeans and rounded the corner of the house, heading for the front door. It seemed funny to call it a house. It still looked like a school. Still had the swings. He didn't suppose the school yard would have had a garden, though. The frost-shriveled squash vines brought back his own memories of a time before he'd gone off to mission school, when he'd spent his summers out in the country with his grandparents. He'd hated squash. Hated cucumbers, even to this day. He hoped this woman had used up all her cucumbers by now.

The door flew open, and she appeared with a big, welcoming smile in her blue eyes that seemed to lift the whole yard, taking him with it. She gave such a smiley feeling that he couldn't help offering one of his own. And not the stamped-on version. The real thing.

"Have I got a surprise for you," she said, as she let the door swing closed behind her. "Do you like surprises?"

"Sometimes." He could go for a steak.

"Only the good kind, huh? Isn't it a gorgeous day?"

The weather usually didn't mean much to him one way or the other, but she offered the observation with arms outstretched and real enthusiasm for the autumn sunshine. It was the kind of gesture that invited a flash of fantasy, a crazy thought of walking into those arms and turning them into an embrace. He cleared his throat. "Is that your surprise?"

"A warm day this time of year in North Dakota always seems like a gift."

"We've been lucky this year." He perched one booted foot on the first of the three steps to her door and read the sign above her head. "What's Coyote's Call Creek? A ghost town?"

"That was the name of the school district, before they consolidated with Glover. I used to go to school here." She reached back, pulled the storm door open and stepped inside with one hand extended to him, beckoning him.

He glanced over his shoulder, took a deep breath and followed, trying to keep up his end of the conversation while he batted down thoughts of being lured into some kind of lair. Hausauer made her sound like a sorceress, but he had to remember that Hausauer was full of it.

Inside, it still felt a little like a country schoolhouse. High ceiling. White walls. Polished wood floor. But that was only the beginning. "You must have a real sentimental streak," he remarked.

"I don't know if it's that so much. I ran across the idea of a converted schoolhouse in a magazine. When I moved back here, I thought, why not turn this old place into something wonderful? It was big enough, pretty well built, and it was for sale." There were two rocking chairs near a woodstove at the front of the building. She touched the high back and set one rocking as she walked past it. "I'm into recycling."

"You did a nice job. I guess I really didn't look around when I came stomping in here before. And it was dark." He nodded toward the two floor looms. "This is where you do your work?"

"Some of it, yes." She could see she wasn't going to get him past her studio until he'd checked everything out.

The shelves that separated the work area from the living area were filled with big, bulky spools of thread in an array of colors that would have made a painter drool. Wyatt surveyed the raw materials, then moved from Lavender's loom to Teri's, following the warp from the part of the cloth that was finished through the heddles and back to the warp beam. His primary interest seemed to be in the mechanics of the loom, and he asked no questions at first. She could see his mind at work, envisioning the process for himself first, just by the way the machine was set up.

"Have you ever seen a loom before?"

He squatted beside the machine and examined the web of strings from the underside. Lavender remembered her own fascination the first time she'd seen a big floor loom. It was like looking at a harp and hearing the music she might make on it in her head.

"I've seen the ones the Navaho use," he said as he stood up again. "They're not like this."

"They use the upright loom. These are floor looms, with a few more moving parts, but the principle is the same." She circled the loom slowly, pointing as she explained. "The warp threads are stretched taut, from here to here, and the heddles lift and lower some of the threads, like so, so that the weft threads can be slipped crosswise, over and under the warp threads." She demonstrated, then turned to him with a smile. "A process almost as old as the hills."

"But speeded up by factories."

"Ah, but faster is not necessarily better." She led him to her desk and handed him a sketchbook, smiling like the kid who was handing in a report she didn't doubt was worth an *A*. "Here are some of the things we make."

He sorted through her design sketches and flipped through two albums filled with photographs of models wearing dresses, suits and wraps in beautifully blended colors. They were the color blends of earth and sky— fields of spring wildflowers, late summer harvest, the hills in winter and setting-sun skies.

She showed him bolts of fabric and his hands were drawn to the variety of textures—blends of cotton, silk and wool—but what struck him most was the distinctive feel of the cloth. It wasn't machine-crisp. He could almost feel the *hand* part of handwoven, as though the fabric had been touched, smoothed, skin-softened to lie easy on the wearer.

Wyatt was not a man to notice such things, but there was an element of hominess in the fabric that drew him to turn, touch Lavender's sleeve and note, "This isn't something you made."

"No," she said. "Not this blouse."

Then he touched her easy-fitting slacks. Not her hip, but the relaxed cotton fabric that covered it. "You made these," he said.

"Yes." She smiled. The intimacy was not threatening. He was permitting a tactile moment for the child within him. She welcomed the artlessness of his gesture.

"They feel nice," he said.

The look in his eyes hardened as the man caught the child and pulled him back out of the way. He moved his hand differently, seeking the hip now. Lavender stepped back, leaving him with a handful of air. They assessed one another for a moment before she lightened the mood with a smile and spun away, moving beyond the divider and into the living area.

"I have dinner ready. I also have a backup, in case you really hate everything I cooked." Not that it would bother her, but she hoped he was more discerning than most. She hoped he was the kind of man who would give something new a chance, but she allowed, "I can make you a pressed turkey sandwich."

"If that's apple pie, I'll clean my plate no matter what." He made a production of expanding his chest on a breath of cinnamon- and allspice-scented air. "Apple's my all-time favorite."

"Good." She sent up a quick prayer that the crust was done on the bottom. "My trees are overflowing this year. Would you like to take some apples home with you?"

"Sure." The table was set with homespun cloth napkins and crockery, and he spied the pie sitting on a rack on the counter. The reluctant choirboy he once was hit a high note inside his head, and his eyes danced to the tune. "Especially if they're baked in a crust."

Like the room in which they shared it, it was an earthy dinner, full of leaves, roots and fruits. Some bunches of dried foliage suspended from a string here or a bit of wire there had probably contributed flavoring to the soup. Or maybe to *his* soup. So far, no sign he'd been slipped an aphrodisiac. If she offered chokecherry wine, he decided he would refuse, even though he didn't think she had a basement to bury his body in. He kept thinking that pie would end the meal on a heavenly note.

As the meal progressed, he almost mistook the soy-based entrée for chicken-fried steak, and she was delighted. She'd nearly fooled him. When she served the pie, he felt mellow enough to pass out compliments. "Some of this stuff wasn't half bad."

"Thank you." For that, she sliced him a generous piece.

"I'm not much for cooked vegetables, but that soup was tasty." He told himself to quit while he was ahead, but he couldn't resist adding one small dig as he picked up his fork. "Although, there were some things floating in it that I didn't recognize."

"Are you asking?"

"Uh...no. That look in your eye says I don't want to know." She laughed and took only a sliver of pie for herself.

"You trying to make weight?" he asked.

"No. I understand that can be a pretty tough challenge all by itself." She spared him a quick glance. "Especially for that most ravenous of all animals, the teenage boy."

"I don't let them overdo it. Some coaches make them take off almost a weight class. I don't think that's healthy."

"Neither do I."

He forked up the tender, three-cornered tip of his pie. It was, m-m-m-m, so tart and spicy. Maybe she would make some for the team, after they won the state championship. Some women loved to cook for a crowd. He'd known at least one woman who was like that, and before he realized it, he'd voiced a recollection. "My grandmother would have known what was in that soup. She always had a big garden."

"Did she dig wild turnips and—"

His warm thoughts cooled. He knew better than to open that door. Right away the woman was seeing star blankets and buffalo. "My grandmother grew beans and potatoes, like everybody else."

"I just thought she might..." She shrugged. "Because I do. I love to forage for turnips. Onions in the spring, and burdock and curly dock. Wild things."

"She dried turnips, I guess. Sometimes." He wouldn't tell her about helping with the braiding, about putting them in soup with dried meat and corn. Not that those things were secrets. They were just ancient history.

Beneath the table, something took a turn around his boot tops and gave him cause for diversion. "Speaking of wild things..."

Lavender peeked over the side of the table. There was the long black tail, held high in the air and hooked at the top like a shepherd's crook. "Jasper's just checking you out. Seeing whether you're fish or fowl. If you're neither, he won't be interested."

"Sorry, guy. I didn't sneak anything in for you." But he reached down and scratched the white triangle under the black cat's chin. Jasper purred loudly.

"Well, that's a switch. He's usually pretty stuck up."

"He thinks I'm chicken, maybe." Lavender laughed. Wyatt didn't. "He's dead wrong."

"Poor Jasper. After five years with a vegetarian, he can't tell anymore."

For long moments they gave their own silence over to the sound of the blower on the living room woodstove and an occasional drop of water plunking into the sink. She was a slow eater, a fact that he suspected might drive a guy crazy if he were anxious to get on to something else. He wasn't. He had all afternoon. All evening, too, if she wanted that much of his time. It was nice to be with someone who didn't seem to be taking notes on his every move.

"This is great pie," he said, finishing his second piece.

"Thank you."

He pushed his plate back. "So, what's next? You want me to wash or dry?"

"Dishes are definitely not next. On a day like this a walk along the creek is next." She stacked his plate on top of hers. "I want to share something with you that I think is very special."

Sharing was a popular cozy-up word that grated on him more than a little, but he didn't let that show. She had the eyes of a little girl who was bursting with a secret, and they softened him. He decided he could stand a little sharing. "More special than apple pie?" he asked.

"I think you'll find this even more delightful than apple pie," she promised as she deposited their plates in the sink and took a fringed, kitten-textured mohair ruana from a fat plastic hook near the back door.

"You'll have to go some to beat that pie." *Like, all the way, pretty lady.* "But lead on."

They swished through the tall brown grass, gravity urging them downhill toward the sluggish little creek. The sky was bright blue, and the air was clear and crisp. A late-afternoon topaz sun burned warm enough to keep November's chill at bay. Lavender led the way through the creek-bed stand of cottonwoods, willows and ash. The crackle of dry leaves drew Wyatt's attention to her sandaled feet, and he imagined returning to the house and warming her toes in his hands.

He shook off the thought. That wasn't his kind of sharing. "You ought to wear some decent shoes. It's getting too cold for those."

She laughed. "Is that the teacher in you speaking, or is that what your mother would have said?"

"It's plain good sense." And he had no idea where it had come from. Sure as hell not from his mother. "Is that shawl thing very warm?"

"Very." She extended a hand, and when he reached her side, she tucked her arm in the crook of his. His brown leather jacket was not zipped, and he had his hands in his pockets. "If you're cold, I can run back and get one for you."

"I'm not cold," he said quickly, and then he allowed himself a chuckle. "Think I'd look like Clint Eastwood wearing one of those?"

"With the right hat and two days' growth of beard."

"It'd take me longer than two days. Indians don't have much beard."

Impulsively she touched his cheek with her free hand, catching him by surprise. Something warm quickened in him at the touch of her hand, and he sought some suggestion of similar quickening in her eyes as they walked. One minute he saw it, and the next it was gone, replaced by an innocent smile and presumably a simpler pleasure. She was the epitome of the tension between guilelessness and sexual knowledge, which excited him as much as her touch did.

"I guess you don't," she said. "That must make your life a little easier."

"Easier than what?"

"I don't know. Easier than shaving." She squeezed his arm. "Lighten up, Wyatt. There is no hidden meaning in anything I say. Hiding your message is wasted effort, as far as I'm concerned."

"So I can take everything you say and do at face value, huh?" She nodded. "Do you shave your legs?"

She laughed. "Sometimes."

"When was the last time?" She looked up quizzically. "Well, guessing about these things takes a lot of effort, too, and I've only seen you in thick stockings and pants. I'm trying to picture your legs."

"Last night." Her sails floundered slightly as she stared straight ahead. "They're spindly."

He doubted that. He'd gotten a good feel of the hip they were attached to. At the moment, it was holding its own, bumping against his.

She stopped walking and stuck out her hand. "Here it is."

A good-size clearing, a hill, a creek and some fading grass and trees. And a scattering of rocks, most about the size of bowling balls.

"Rocks?"

She squinted up at him. "Don't you see the pattern?"

"Looks like..." The woman had some funny notions, but he was beginning to like her enough to play along. He surveyed the field and gave the game an honest shot. "One of the constellations, right?"

"You mean stars?" She stepped to the right, angled her head and reconsidered.

Wyatt withdrew his hands from his jacket, slipped them into his hip pockets and moved behind her, really looking, really trying to figure out what she saw. "The Big Dipper's the only one I know. If you tell me this is a map of the sky, I'll have to take your word for it."

She started laughing, and he wondered what had happened to all that openness she claimed. *Don't you get it?* were fighting words to him.

He covered by switching to offense. "You're going to tell me that some aliens put these rocks here to show you where they live. And they don't eat meat, either."

"Of course not."

"And their superior intelligence can be attributed to that fact." He would get his digs in before she told him the joke was on him.

"Undoubtedly." Smiling, she stepped closer for a face-off. The fact that she had to tip her head way back didn't seem to intimidate her. "You must really think I'm loony."

"Where would I get an idea like that?"

"You've heard rumors."

Impulsively he touched a red-gold glint of sunlight in a curl that turned away from her forehead. "They say you know how to cast spells on people."

"Do they now?"

It was his turn to touch her cheek to test, but not as she had tested. He knew he would find softness, but forbearance in being touched was another matter. He spoke in a hushed tone. "I think it might be true."

He meant it to be a line, but he realized as he said it that he was at least half serious.

"I think I ought to tell you that Jasper used to be a tomcat, too, until I had him fixed." She let that "too" sink in before she elaborated. "He was making a fool of himself with all that caterwauling that males do when they're on the prowl."

"Caterwauling?" He withdrew, laughing in spite of himself. "Okay, tell me about the rocks while I fall back and regroup."

"I think this might be an Indian spiritual center." She looked to him, hoping for confirmation. "I feel power here. Don't you?"

"Seriously?"

"Seriously." She moved backward around the edge of the ring, demonstrating with her hands. "It's shaped like a medicine wheel. This points due north." She pointed. "South, east, west. It can't be just coincidence."

He watched, listened, shrugged. "I might as well tell you, I don't know much about traditional beliefs and practices, other than what I learned in college history classes. I went to boarding schools when I was a kid, and they didn't teach that stuff."

"What about your family?"

"My family is—" he turned away as he tossed off what seemed to be an easy reply "—just like any other family. They live in houses, eat frozen food and occasionally go to church."

"I've seen the big medicine wheel in Wyoming, way up in the Bighorn Mountains. They don't know who made it, but lots of Indian people make pilgrimages up there, and you can just feel the power. I think this could be something like that."

The excitement in her voice drew him around again. Her face was bright, burnished by the sun, as was her tawny hair. Every wild wisp of it. He wanted to touch it again, crush a handful of curls in his palm and watch it spring back to life when he opened his hand.

Obligingly, he looked her find over once more. "I don't know. It takes a pretty big stretch of the imagination to see—"

"There used to be a cottonwood growing right there. See that depression? With the tree there, you didn't notice the pattern. But it got hit by lightning—smack!" She gave her own palm a karate chop. "Split right down the middle."

"Now that sounds like power." He grinned. He couldn't resist her sparkle. "Electricity."

"But free and unbridled and natural and, and..." Flapping her arms under the long, loose wrap, she reminded him of a pretty little hen. She would never make it into the air, but she was trying hard.

"Anyway, I cut the tree up for firewood, and now look," she entreated, approaching him again. "Come on, you're a history teacher. Just imagine the possibilities,

right on this very spot.'' Her open arms might have en-
compassed all time and the river flowing. "People. Hun-
dreds, even thousands of years ago..."

"Then they weren't Sioux," he told her. "The Sioux
migrated here, chased out of Minnesota by the Chippewa
before they got the horse."

"So what if they weren't Sioux?"

"I'm Sioux. If it was that long ago, these weren't my
people." He shook his head, chuckling. "What am I saying? I'm not into this *my people* stuff. I'm just—"

"The point is, *some*body put these here."

"How about some*thing*? Like a glacier."

"No, Wyatt," she insisted, illustrating with expansive
gestures, "this is definitely a circle with a cross inside. Or
an *X*, depending on how you look at it."

"Could be." She surely wanted it to be. So why not?
"Yeah, I guess it could be. You should call the state historical society. They could probably tell you more."

"It shouldn't be disturbed. It's a mystical place. It
doesn't matter when it was built or what kind of technol-
ogy the builders had or what they wore. Some form of
give-and-take between man and earth happened here, and
it's important to let it be." Her voicing of the word *man*
surprised him. Surprised her, too. He could tell by the
twinkle in her eyes. "Man, *wo*man and earth. Don't you
feel the energy?"

"I feel something, yes." He stepped close to her. "A
strong attraction."

"Between us?"

"Between man and *wo*man. Don't you feel it?" Closer
still. "You're the one who had the feeling you were supposed to answer that letter." He took her shoulders in his
hands. Soft wool. Soft eyes. No resistance now. "Some
kind of magnetism, don't you think? Let's test it out."

He tilted his head to the side and lowered it slowly, watching her eyes as she watched his. She closed hers first. Acceptance. She tipped her chin up. Willingness. His kiss acknowledged those things. He felt the stiffness in her shoulders and the hunger in her lips, and the contradiction aroused him. He tasted cinnamon and the tang of apples, and he deepened the kiss for the sweeter taste of warm promises.

She knew better than to let this happen, but her heart was so hungry, her lips anxious for the taste of his, just one taste. She put her hands up to keep herself safe, resting them on the pliant leather of his jacket. With her arms as space makers between them, she welcomed his lush, open kiss. Already the mingling was complex. Sweet and seductive. She gathered two handfuls of leather and held on for dear life.

He lifted his head, kneading her shoulders to relieve her tension. "What do you think?"

"I don't deny the, um..." She gave her head a quick shake, clearing cobwebs. This man would pull out all the stops if he could. If she would let him. "But I don't think we're supposed to sleep together."

"Who said anything about—" He stepped back, staring. What a way to kill the mood. "According to who?"

"Me. My instincts." Her face was full of aggravating innocence and insight, which had no business getting mixed up together as far as Wyatt was concerned. And she spoke too damned matter-of-factly. "I just thought you should know, in case that's all you're interested in."

"In case..." He didn't know what to do with his hands, so he clamped them under his armpits, arms crossed over his chest, and scowled. He took some satisfaction in the fact that he was looking down at her. "Who are you trying to kid, lady? And who the hell are you *supposed* to sleep with?"

"The kiss was nice. I liked it. I'd even like another one."

"Yeah, well, I don't give them out to be analyzed."

"I wasn't analyzing. I just had this feeling that inside your head you had me half undressed, and I thought you might want to know that..."

Was that a patronizing smile? Another kiss would take care of that. But it wasn't cold enough, and this wasn't hell. He was still in North Dakota, right? Where men were men and...

"...it's not supposed to happen. It would ruin our friendship."

"What friendship?" He was looking for a woman, not a friend.

"I think we might complement each other quite well, if you got your priorities straight. I think we could learn a lot from each other." *About each other,* she amended. About all the stops and how ripping them out would strip the magic away.

They stood toe-to-toe, and he was bristling. "There's nothing wrong with my priorities."

"We can talk about that another time. You're not ready for an honest discussion of—"

"I'm not ready for—"

She laid her hand on his arm. "There, you see how much energy flows through this place? You're fairly bursting with it."

"You *are* a crazy lady, you know that? People don't talk to people the way you do right off the bat. People don't just assume..." He groped for the words. "They don't just *tell* somebody..."

"I do. It makes more sense." Her hand slid away, and her smile—oh, that smile was a cute touch, he thought. "But things could change. Those feelings don't always turn out to be right." She tipped her head like a curious cat. "You have a stiff neck, don't you? I could help you with that."

"How?"

"With a fifteen-minute massage. You'll forget where the pain even was."

"No thanks." He started up the hill, figuring there must be a diagonal shortcut back to the house. Back to his car. "I think you'd better keep your hands to yourself, as long as we're just going to be friends."

"There, you see." He could hear her marching up behind him in the grass. The little skips she had to take to catch up to him gave him a *real* surge of energy. "Your priorities are a mess," she insisted. "Do you like to play *Sorry?*"

He spared her a glance. "Is that what this is?"

"No, you know, the game."

"I hate games." He took long strides.

She took quick ones. "I've got others. How about Chinese checkers?"

Wyatt had turned down her offer of a last cup of coffee before he left, but he did accept the leftover pie. He'd said nothing more about the kiss they'd shared, and she was glad. It was soft and sweet, and it had made her feel the way Teri had sounded when she spoke of John. A kiss to take a woman's breath away and make her forget all she'd ever learned about taking care of her heart. Maybe she'd been too quick to set him straight, but Wyatt Archer was certainly more in need of a massage than sex. He was barreling right past life's roses. He was in no shape to ap-

preciate what she had to offer a man, and she had stopped
casting pearls before swine some time ago, figuratively
speaking.

Literally, the man was not swine. Chauvinistic, maybe.
Spiritually impoverished, definitely. And, like most men,
he was driven to win, even when there was no contest. He
really wasn't ready for her.

But his time was coming. He was on the brink of en-
lightenment. She could feel it.

Teri's call came just before Lavender went to bed that
night, and she could tell by Teri's hushed tone that the girl
had waited until the house was dark and quiet before she'd
gone to the phone.

"I had a problem with John tonight," Teri confided.

Lavender sat in the middle of her big round water bed
and poised the nail clipper over her big toe. "What kind
of problem?"

"We went to Brinker's for a Coke, and we saw Heidi
and Kirby and Mark, and we were just talking, you know,
joking around. All of a sudden John got mad and dragged
me away. He said I was flirting with Mark. Mark Christian, of all people! He's way shorter than I am."

Imagining the scene, Lavender set the clipper aside.
"Did John hurt you, Teri?"

"Oh, no. He wouldn't do that." There was silence, then
a small sigh. "Well, he pulled me by the arm, kind of
rough."

"What did you do?"

"I jerked away, but I went with him, and I tried to tell
him he was being ridiculous. He yelled at me, and that's
not like him." More silence. Lavender waited. Finally, a
small voice shared the fear. "I thought he was going to hit
me."

"Did he?"

''No. It was like he was having a hard time controlling himself. Then he just walked away. I went after him, but he wouldn't get in the car. He told me to leave him alone.''

''Good advice. Did you take it?''

''Yes. I didn't want to, but I did.'' Lavender heard the anguish in the girl's tear-thickened voice. ''I don't want him to be mad at me, Lavender. I must have made him think—''

''You didn't make him think anything, honey. His thoughts are his own. Had he been drinking? Do you think he was high on anything?''

''No!'' It was female defense so pure, quick and automatic that it made Lavender's stomach tighten. She'd counseled against it, but there had been times when she'd practiced it herself. Those times had not been good. ''John is a wrestler. He would not jeopardize—''

''This isn't Coach Archer you're talking to, Teri. This is Lavender.''

''He wasn't drinking. I think he's just pushing himself too hard. I think he's tired.''

''You won't let him take it out on you, will you?''

When she heard a soft, tentative ''no,'' she knew Teri wasn't going to risk losing a boyfriend, either.

''Let's encourage John to talk to Mr. Archer. As long as John isn't breaking the rules, I think he's the man who could help.''

''Okay.''

''Can you stay for supper tomorrow? I've got apples, any way you want them.''

''Sure.'' Sniff. ''Thanks a lot, Lavender.''

''See you tomorrow.''

Chapter 4

Glover should have won its meet against Alma High School, particularly on home turf. Alma was strong, but Glover should have outclassed them. Lavender found herself mentally withdrawing from the hyped-up hometown crowd and simply watching the way each Glover wrestler met his challenger. Those who had been on the team the previous season had learned a lot since then. They had more moves. Some of them had newfound control, and those boys won their matches. But there was a kind of desperation in some of the boys' eyes that bothered Lavender. She wasn't sure why. They looked so eager, but the eagerness seemed to turn into an almost unnatural urgency, and their timing was off. Their control was not tight, and the points slipped away.

It was the first time she'd seen John Tiger wrestle, and even though he had all the right moves, Lavender could feel his defeat coming. His match came toward the end of the close-scoring meet. Teri's confident cheers rang in

Lavender's left ear. "Lookin' good, John. Oh, yes! Lookin' great."

He was looking strong, certainly. He was looking to Wyatt, who knelt beside the mat and offered encouragement. But there was something about the way he approached his opponent, the way he stole those uneasy glances, that told Lavender what the outcome of the match would be. Not that she understood the dynamics of the sport that well, but she understood body language, and John Tiger's was saying, "This isn't my night."

The pin came with John two points in the lead. The blond boy in the green-and-gold singlet mounted a desperate charge. John hesitated just long enough to lose control of his center of gravity, and he went down under a half nelson, the most elemental of pinning holds. It was as though for a moment John had gone to sleep. Rather than look away from the hold and free his head, he gave his opponent the leverage to turn him on his back and pin his shoulders against the mat.

Wyatt hid his disappointment well as he consoled John with a pat on the shoulder and turned his attention to the upcoming 185-pound match. He didn't even glance at the scoreboard when the six points were added under "Visitors." On the floor he maintained a cool head—unlike Alma's red-faced, spit-spewing head coach, who was a good candidate for a stroke. Win or lose, Lavender had to hand it to him; Wyatt modeled marvelous sportsmanship.

"Some of you guys were *asleep* out there. You let a bunch of scrawny little *sissies* beat the *pants* off you." Wyatt didn't have to raise his voice in the locker room. His deep tone and the dark chill in his eyes were menacing enough. "How does it feel? Huh? How does it feel to get beat by a bunch of..."

He almost said *winyans*. Girls. Old Uncle Roscoe's favorite way to shame a guy if he ran from a fight or let any tears show. Call him a *winyan*. You couldn't say that anymore, though, not even in the boys' locker room. Women got all huffy over slips like that, and the Glover school board was more than half female. There was a whole list of words he had to be careful not to use if he didn't want to get on the wrong side of the school board in this town. But this sorry-looking bench full of dejected boys deserved to be hanging their heads, and he groped to find the words that would keep them humble. Hair sticking out at all angles from sweating under the protective headgear, shoelaces dragging, elbows planted on their knees and shoulders sagging, they were looking like losers. That look was what angered Wyatt the most.

He paced. He wanted to walk out and leave them to their self-pity, but this was his team. They were young and impressionable, and he was determined to make an impression. There was humility, and there was *humiliation*. Alma had handed them the latter.

"They were just a bunch of farm boys," Wyatt said disgustedly. Hoss Sandland glared at him. Wyatt could hear the school-board president now, but the gauntlet was down. "What's wrong, Sandland?"

"My dad has milk cows. Does that make me a farm boy?"

Maybe *winyan* would have been a better choice. "Yeah, it does. Where I come from, everybody knows you get a big farm boy on his back, he's just like a turtle."

"He didn't get me on my back. He got me on points. I ain't no turtle."

"Glad to hear it. Stand up for who you are, Hoss. You've been throwing bales all your life, and it's put some muscle on you. But all that milk and potatoes you've been putting away is slowing you down." Wyatt tossed Hoss a towel. The boy caught one end and whipped the other over his shoulder, as if to punish himself.

Wyatt continued dutifully. "Alma is not that good a team. You keep letting yourselves get beat by second-class acts like that and you can kiss the state tournament good-bye. Now go wash off that stink of defeat and go home to your disappointed families. They'll probably say stuff like, 'You gave it a good try.' Don't believe it for a minute. We know damn well we could have done better. Come Monday, you can plan on a workout you won't believe, either."

He didn't hear much chatter in the showers. He sat on the desk in the instructor's office and went over the score book. They didn't waste much time. By twos and threes the boys soon shuffled on their way, slick wet heads still hanging. Their mumbled farewells were polite acknowledgments that the coach was still the coach.

"'Night, Coach."

"See you Monday, Coach."

Beyond the locker-room door there were other voices fading out the side door of the gym and into the night, leaving, finally, only John Tiger in the locker room with Wyatt. He'd been the last to shower, and he'd dressed with the slow deliberation of one who had just learned about buttons and shoelaces. It was as though the boy felt he hadn't gotten his full share of comeuppance. Wyatt stood there with his hands in his pants pockets, watching John pack his wrestling shoes in a battered duffel bag.

Nobody expected an Indian kid to be able to wrestle. He was supposed to ride bucking stock or shoot buckets on the elementary school playground. And he was supposed to hang his head all the time, the way John was doing now.

There was humility and there was humiliation. Not looking an elder in the eye was a sign of proper humility. Losing out because losing had become a way of life... damn it, that was humiliation. John had to learn the difference before it was too late.

Wyatt stepped closer to the bench as John zipped his duffel bag. "What happened out there, John?" he asked.

John straightened slowly. "I blew the match."

"I saw that. I want to know why."

The big boy in the letterman's jacket shrugged. "I don't know."

"Try again."

John injected more volume, as if he thought Wyatt hadn't heard. "I don't know." He snatched the duffel bag off the bench and fidgeted with the handles, still refusing to look at his coach. "That guy was good."

"Not that good. You're stronger. You're faster. But you were doing the same thing with him you did with me." It was time to see what kind of backbone the kid had going for him. Wyatt knew it was there somewhere. John had grown up on the reservation. He had to have some sass in him.

"Excuse me," Wyatt mocked. He swaggered a little, hands on his hips, challenging John's defensive stance. "I'm here to wrestle. I mean, I *think* that's what we're supposed to be doing here, but I don't want to step on any toes. Would you mind if I went for a snatch and dumped you for the takedown now, or would that bother you? How about a lateral drop? I could flip you over like a pancake, but would a pin inconvenience you right off the bat like that?"

John lifted his chin, and his eyes narrowed slightly. "I wouldn't say stuff like that."

"Maybe not with your mouth, John. You said it with your eyes. Your body. You let that guy pin you. You rolled over on your back for that boy. At least four different times you could have had him, easy, but instead you played with him a little. Then you gave him a pin. You *gave* them six points."

"I didn't *give*—"

"You *did*. Were you feeling like a big Indian? Huh, John? Kid from the rez playing the white boys' game by the white boys' rules?"

"No!"

"I taught you your *own* game. You didn't use it." A spark flashed in John's eyes. Good sign. Wyatt pressed. "There's nothing wrong with your strength or your speed or your skill. It's your attitude. You're thinking like a second-class citizen, backing off, letting a guy with half your talent show you up."

"I'm not thinking like that. I'm just as good as—"

"Better! You *have* to be *better*. You have to work harder to prove yourself."

"To who? To you?"

"To *them*. And to yourself. I know you can be good, Tiger. You've got everything it takes except . . ."

John was ready to fight now. "Except what?"

"I don't know whether you've got the heart." Wyatt waited for John to make a claim, but none came. The boy stood there, isolating himself inside his own head, peering out at the man who could make the decision for him. Heart. No heart. He wanted Wyatt to call it for him.

"I'm not God," Wyatt said quietly. "I'm just a coach."

A silent moment passed between them.

"Can I go now?"

Wyatt nodded. He hadn't told the boy to stay. He had one last offer before John reached the door. "Six a.m. every morning, I'm here in the gym for a workout."

John stopped and took a moment to put together an attitude. He even managed a sneer. "So what does that make you? Supercoach?"

"Kirby's been coming over. So's Donny."

"Good for them."

"The door's open for you, too."

"Ally's right. You oughta get a life."

Defiance was better than defeat in Wyatt's book. He could turn defiance into determination. He slung his jacket over his shoulder and followed John into the gym. The janitor was collapsing the wooden bleachers back into place against the wall, and the clank-click-clank of the mechanism echoed in the rafters.

Teri was waiting across the floor, next to the far door. Wyatt watched John home in on her, as though her arms were open for him. She spoke to him, he nodded in response and pushed the side door open for her.

Wallow in female sympathy tonight, kid, Wyatt thought. *Tomorrow you make up your mind whether you've got it in you to be a wrestler.*

"Do you have time for a cup of coffee?"

Wyatt started and turned toward the sound of the familiar voice. Lavender had been waiting, too, on the bleachers closest to the locker-room door, about seven rows up. She descended now, tripping lightly from bench to bench as only a slender sprite could do. Her voluminous woven coat trailed behind her like a silver blue billow of smoke.

She smiled as she hopped from the lowest bench to the shiny wood floor. "Actually, I need a ride home. I let Teri take my car, because she didn't want to go home with her mother, because then she wouldn't get to see John...and you know how those things go."

Wyatt slipped one arm into his leather jacket. "Not really. If I lived fifteen miles outside of town, I don't think I'd let somebody take my car, even if I did have the urge to play Cupid."

"John needs a friend right now." She resisted the temptation to add *so do you,* but reached up to turn his jacket collar out for him because it was something a friend would do. "Besides, I thought I could tempt you with the promise of apple pie."

"Guess I could use a little comfort food, too." He wasn't going to say *friend.* No way. Company, maybe. And as long as she seemed to be offering and no one else was looking, he might enjoy some of that female sympathy. He could easily get lost in those big blue eyes. "We shouldn't have lost this one."

"It was close," Lavender offered.

"Close doesn't count in my book."

He spoke little during the twenty-minute drive to her house. He appreciated the fact that she let him be silent, but that she was there. That surprised him. When he felt down, he usually preferred to compound it with feeling lonesome, too. But he was glad she'd waited for him. He figured she had her reasons, and if he asked, she would probably tell him. He wasn't going to ask. He was just going to let it be. The road was dark and quiet, and it invited him to play the match out again in the spotlight of his car's headlamps. The silence between them was comfortable.

The schoolhouse was comfortable, too. There were accessible places to hang your jacket and sit and put your feet up. Even before she made coffee and heated up the pie, pleasant scents pervaded. Wyatt figured it must be the

little bunches of dried plants that filled containers here
and there and dotted the rafters. He was half tempted to
ask her what the stuff was. The scent gave the place char-
acter, which was something his own apartment lacked. He
decorated in black and white.

He added a couple of logs to the still glowing embers in
the woodstove and ignited a flame with a few puffs from
a handy bellows. He associated woodstoves with a lack of
central heating, but he knew that wasn't Lavender's
problem. She would be the type who preached about al-
ternative energy sources. Still, he was finding the whole
scene pretty homey and the memories it conjured unusually welcome.

Lavender served up dessert and sat near him on the
sectional sofa. She tucked her bare feet to the side and
covered them with her heather-tone skirt. He watched her
take bird bites from her pie, while he devoured his. Every
time she tossed that mass of honeyed hair behind her
shoulder he saw his own fingers brushing it back against
a white pillowcase. The image prompted him to uncross
his booted ankles on the hassock, shift a little and cross
them again in her direction.

She set her plate of half-eaten pie on the floor and
turned to him, propping one elbow on the sofa's backrest
and signaling time to talk. "I'm a little worried about the
desperation I saw in some of the boys' eyes tonight. It almost didn't look . . . natural."

He'd been watching arms and legs rather than eyes, but
he thought he knew the look she meant. "It isn't natural.
It's an acquired taste. You learn to want success. You get
a taste, you hear yourself called the winner, and you start
thinking like a winner. You're hungry for it." Jasper
popped his head above the hassock. Wyatt returned the
cat's glance—sort of a mutual male acknowledgment—

then continued. "That's what you see in their eyes. Hunger for more of that sweet taste of victory. They have to learn to control it better, though. Use it to their advantage."

"Maybe," she said, unconvinced.

"They were trying too hard," he decided. "Sometimes you want it so bad, you lose sight of what you have to do to get it."

"And you do whatever you have to do to win?"

"Well, you follow the rules." He looked at her pointedly. "There are rules for every game. It's not a real victory unless you're playing by the rules." He smiled slowly. "Even if somebody else is making them up as she goes along."

She wasn't buying it, but she was smiling. "You know, I truly believe there's a real human being inside you somewhere, just dying for a chance to come forth and shine."

Hell of a generous break, just when he was getting comfortable. "That's *truly* flattering."

"I mean it. I think you know there's more to life than acquiring trophies." She tapped her forefinger against his chest. He had to glance down, just to make sure. "Somewhere, deep down inside."

He looked up, and she retracted her advance. "Well, I'm keeping that secret to myself, which means you asked the wrong man to give you a ride home. Because in practice, lady, I'm looking for those trophies. In the real world, everybody wants to see your trophy case." She looked doubtful, and he shook his head. "You don't live in the real world."

"I don't?"

"Nah." The cat was nosing around her plate on the floor. He hated to see that pie go to a cat, but Lavender did nothing to shoo him away.

"Where do I live, then?"

"You're kind of an artist, and artists don't live in the real world. Look at this." He gestured toward the rafters. "You live in a schoolhouse. You don't have to deal with people because you do your own thing and people like it, so they buy it. You're an artist." He laid his hand on the handwoven skirt that covered her knee. "I'm not an artist. I can't make my trophies. I have to win them."

He could have sworn his hand was going unnoticed.

"Who do you have to impress?"

"The people I work for. The people I might *want* to work for." The woman he wanted to get closer to for the duration of his sojourn in Glover, North Dakota.

"Aren't you a good teacher?" she asked.

"Yeah." He swept his thumb slowly over the nubbly fabric. "Yeah, I'm a good teacher, but that's not enough. I'm a good coach, too. I was a good wrestler."

"I understand you still are." He liked the sound of that. The clink of fork against plate drew her attention to the floor, and she clucked to the cat. Apparently she wasn't one to refuse a little nibble. "The boys on the team are really the competitors, right? You're there to show them how. Then you stand back, and you let them enjoy the sport."

"They don't have much fun if they lose. You saw John Tiger tonight. He didn't feel too good about blowing a match that he should have taken easily." The hand on her knee became a fist as he forgot about his own advance and remembered John standing next to the bench, hanging his head. "He's got so much raw talent, so much . . ."

"Are you riding him harder than the other boys?"

"Hell, no. Is somebody complaining?"

"Hell, no," Lavender echoed saucily.

"The girlfriend, huh?" Wyatt chuckled as he wagged his head at himself as much as at the thought of John. "Women can make you soft."

She squared her shoulders and lifted her chin. "That's the most sexist comment—"

"Sometimes you don't mind taking a little time out for soft," he assured her. "But if you start feeling sorry for yourself, you're done."

"Done with what?"

"You've lost your shot. If John Tiger works at his sport, it could pay his way through college. If he doesn't, it could become a flash of glory that he recounts five, ten years down the road, while he's passing the bottle with his beer-bellied buddies."

"That sounds..." she scooted a little closer, as though she needed to physically help him put this into perspective "...like a caricature, Wyatt. Why would you think—"

"Because I know it, and so does John." And pretty, blue-eyed Lavender Holland hadn't a clue. He didn't ask himself why it was up to him to give her one. "There are a lot of *real human beings* who had one shot—*one* shot— but they didn't see it for what it was, so they let it pass them by."

"People get more than one shot."

"Some people, maybe." She would, if she wanted it. She didn't have to get it right the first time. And he really didn't want to get into this with her, but she had some influence where John was concerned, at least indirectly. And, surprisingly, her naïveté galled him. "Some don't even get that. Depends on who you are."

"John Tiger lost one match, Wyatt. If you let him think that's all—"

"He *blew* the match, and he knows it. Lost his confidence and let that kid walk all over him." She was ready to object, but he cut her off. "John's strong. Do you see how strong that kid is? He's so close, but he doesn't see himself there yet. You've got to be able to see yourself there, you know what I mean? You've got to visualize it."

"I do know what you mean." He doubted that, and it showed. "Really, I do," she insisted. "I practice yoga."

"You mean you visualize yourself..."

"Yes. I visualize. It brings me inner peace."

"I don't know about yoga, but visualizing brings me confidence." This newfound common ground was encouraging. He believed strongly in envisioning an achievement. He'd built a career doing it. "You need confidence, you know? You need to believe in yourself."

"John Tiger believes very strongly in you."

"He's gotta believe in John Tiger."

"He will. He's a teenager, Wyatt. Do you remember what that was like?"

"Yeah, I remember." He tipped his head back and grinned at the ceiling. "You can't look at a girl without breaking out in a cold sweat. If you work up the nerve to try to talk to her, your voice cracks."

"And if you're a teenage girl, you're dying to hear that voice, and you don't hear that little warble, because you're trying to control that stupid giggle that always creeps up on you when you're nervous." He laughed appreciatively. "And you're living on french fries and orange pop, even though you've heard junk food causes pimples." She put her hand on his arm, and he glanced down, noticing the contrast between his tan sweater and her pale skin. "You know, maybe John isn't eating right," she suggested, as though the possibility had just occurred to her.

He sat up, frowning. "Hey, I stress diet. We talk about food groups, and how many servings they need from each group every day, how much water, all that. If I think they're cheating, I make them tell me what they've eaten that day."

"But you don't see them actually eat it."

He shrugged that off. "You can just tell. Besides, they're too big to be spoon-fed."

"Teenagers are apt to take shortcuts," she said. "They're impatient for results, so they'll ignore your best advice in favor of the fastest—".

She hadn't *just* thought this up. "I get the feeling you know something I don't know."

"I think some of the boys on your team . . ." She fidgeted, as though her feet had gone to sleep under her fanny. What she'd really been sitting on was a confidence, and it was jabbing at her. "Maybe they just aren't eating right. Maybe they're starving themselves before a meet, trying to get last-minute energy from a sugar fix."

"They know better."

"I used to be a social worker." She gave the sigh and the openhanded gesture of one owning up to a bad habit. "In another life. I worked with lots of kids. They don't think any of the warnings apply to them."

"Who? John Tiger?"

"I didn't say—"

Wyatt offered an indulgent smile as he stretched his arm along the top of the sofa. "John's biggest problem right now is puppy love. He's thinking about the wrong kind of clinch."

"Another case of screwed-up priorities?"

"For a kid, yeah." He ventured to rest his hand on her knee again, half surprised that she didn't pull away. "I'm not a kid."

"And you know exactly what you want," she said quietly.

"Pretty much." His thumb stirred. He figured with a few deft strokes he could edge that skirt up over her knee and touch her skin. Then she'd probably bolt. "But sometimes something unexpected comes along. Something that wasn't in the plans."

"And you're not quite sure where to fit it in."

He smiled, mostly at the progress his thumb was making. "I'm not totally without ideas."

"Neither am I."

"Care to compare them?"

"I think yours would pale by comparison, Wyatt Archer."

Whoa. He glanced up and got a dose of all-seeing, all-knowing woman, and he imagined the heat behind those rosy lips. He reached the bottom of the skirt, but her knee was still covered. *Damn tights.*

She almost smiled. "But, then, we're not supposed to sleep together, anyway. That leaves us with…envisioning those ideas."

"And your love of games." A tease and a half, this woman. But he enjoyed being teased. He enjoyed the starshine in her blue eyes.

"Mmm-hmm. So, how did you get interested in wrestling?"

He laughed. "You don't get *interested* in wrestling. You get taken by it. Sucked in. You get out there, and you take on somebody who thinks he's pretty tough, and it's just you and him. One on one. You beat him, and you get ready for the next guy." He gave her knee a single pat and reached for the remainder of the coffee he'd all but forgotten.

"Can I warm that up for you?"

He chuckled and sipped it cold.

"Then tell me how you got started," she coaxed.

"I was sent to a boarding school back East. Prep school, they call it there." He drained the cup, set it aside and realized that she was interested. She actually wanted to hear him talk about this stuff. "Run by a church. Real strong wrestling program."

"Who sent you there? Your parents?"

"The church sent me. A man named Edgar P. O'Connell from Worcester, Massachusetts, footed the bill for the first year."

"Friend of your family's?"

He watched her pull one leg out from under her and hook her heel over her knee. "Never laid eyes on him." Strange way to sit, he thought. The tights were dark brown. Her skirt was like drapery, and her hands, her eyes...she was waiting, listening. She wanted to know these things. He wanted to tell her.

"He had a thing about Indians, and I had a thing about getting off the reservation. Some church network matched us up. All I had to do was write a letter and send a picture. Small enough request, right?"

"I don't know," she said. "Was it?"

"I had to write the letter three different times. Everybody had a say—the school counselor, the priest, the English teacher. They wanted me to tell this guy how, uh...how anxious I was to better myself, and how generous his offer was. So that's what I wrote."

"Whatever it took?" she asked.

"Yeah. I gave him a nice star for his crown." He glanced away. "Once I got into wrestling, there were all kinds of scholarships available. And not for being a scholar, which I wasn't, or for being poor, or for being an Indian." Suddenly he wanted her to know him. Damn right. He was good. *Look at me, lady.* "For being a winner in my sport."

"I see." She brought up the other leg, bunching her skirt in the cradle her legs made. "But didn't you ever blow a match?" she wondered.

"Seldom."

"It must have happened, though."

"If it did, I made whatever changes I needed to make, and I won the next one." That capacity was the source of his strength and the essence of what he wanted her to know about him.

The tights took nothing away from the slender curve of her ankles. He wondered how much closer she would scoot to plead the case she was making for John, and he smiled. "Don't worry. I'm not going to hang Tiger out to dry. He knows where he went wrong. He'll lick his wounds tonight, and tomorrow I'll show him how to make the changes."

"That's good. It is a sport, after all. A game. I think you should share your visualizing techniques with the team. Maybe I could offer a yoga demonstration sometime."

"Sure." Wasn't that what this was? "Maybe you could bring along some tasty health food, and we could get them back on a high-performance diet."

"Apple pie?"

"No, you save that for me." Teasing her with a grin, he ran two fingers over the bottom of her upturned foot. "Okay? Nobody else gets the apple-pie treatment."

The delight that shimmered in her eyes plowed into his belly. She was a far cry from the kind of woman his imagination had him teamed up with on a permanent basis. She was hardly Miss American Pie. But she sure made him hungry.

"I have other visitors sometimes," she told him. "I'll have to serve them something."

"Give them rhubarb. I hate rhubarb."

She laughed, and he heard those sweet bells again. "The coach has all the lines here."

"This is all unrehearsed." He was petting her foot now, as though it had fur. He realized he must look as silly as she did, and he didn't really care. "Actually, I don't usually do this much talking."

"I don't usually do this much baking." She leaned closer to confide, "And I really don't have many other—"

A car slowed down out front, which, for a rural dweller, was a signal as sure as a doorbell. Wyatt straightened as Lavender unfolded her legs and hopped over the plate on the floor. Peeking out the window was an automatic response, although she could see nothing but headlamps. She knew the sound of her own car. "You'll give Teri a ride back to town, won't you? Maybe John's with her."

"I'm the last person John wants to see right now," he said, but he was thinking more about how little he wanted to see either kid right now. He shifted his hips to redistribute an ache he'd been building up.

"Well, I'm glad to see my car back this early." She swept the plate up off the floor. Jasper had cleaned it. "You worry a little when you help facilitate these things, you know?"

"Not being much of a Cupid, I guess I don't know."

Lavender met Teri at the door. The girl was agitated. "Oh, Lavender, I need your help. I'm really—"

Wyatt appeared behind Lavender's shoulder, and Teri closed her mouth and tucked her chin into her jacket. She glanced at Lavender, then Wyatt, then back to Lavender.

"What's wrong?" Lavender said gently.

"Something's wrong with John. He's..." She pressed her lips together and adjusted her coat as though Wyatt himself were a gust of wind. "Mr. Archer, he tried really hard tonight. And now he feels..."

"Where is he?" Wyatt asked.

"I don't know."

"Teri, what happened with John?" Lavender pushed the girl's hair back from her face, trying to get a closer look. "Are you okay?"

"Yes, yes, I'm fine." She offered Lavender her car keys. "He wouldn't talk to me much, so we just drove around. I thought maybe he needed some time to just cool off. He seemed so keyed up after... You know, so upset about the way..."

"The way the match went," Wyatt supplied.

Teri bristled. "You can't expect him to win every time, Mr. Archer. Nobody can win every single match."

"What happened, Teri?"

"He wasn't angry with me," the girl protested, first to Lavender, then to the man she held responsible for all this. "He wasn't. I know he wasn't, even though he sort of *acted* like..." The look in Lavender's eyes made her change her tack. "He told me to stop the car, so I did, because we were close to this place he kind of likes, and I thought..."

Teri gave her head a quick shake and tried to squeeze the quiver out of her voice. "The middle of nowhere! He just got out of the car and walked off. I tried to follow him, but he told me to go back. He shouted at me, kind of mad-like. 'Go on home,' he said, and he just disap-

peared into the darkness." Blinking furiously in a hopeless effort to stem the flow of gathering tears, she turned
to Lavender. "I was too scared to—"

"Of course you were. You did the right thing." Lavender touched Wyatt's arm. "It's too cold for him to be
left—"

Now that the story was out, Teri rushed to supply more.
"We weren't too far from the train bridge near Clausson's place. He likes to go there. He likes to climb up on
that trestle sometimes." Her mouth puckered, and a tear
finally slipped. "Lavender, I'm scared."

"Was there any drinking going on or anything?" Wyatt
demanded.

"No." Teri shook her head. "I swear. But he was pretty
upset."

Lavender reached for the coat she'd hung in the entry-
way, but she hesitated. "Maybe we ought to call the sheriff."

Wyatt was already putting his jacket on. "Let's check
out this train bridge first. It would be better if we found
him. If he thinks the law is after him, he'll hide. Let's take
your car in case we need . . . more space."

Lavender handed Wyatt her keys. "I hate driving at
night," she explained.

"He hasn't done anything wrong," Teri insisted.

"No, but it sounds as though he's in trouble, honey."
Lavender put a hand on Teri's shoulder as they followed
Wyatt to Lavender's car. "And if he's not, at least we'll
know he's okay, and he'll know we meant well."

The narrow county road was deserted. The headlights
played cat-and-mouse with patches of road-hugging fog.
Lavender directed Wyatt, while Teri sat quietly in the back
seat, wishing he would drive faster.

They parked the car on a gravel approach and left the emergency flashers blinking. Lavender grabbed a flashlight from the glove compartment, but Wyatt told her to keep it off. "We'll be better off to let our eyes adjust to the dark."

He pushed two lower strands of barbed wire to the ground beneath his boot and stretched the top two upward, allowing the women to pass through the right-of-way fence. Bright moonlight made a dark but distinguishable shadow of the train bridge, a quarter of a mile away. Shoulder to shoulder, they swished through the tall, dry grass. Wyatt had always loved the prairie on nights such as this. A dearth of living sounds this time of year. Dark. Endless. Barren. You had to feel your way along. If you wanted to disappear out there, no one could stop you.

"He brought me out here in the daytime," Teri said, her voice an intrusion in the vast silence. "Not at night."

"What does he like about it?" Wyatt asked.

"The stream cuts a deep gorge. I think he likes heights. He's such a daredevil. He likes to climb on the scaffolding and..." Teri drew a shaky breath "...kind of play chicken with the train."

"And show off for his girl," Wyatt offered. "I remember those days."

Lavender took Wyatt's cue. Teri needed reassurance. "Without an audience, he probably wouldn't—"

"Shh, listen." The three stopped and stood still. "I thought I heard something. John?" Wyatt took a few steps, tentatively now. The ground sloped only slightly, but he knew the drop-off was just ahead. "John, are you out here? We just want to take you home, okay?"

This time they all heard it. A groan. A faint sound, but for those who searched it filled the night. They stumbled down the steep slope beneath the bridge with Wyatt in the lead.

"John? Answer me, son. Are you hurt?"

Another soft groan gave him direction. He glanced back, assuring himself that the women were with him, and he skittered down, down the embankment, deeper into the shadows below the bridge. Nothing moved. Nothing called attention to itself, but a sense of urgency drew him down.

He nearly tripped over the crumpled body.

Chapter 5

"We can't move him," Wyatt warned as he spread his jacket carefully over John's upper body.

Lavender handed Wyatt the flashlight and took off her long coat to add to Wyatt's jacket. John made another small, desperate sound, which seemed to cause him pain simply in the making.

Teri dropped to her hands and knees and hovered near the boy's head, muttering his name.

Wyatt flashed the light over John's bruised face and then beneath their makeshift covers, looking for blood.

"I'll go over to Clausson's and call for help," Lavender said. "It isn't too far."

"Tell the sheriff to bring a signal light and call for a rescue helicopter. There's no way—"

"He won't die," Teri moaned. "He can't die."

The girl's whining chilled Wyatt worse than the autumn air. "Take her with you."

"I'm sending her back with emergency equipment from my car. Blankets and signal flares." Lavender took Teri by the shoulders and helped her to her feet, speaking gently. "Teri, you come with me. We have to work fast."

"Take this," Wyatt said, and he handed Lavender the flashlight, sweeping its small beam above their heads. "You know where we are now. Don't get turned around in the dark."

"We'll be right back."

"Watch out for gopher holes!" he called out. The prairie was deceptive at night, but he knew it was no use telling them not to run. He strained to keep track of the swish of their retreating footsteps.

If it were him, he would run. He'd sprint across the flat as though the devil were on his tail. He'd sooner have run the original marathon than sit there next to that broken boy and maybe watch him die. He tried to remember all the first aid he'd ever learned, but his mind was a jumble.

"John?" He cleared his throat and made himself sound like *the coach*. "John, can you hear me? Can you tell me where you hurt the most?"

"M-m-m . . ."

Thank God. "That's good, son." He wanted to reassure the boy with a touch, but where? "Talk to me, okay? Where does it hurt?"

"Ev . . . ery . . . where."

"Good." Wyatt tipped his head back and sighed. The bridge was an ominous black thing etched against the night sky, high above them. Forty-, fifty-foot drop, maybe. "Hurting is better than numb," he whispered.

"Coach?"

"I'm here." Grateful just to hear the word, Wyatt touched the boy's hair. He found a patch of warm stickiness, and he searched for the source. "Does your head hurt?"

"Mmm . . . hurts."

"Pretty nice goose egg in the nest here. You know what a hangover is like?"

"N-not me."

Wyatt's quick laugh expressed his relief. The boy still had his wits about him. "You will. I want you to keep your head still, okay? Don't move your head at all."

"Don't think I can . . . stand up, coach."

"You stay put. Nobody's looking for any escape moves right now." John whimpered painfully, and the sound pierced Wyatt's chest. "I know. I know you're hurting, son."

So do *something about it.*

What? God, how can I help him?

Wyatt touched the boy carefully. "Can you feel where my hand is now?"

"Left side." There was a quick catch in John's breath, but he clarified, "Leg."

"Can you move it just a little?" Wyatt felt little more than a twitch beneath his hand. "Great. How about now?"

"Ahhh!"

"That one hurts, huh?" He drew his hand back quickly, his heart pounding so hard he had to remind himself to stay calm, or at least sound as though he were. "Okay. It'll be okay. Just lie real still and don't go to sleep on me. If *I've* gotta stay awake, *you've* gotta stay awake."

The ground was relatively soft here. Sandy. Three feet away there was a pile of rocks. Not a ring. Just a pile. If it had been a ring . . . a circle, maybe a medicine wheel . . .

God, I let this boy down. I was too hard on him, but don't You be. Don't You let him . . .

"Don't go to sleep now, John." *Talk to him. Get a story going.* "I got hit on the head once when I was a kid. My cousin Sheldon and I were staying with my grandma, out in the country...."

"I got a...grandma," John said. His voice sounded a little stronger. "Used to have a place...out in the country."

"They all did once. Head for town once a month. The rest of the time..." They'd both been there, Wyatt thought. Different time, same damn place. End of the trail, U.S.A. "Anyway, Sheldon hit me with a rock. Blood all over hell. They hauled me to the clinic, got me stitched up, and the doctor said, 'You watch this boy. Don't let him go to sleep.' They meant for like a few hours, but Grandma kept me up all night."

He remembered all the coffee she'd made, and the way she'd kept them playing a game of three-handed Hearts until Sheldon had finally fallen asleep. It had been fun to be the center of attention, but staying awake because you had to was no easy chore.

"John? You still with me?"

"Sorry...for what I did, Coach."

"You want to tell me what you did?" Even though, God help him, he didn't want to know.

"Kinda lost it." There was a patch of near silence. Quick, shallow breathing. Then a whisper. "M-my... match."

Blew his match, Wyatt had said. Lost his shot. He'd said that to Lavender. Good God, what had he said to John? What stupid remark had he made that had hit home this hard?

"Don't worry about that. Sometimes I get too—"

"Think I lost...think I fell, Coach." Wyatt passed his hand over his face, wanting to believe. But there was pain in John's voice beyond what was physical. "I think I just...oh, God, what's happening...it's bad...I know it's bad."

"It's gonna be okay, John." To his great relief, Wyatt heard footsteps. "Here comes Teri. We'll get you some help pretty soon."

"Don't tell Teri." John tried to move his arm, but Wyatt immobilized him. "I don't wanna hurt Teri."

"Okay. Stay with me, John."

"Where's my mom?"

A mom? John had never mentioned one. "We'll call your sister," Wyatt promised.

"Find my mom, Coach."

"I will."

Teri skittered down the embankment. "He's talking!" She was nearly breathless, but the terror was gone from her voice. "Oh, thank God, he'll be okay now, won't he? If he's conscious and he's talking, he'll be okay."

"No," the boy groaned. "No, don't let her see me."

"It's dark, son. She can't—" Teri thrust a box in his hand. "Flares?"

"Yes. Put your jacket on, Mr. Archer. You're shivering. I brought blankets."

"I'm all...pinned down...my shoulders," the boy ground out. "Oh, God!"

Wyatt hadn't realized how cold he was until he tried to help with the blankets. His fingers were getting stiff. Teri spread the blankets and crooned to John that all would be well. Then she hunkered down next to him.

"Go on home, Teri," John begged. "I told you..."

"I'm staying with you." She tucked the top blanket around him carefully. "I should have stayed with you. I shouldn't have left you out here alone, John. I'm so sorry."

John groaned, shuddered, trembled, all the while muttering snatches of obscenities. The words, "Incredible Hulk," sandwiched between expletives prompted Wyatt to promise, "You don't have to be anybody but you, John. We don't need any 'Hulks' on our team. We need—"

"Half man, half monster," John muttered. "Feel like that sometimes when . . . don't know what's ha-happening . . ."

"He's going into shock. We've gotta keep him warm," Wyatt said. Teri had handed him his jacket, but he piled it back over John. "These flares will make it a lot easier for somebody to find us. Try to keep him talking while I get one going up top." He reached out to catch himself as he slipped on the scramble up the steep grade. He heard another terrible groan. "Help's coming, John. Hang in there."

Sheriff Ron Christian arrived first, with Lavender showing him the way. He set up a signal light for the helicopter. The distant churn of its blades was the sound they'd all been listening for, praying for. *Please come. Please come now.*

The helicopter brought a rush of wind, a flood of lights and a flurry of activity. Those who had kept the vigil were asked to step aside and make way for those who knew how to help. The paramedics deftly immobilized John's head and lifted him onto a stretcher in a matter of moments. Sheriff Christian volunteered to notify John's sister and to tell Teri's mother that she was going to drive up to the hospital with Lavender. There were an emergency-room nurse and an anesthesiologist on board, but Wyatt was allowed to ride to the hospital with John in the helicopter.

After midnight the hospital was a quiet place where hushed voices and footsteps echoed along shadowy corridors. Lavender and Teri were directed to the surgical floor, where Wyatt waited in a cozy seating area. A young woman was asleep on the overstuffed sofa, and a slack-jawed older man had dozed off in a corner chair. A vigil already in progress, Lavender thought, and ours has just begun. Then she saw Wyatt at the nurses' station, apparently seeking information. A nurse was shaking her head. He turned away, ready to sip from the paper cup in his hand when he realized that Lavender and Teri were there.

He came to them, and they moved away from the sleeping man and woman, not so much to avoid waking them as to keep their own concerns to themselves. For now, they were John's family.

"They just finished up in X-ray, and now they're taking him to surgery. They said they've got him stabilized, whatever that means."

"Will he be all right?" Teri asked.

"They don't know how bad it is just yet. Some bleeding. Some broken bones. He was conscious most of the time." He jerked his chin in the direction of the nurses' station. "They say that's a good sign. The sheriff's bringing his sister up here, but John keeps asking for his mother."

"Poor kid." Lavender saw the look in Teri's eyes. She wanted to be the one for whom John asked. "He knew you'd be here, honey. But, of course, he wants his mom, too."

"Well, I'm going to be here no matter what."

"Sheriff says *your* mom is pretty upset, too," Wyatt told Teri. "Worried about where you were, I guess. You probably should call her."

"I know what she's going to say."

"Wyatt's right," Lavender said. She glanced from the waiting area to the elevators, finally spotting a phone near the drinking fountain. "We might have to wait quite a while before they're able to tell us anything."

Teri wrapped her arms beneath her breasts and hugged herself. "I'm not going home until I see him, no matter what she says."

"Call," Lavender ordered.

They stood quietly for a moment, watching Teri drag her feet toward the pay phone. Lavender sighed and shook her head. "Marge Nordstrom can be a little unpredictable."

"We've met." Wyatt studied his cup for a moment. "Listen, John says he *fell* off that bridge, but I don't know...."

"You think he might have jumped?"

He looked up, his eyes hollow with weariness. "I think it's a good possibility. Why the hell else would he climb that thing at night?"

"Could you tell...had he been drinking?"

"I didn't smell anything."

She shook her head. "You weren't in any frame of mind to play detective, anyway. Teri said he was kind of a daredevil sometimes. Maybe he was just..." She gave an exaggerated shrug, letting her shoulders sag at the end. "Being a kid."

"A kid who'd just lost a—"

"Wyatt, you can't assume one loss drove that boy off a train bridge." She held up both hands in a gesture he could interpret as he would—protest or surrender. She didn't want to debate. "Right now, let's just worry about him pulling through this. There'll be plenty of time to find out what happened later."

"You're right. Of course, you're right. They'll have all kinds of test results, and we'll know...." Closing his eyes, he hung his head, a gesture that reminded her of John. "God, I hope I didn't push him too far."

"And Teri wishes she hadn't left him out there alone." She stepped closer to him and laid her hand on his arm. She had heard him talk about winners and losers, and she knew how heavily that talk weighed on his mind now. "It happened. We can't change that now. And it wasn't anything you or Teri could have predicted."

By the time Ron Christian walked in with John's sister, Marla, the other vigil had moved down to the coffee shop. Teri was now asleep on the sofa. Lavender greeted Marla, but Wyatt assumed the spokesman's role. He owed John's concerns first voice.

"He keeps asking for his mother. Have you had a chance to call her?"

The small, dark-eyed woman spoke softly. "I'm not sure where she is. She has a sister in Pierre and one up in New Town. I haven't seen Mom in a while. Neither has John. He stayed with my brother last year."

Wyatt had knocked around a lot himself as a kid. He knew how that went, and he knew how it felt to be sick or hurt and to wish you had a mother close by to hold your hand and tell you it would be okay.

"We should get hold of her somehow. He's hurt pretty bad. They're operating on him now, but the nurse over there can probably help us locate Dr. Volk from the emergency room. He can tell you more than I can."

"The sheriff—" Christian was standing behind Marla, waiting to be acknowledged. She spared him a glance, as though inviting him to corroborate. "The sheriff says he fell off that train bridge over east, near the river."

"Yeah, that's right," Wyatt said. "John wasn't able to say much. Just that he fell." With a look, John's sister and his coach shared memories and fears. How deep was the despair in John's life? Deep enough to make him another statistic in the long list of reservation lowests and worsts? "The hospital needs your signature on some papers," he said.

Marla repeated the question they'd all asked. "Will he be all right?"

"He was talking to me right along." Wyatt's sigh came from a terrible empty place in his chest. "I don't know what kind of damage there might be. It was a long drop."

"I've got kids at home. My husband can't be watching them, and I don't know anybody well enough to ask—"

"I can help," Lavender offered.

"I'll look in on him as often as I can," Wyatt promised. He knew Marla wouldn't call on Lavender. Cut off from her family, Marla thought of herself as a raisin floating in a bowl of milk at times such as this. An Indian in a white man's world. He knew that feeling, too, but they'd made choices. Nine days out of ten, there were no regrets.

"He probably won't be wrestling no more," Marla said.

"Not this season. He's got enough of a fight on his hands right now in that operating room." He gestured toward the seating area. "Have a seat and I'll get you some coffee." She stood her ground, waiting for something more. "I'll stick by him," Wyatt promised. "You try to get hold of your mother for him, but if she doesn't come . . . Well, we'll tell him something."

"She'll come," Marla said. "I'll find her, and somebody'll bring her." She chose the straight-backed chair in the corner. "I'll have coffee now."

By late morning John had been bound in leg and shoulder casts and moved into the intensive-care unit. His surgeon, Dr. Hagberg, introduced himself but kept his distance, as though he'd only allotted a minute and a half in his schedule to make his report to John's family. He judged that all "visible" damage had been repaired and that John would heal.

"Physically," Dr. Hagberg hastened to add. Wyatt and the three women stood together like a little tour group, waiting to be enlightened further. "Go home and get some rest," the doctor suggested. "It'll be twenty-four hours before that boy cares anything about who's here and who's not."

The little man in the green suit wasn't going to be able to brush Wyatt off that easily. He followed the doctor to the nurses' station.

"So, what's the *in*visible damage, Doctor?"

Hagberg turned and peered over the glasses that had slid halfway down his nose. "You're family?"

"I'm his wrestling coach. John's living with his sister, who's—"

"Wrestler, huh?" The doctor signaled the nurse, pointed to a rack and mentioned a name. Then he turned his attention to Wyatt again. "I can tell you he's out for the season, anyway. You'll be back up to see him?"

"Will he care who's here by tomorrow night?"

"I don't know. Depends on how this happened. I'm sure you've got some questions—I know *we've* got some questions—but we're all going to have to save them until his mind's a little clearer." A nurse handed him a chart. He gave it a cursory glance, then looked up at Wyatt, as though in passing. "John's lucky to be alive. Let's leave it at that for now."

Why didn't the guy just say what was on his mind? Wyatt thought better of trying to shake some straight talk out of the man as he watched him disappear down the corridor.

Lavender drove Wyatt, Teri and Marla as far as her house. It seemed as though it had been a week since Wyatt had left his car there. She was almost surprised to hear the motor kick over so easily. Teri and Marla emerged zombie-like from one car and piled into the other one. Little was said as they took their leave.

In the pink morning light Lavender watched the silver gray Toyota disappear over the rise, then pointed herself toward the wrought-iron spiral stairs that led to her loft bed. She got as far as the living room sofa, where she paused to unbuckle her shoes. The sofa pillows looked soft. The steps looked far away. She leaned over, snuggled down, drew her stockinged feet under her skirt and drifted off.

The knock came first as a distant irritation, which she managed briefly to ignore. But it wouldn't go away. Lavender groaned, sat up and glanced at the kitchen clock. She'd actually been sleeping for almost three hours, but she could have sworn she had just been on her way upstairs.

"I'm coming!" she shouted. She noted she hadn't even taken her coat off. The front door creaked, and she strode quickly toward the weaving studio, tossing her coat over the back of a kitchen chair as she passed.

"It's Wyatt," came the reply. He stood there looking a little sheepish, with his hands in the pockets of his leather jacket. "You, uh . . . got a few minutes?"

"Wyatt, for heaven's sake. You oughta be—" But the look on his face made her change her tune. "Is something wrong? Did you hear from—"

"No. John's still the same." He closed the door behind him. "I called up there."

"Why are you awake?"

"Why are you asleep?" They assessed one another for a moment, presuming answers. He glanced away. "I'm sorry. I shouldn't have come over here to bother you."

"It's no bother. I'm glad you came." She brushed her hair back from her face and offered a smile. Then she extended her hand. He stared at it for a moment, then took it, held it, made it warmer than she'd anticipated. She knew he had tried not to come to her for this. It was not his way.

"I can't shut my mind off. I needed to talk to somebody." He squeezed her hand and spoke softly, like a man ill-at-ease in the confessional. "You," he admitted. "I needed to talk to you. Lavender, I pushed him too hard. We both know he jumped off that bridge."

Chapter 6

Lavender saw the sadness in those dark hooded eyes, and she knew there was nothing to do but hold him. She slid her arms around him, underneath his open jacket, and pressed her face against the side of his neck. He hesitated for just a moment, as though he might punish himself by denying the closeness he'd come looking for, but then he enfolded her in his arms and nestled his cheek in her hair. She knew it was hard for him to expose himself this way, and she wanted to shield the most vulnerable part of him.

They stood in each other's arms and lifted one another from lonely solitude. It had been such a dark night. He drank in the scents of wood smoke and dried herbs, and she inhaled the smell of cold autumn on warm skin.

Lavender offered Wyatt no argument for his assessment of what had happened. No assurance that John was a great kid who had everything going for him, so there was no reason to assume he'd jumped off that bridge. Well, he thought, if he'd wanted happy talk, he should have known he'd knocked on the wrong door. He hadn't really known what he wanted when he'd knocked, but he knew now. He wanted to feel something besides a heartsickness too thick for words to cut through. He wanted Lavender's arms around him.

Don't let go yet, he thought when she shifted in his arms. But she didn't. She only moved closer, pressing fully against him. He was exhausted and drained, and she lent him support because he was not ready to give in to those things just yet. He felt too much, and now, as his feelings expanded even more, she helped him sustain their weight.

"I thought I'd forgotten how to pray," he said. "It's been so long."

Her breath warmed his cheek. "But you haven't, have you?"

"No." He leaned back and looked into her eyes. They were morning-soft and misty. "Do you think anyone's listening?"

"I believe so." She brushed the tuft of dark hair at his temple with her fingertips and touched the pad of her thumb to the smudge of fatigue beneath his eye. "Sit with me for a while?"

He nodded, and she led him to the sofa, where they sat for long minutes, their hands knotted together in her lap.

"John and I come from the same place," he told her finally. "The same people. Good people, mostly, who get caught up in a lot of depression because there's not much there for them. I couldn't wait to get away. And I haven't spent a whole lot of time looking back."

"Do you think you need to?"

"Sometimes." He felt something rub against his leg. Next to his knee he saw the points of two black ears. He extricated his left hand from Lavender's to reach down and greet Jasper.

Now was a good time, he thought. He put himself in the boy's place by remembering another boy in another place. "If this had happened to me, they'd have called my grandmother. She would have come. And I would have been ashamed for her to see me." He knew, because he'd thought it through, more than once. "There were times when I lived back East...you know, when I was a kid, away at school...that I felt so alone...."

"So alone that you thought about jumping off a bridge?" she finished gently.

"Something like that." That, and worse. "Wrestling gave me something to hang on to. Winning gave me a sense of pride. I got so proud I didn't want—" and this was the worst, because it made him feel so small "—didn't really want to be seen with my grandmother. She's a full-blood, and I'm...not." He turned his head to look at her, thinking he would find disgust in her eyes. Disgust for him. Because it wasn't there, and because she truly listened, he told her honestly, "You know, when you said John Tiger believed in me, I felt a little queasy about that."

"You said he had to believe in himself, which I think is true."

"I'm too damn proud." He dropped his face to his hand and rubbed the bridge of his nose. He was tired, but there was more to tell. "After the meet, I chipped away at that boy's pride because he'd let me down. I figured, if you're gonna come over on this side of the river, you'd better be ready to live up to *my* standards. We've gotta prove ourselves here." Dropping his head against the backrest, he sighed. "Oh, for what? For what?"

"Good question," Lavender said. "What are you looking for on this side of the river?"

"Respect. Security." He stared at the rafters. "The stuff you people have."

"You have those things now, but you're not content."

"I want a home and a family, like most people do." He gave her an unabashedly plaintive look. "I'm just like most people."

"In some ways. In some ways not." She laid her hand on his arm. He was still wearing his jacket, and she kneaded the leather to comfort the flesh beneath it. "You were wrong about people getting only one shot. If John pulls through this, he'll have another shot at life. Not the same kind of chance, because this changes things, but a different chance. Something he didn't plan, and you didn't plan for him."

It was probably a fair indictment, but his first instinct, still, was to stiffen his resolve. The problem was that he had no resolve. He was too damn tired. He made a half-hearted attempt to sit up, but she tightened her hold and looked earnestly into his eyes.

"You're thirty-six years old, Wyatt, and you're still not content. You're still trying to prove the same points you were making when you were John's age. You've won respect. You've won security. But what are you losing?"

He closed his eyes and let his back turn to jelly. "I'm sure as hell losing a lot of sleep lately."

"Then rest here," she said, permitting the real answer to her real question to hover where it would in his head.

"I'll be okay." He covered her hand with his. "I could really use a cup of coffee, though."

She smiled. "What was the last thing you had to eat?"

"Apple pie."

"Then my offer is coffee with food."

"Sounds like a damn good deal."

He had coffee while she made vegetable soup, and they shared a Saturday afternoon lunch. He hardly missed the meat. Lavender's whole-wheat bread tasted pretty good, and he agreed to try the tea she'd brewed from some of the dried herbs she kept hanging around the room. Still, he couldn't take his mind off John, and a call to the hospital wouldn't suffice.

"I'm going back up there," he said finally. "Just to see for myself."

Lavender nodded and took his jacket and one of her ruanas down from a hook. It was a long drive for the few short minutes they were permitted at the boy's bedside. But it was worth it to hear John's voice, feathery though it was, offer the barely coherent assurance, "Doin' okay, Coach."

When they left the hospital, each slipped an arm around the other as they walked to his car. Nothing was said when Lavender went to the driver's side. Wyatt simply handed her the keys, took the passenger seat and dimly counted traffic lights. He was asleep before he got to three.

"What were you doing out by Clausson's bridge?"

Under the pressure of her mother's interrogations, Teri could never remember all the great answers she'd thought up for such occasions. All she could think of when her mother's lips thinned and her eyes narrowed was, "Nothing."

"At that time of night." Marge planted her hands on hips that were cocked first to the left, then shifted right. "With *that* boy."

"It wasn't that late, Mom."

Drake Starky stepped out of the shadows where he'd been lurking, just beyond the kitchen doorway. He crushed a silver beer can between his palms as he toed the lever that popped the lid on the trash can. "That's not what the woman's asking you. What were you doing out with that Indian boy?"

Quick anger made Teri's face feel hot. "You are not my father."

Marge folded her arms beneath her breasts. "Well, *I'm* your mother, and I want an answer." She took a step to the side, putting her closer to Starky, who was going after another cold beer.

"We're friends." Teri flinched when the refrigerator door whacked shut, but she stood her ground. "Mom, John's lying up there in that hospital bed, maybe dying, and all you can think about is—"

"Your reputation, which is something you seem to have forgotten all about." The metallic whisper of Starky's pop top punctuated the rising tide of Marge's ire. "Was he drunk? Huh?" She allowed Teri half a second to reply. "Answer me, Teri. People don't just fall off bridges in the middle of the night."

"He wasn't drinking at all."

"Then he must have—"

Oh, God... "I don't know how it happened! I just know John's hurt."

Marge scowled a moment longer. Starky offered her his beer, and she sipped, grimaced and shook her head as she handed it back to him. "I feel bad about that. Really. He's just a kid, and he *was* a good wrestler. But I don't know what gave you the idea you could go out with him."

"Mom..."

"Except that that *Lavender Holland* let you use her car." Marge made Lavender's name sound like a reason to buy a disinfectant. She opened the refrigerator and passed over Starky's beer for her own brand. One with fewer calories. Eyeing her daughter suspiciously, she opened the can. "Did that woman arrange this little match?"

"Would you *please*..." Teri cast about in her head for a possible diversion. "Ally told me *you* were flirting with—"

Suddenly Ally was standing in the doorway. Starky, his stubbled chin jutting out like a pointer's muzzle, waited for the name. Teri clamped her jaw tightly. "Flirting with who?" Starky demanded.

"Never mind," Teri said quietly.

Starky turned to Ally. "Who was she flirting with? That new coach? She's been sniffing after that new coach, hasn't she?"

"Yeah, kind of," Ally admitted with a shrug.

"Talk about letting your reputation go to hell." Bracing his arm on the doorjamb, Starky confronted Marge. It was as if Teri's face had been suddenly relieved of the heat of a spotlight, but she took little satisfaction in the way Starky was able to make her mother squirm. "You want me to leave?" he bawled in Marge's face.

"No," Marge snapped back. "I'm not lookin' for you to leave."

"Because I can be outta here—" he snapped his finger in front of her nose "—just like that."

Marge wagged her finger at her son. "Ally, that's ridiculous. The coach—what's his name? Archer? He broke up that party she had for Teri, and I wanted to make sure she wasn't up to any of her crazy voodoo with you kids. So I asked him about it. That's all."

Teri was quick to defend her friend. "She doesn't practice voodoo or anything of the kind. She's very... centered." She glared at Starky. "You wouldn't understand that, but she is."

"Centered?" Marge countered. "If she's centered, then I'm—"

"Are we going bowling or not?" Starky took a long pull on his beer before looking to Marge for an answer.

"It's Saturday," Marge told Teri. "My day to go out and enjoy myself. I'm not going to have to worry about what kind of mess you might be getting yourself into while I'm not looking, so you are grounded, girl. You're not using the car. You're not going to Lavender's *den*." She allowed a pause for effect. "And you are *not* going to Bismarck, because you..." She had to think for a moment. She had a reason somewhere. "You have things to do here. Get your room cleaned up, for one thing."

Her room *was* clean. Watching her mother leave the house with that stubby little bug-eyed boyfriend of hers made Teri's eyes burn. John had almost died a few hours ago. Couldn't her mother understand how scary that was?

"So did he jump or what?"

Teri turned to her brother, who'd brought a glass of milk and a package of Oreos into the living room and dropped himself into Drake Starky's favorite slipcovered easy chair. "That's a very good question, Ally. What do you think?"

"How should I know? Crazy Indian, he probably did." Ally grinned. His teeth were caked with Oreos. "The flying Tiger."

"It's those pills, isn't it?"

"What pills?"

The idea had just occurred to her, and Ally's mock-innocent expression struck her as a confirmation. She'd heard the boys talking about something they were taking to build muscle, and when she'd asked John if they were vitamins, he'd been evasive. But she'd heard him tell Ally once that he was out of "muscle makers." She'd told herself that Ally was the team manager, and they'd probably latched onto some kind of super vitamin. He was her brother, and she'd never known him to do anything really...

The look on his face made her feel a little sick.

"I know he's been getting some kind of drugs from you," she ventured, baiting him. She didn't know. She hadn't *wanted* to know. Now she had to put the pieces together. "He's not the only one, either. John and Mark and—"

"What are you talkin' about? You mean the 'roids? Hey, they help build muscles, is all. They're not drugs— not like, *drugs.*"

"Of course they're drugs." She wasn't sure what he was talking about, but she wanted him to think she was. "When is a drug not a drug, Ally? What else do they do to people? Do they make them act any different? Because if they do..."

He gestured innocently, cookie in hand. "They don't do anything but build muscle, but the FDA controls them just like everything else because drug companies can make more money if they—"

"Who's been telling you all this?"

"Anabolic steroids are perfectly safe." Ally straightened up a little and brushed a few crumbs off the moose that graced his T-shirt. "Otherwise they wouldn't treat diseases and stuff with them, and in a lot of countries you can just walk into a drugstore and buy them."

She folded her arms and stood fast, trying to hold on to herself, trying to appear more self-assured than she felt. "Obviously not in this country, so where are *you* getting them?"

"That's not your business, Teri. And you'd better keep your mouth shut about it, or you could cause a lot of trouble for your friends, not to mention your brother."

He reached into the bag for another cookie, and she wanted to snatch the package away from him and hold them hostage until he told the truth, the way they had when they were younger. But this wasn't some silly escapade of his, even though he didn't want to admit it. Maybe she should just slam the lid back on this can of worms and hope it would all go away.

Ally dunked the cookie in his glass of milk and let it drip on his jeans while he gave her that innocent look again. "They're safe, I'm tellin' you. They're just not that easy to come by."

"Maybe I should find out just how safe these—"

"Just keep your nose out of it, okay? Your boyfriend was just bummed out over losing a match, breaking his winning streak." He waved the whole matter away with his dripping cookie. "Indians are touchy about a lot of things, you know? They can't handle pressure like us white guys can."

"You sound like Mom."

"It's not that I've got anything against Indians, Teri. You know me. Maybe I'll even go up and look in on him after a few days, see how he's doing."

"Why? You couldn't care less whether he lives or dies."

"Go on, you're makin' a big federal case. I like ol' Tiger. I tried to help him out because he really wanted to show the coach what he could do." He finally popped the soggy cookie into his mouth and talked around it in a revolting way that only Ally could manage. "And he was lookin' real good. Those 'roids work nice. But it's just like Coach says, you've gotta have that winning attitude."

"Does Mr. Archer know about these . . . these anabolic steroids?" Ally gave her a get-outta-here look. "I didn't think so. They'd all be kicked off the team, wouldn't they? Whoever's taking them. Just like for drinking or smoking."

"Well, you know, they've got different penalties for—"

"What about you, Ally?" she challenged, closing in on him. "Couldn't you get arrested for this?"

He laughed and shook his head. "You're turning out to be a real narc. My own sister."

"I'm not. I just don't want you to get in trouble." It was true. Her head was spinning with facts that weren't facts, drugs that weren't drugs, and loyalties that had to be put into some kind of order.

She sank into a big brown corduroy beanbag chair and hugged her knees. "You should have seen him, Ally. Lying there in the dark like that. He was suffering so much pain." The memory made her hurt, too. "I don't know why he'd do a thing like that, unless . . ."

"I'm really sorry about Tiger. But take my word, Teri. It has nothing to do with the 'roids. That guy's got problems. All Indians got problems. Drake says he used to live on a reservation, and they *all* got problems."

"I don't believe that. John's such a sweet . . ." She crossed her legs Indian-style and leaned over her ankles, pressing her point with convincing evidence. "Just look at Mr. Archer. Mr. Archer doesn't have any problems."

Ally folded the top of the cookie bag over and set it on the lamp table next to half a glass of milk polluted with cookie sludge. "I wouldn't bet on it," he advised as he rose from the chair. "Some of us guys tried to find somebody to go out with him, but all he thinks about is—"

"You're such a jerk sometimes. Put that stuff away," she demanded, pointing at the remains of his snack. He ignored her. "And you had no business talking to Drake about what happened to John, either."

"Hey, we've all been talking about it ever since Ron Christian called to tell us where you were. And was Mom steamed."

"I don't care. I'm going back up to see him as often as I can. She can't stop me."

Ally shrugged and gave the bottom of his sister's tennis shoe a playful tap with the toe of his own. "Just keep your mouth shut about the 'roids, okay? If anyone starts asking questions, we don't know nothin' about nothin.'"

It was after nightfall by the time Wyatt and Lavender returned to her schoolhouse. Wyatt gripped his knees, stared at the words "Coyote's Call Creek" above her door and listened to the motor idle. A woman who lived in a schoolhouse in the middle of beef country and refused to eat meat. This was not the girl next door. She was going to say good-night, and he was going to drive away.

"Coffee?" she asked.

He looked at her and forgot his list of rules and requirements. "I don't want to go back to my apartment tonight, Lavender."

"Then you're welcome to stay."

"I just want some company. That's all."

"That isn't quite true." She pulled the handle and pushed the car door ajar. The dome light illuminated her smile. "But I think it's mostly true. I want to give you a gift, Wyatt."

The idea made him uncomfortable. He didn't need gifts. He wasn't sure what he needed now. He only knew he wasn't ready to leave her. "You make a damn good cup of coffee. That's really all I'm asking for."

"That first. Along with maybe a sandwich."

"Sounds good. I won't look inside the bread."

They were out of the car, climbing the front steps together. She linked her arm in his. "And then total relaxation. I promise. That will be my gift."

"All natural?"

"Absolutely organically grown."

He hardly touched the food she prepared, and when she suggested that he go upstairs and take a hot bath, he laughed.

"This has to be done my way, Wyatt. Otherwise it won't work at all." She took his plate away. "It starts with warm water. Just like new life."

"Meanwhile, what will you be doing?" he asked as he pushed his chair away from the table.

There was something inside him that was inexplicably drawn to her. In the past, when he'd made advances, she'd turned away. Rather than advance on her again, he was inclined to let himself be led tonight. Mothered a little more, maybe, the way John wanted to be mothered. And then after that...she was right. Company wasn't quite all he wanted from her.

"What I need to do." She offered an enigmatic, soft-eyed smile. "It'll be good for you. You'll feel so much better."

He didn't like the idea of taking his clothes off solo, but the idea of a tub of hot water took precedence. A tub of hot water, and then Lavender. The wrought-iron steps with the curving brass rail promised a journey to heaven, but he wondered what the brass fire pole next to them signified. If he failed to satisfy her, would she send him down the pole?

The idea made him chuckle. "You ever use this fire pole?" he called down to her.

"When I'm in the mood. It's an antique. Came with the steps, which I bought at an auction when I was having the place remodeled. The loft was a major architectural achievement." He made a turn around the pole that secured the steps and caught a glimpse of her teasing smile as she continued to expound. "I'm sure that pole has been polished by the seats of many firemen's pants."

Firemen or lovers? He told himself it didn't matter, but that bright, sweet look on her face made him want to believe she'd had no lovers, and that once she got him into her bed, it would be he who would coax her gently.

The stairway to the loft reminded him of the steps in the school library that had taken him up to the stacks where the historical novels were shelved. It was a stairway to a place where a boy could happily lose himself, which was okay for a boy. For a man, there were other pleasures, but never the total retreat that might be found in fantasy.

It was the first time he'd seen Lavender's bedroom. It lent itself to fantasy. He could imagine her waking up in the round bed in the center of the room, stretching, emerging like Venus from misty lavender sheets. She would take her clothes from the closet and the drawers that were built in beneath the rafters on one side, then parade past the railing to the other side. There the steeply pitched roof had been bumped out for the bathroom.

Well, not exactly bath*room*. The loft was all one room. The toilet and sink were hidden behind a partition, but the cedar-decked garden tub with its hand-held shower took up a whole corner of the loft. The room was not frilly. But appointed in shades of purple and rose with handwoven accents, piles of pillows and bleached pine woodwork, it was distinctively female. And it was Lavender. Through the skylights she would almost be able to touch the stars.

The whole house was one big room, he realized. Just like his grandmother's house, where he'd bathed in a galvanized tub in the kitchen. He remembered describing it to his roommate at school. Big mistake. The kid had laughed and told the guys next door that Wyatt was going to be looking for a toilet out behind the dorm. After that, he'd seldom spoken of the place and the people who had been home to him.

"If you're shy, there's a privacy screen over by the closet," Lavender instructed from below. "Do you see it?"

"Yeah." It was another artsy-craftsy thing made of woven willow and panels of her purple cloth. He unfolded it and set it around the tub. "Why didn't you just put in a bathroom with real walls?"

"Silly question," she said. He heard a clatter of plates, and then she added, "Why would I want walls?"

"I don't know," he muttered to the faucet, as he let the warm water flow. "Privacy, maybe?"

She couldn't have heard him. She was obviously thinking along other lines, anyway, and she sang out, "There's a bottle of bath oil on the shelf near the tub. Got it?"

"I see it."

"Put about half of that in the water, okay?"

Half a *bottle?* He opened the cap and sniffed. No flowers accosted him, so he decided to humor her. He watched the oil stream into the rising steam.

"We could do this together," he suggested. He could hear more rustling around downstairs, and he figured she probably had something of the kind in mind. It was better if he said it first.

"No, we couldn't. That would be a distraction, I'm afraid. What kind of music do you find most relaxing? I'm trying to find just the right—"

"Any kind." Music was music. He could listen to anything and often did, just to get some noise going when his apartment seemed too quiet.

She chose classical guitar, and the soothing melody floated to the rafters.

He lowered himself into the tub, letting the satin-textured water slide over him. The scent of mineral oil melted into the earthy vibration of strings, inviting him to close his eyes and drift. But when he did, he saw John Tiger's black hair against white sheets, and the plastic tubes and the metal rail along the side of the bed.

Wyatt's head throbbed. He opened his eyes and searched for soap.

He heard Lavender on the stairs. She'd been busy. He'd already made up his mind what he was going to say if she offered him a joint. He wasn't into that kind of relaxation, but if she was, she could suit herself. Through the screen he could see the movement of her shadow mixed with slivers of lamplight beyond the bed. He resisted the temptation to ask her what she was doing. She was setting him up for seduction, sure as hell, and that almost amused him. Total relaxation was an interesting term for it. He had to admit, she was an interesting woman. *Unusual.* He should have known that run-of-the-mill advances by the old stream wouldn't cut it with her.

He closed his eyes again, and this time he imagined the way she would look when she suddenly appeared on his side of the screen, her nudity intended to be a pleasant surprise. He would give her the appreciative response she would be looking for as he made room for her in the tub. This would be easier to handle than the talk they'd had earlier. In one morning he'd talked enough to last him a year. He was ready for whatever kind of seduction she was cooking up for him, and knowing Lavender...

He heard the snap of a length of fabric, and he thought, nice touch. She was even changing the sheets.

"I might as well tell you," he said dreamily, "I don't like the smell of incense. Makes me think I'm at a funeral."

"That's interesting." There was a moment's pause. "Do you have any objections to potpourri?"

"Mmmm, I might," he said, smiling to himself. "If I knew what it was."

"Dried flowers and herbs."

"Burning?"

"Simmering in water."

"No objection."

"What associations do you have with candles?"

He chuckled. "No electricity."

"Are you afraid of the dark?" He laughed that one off the way any man would. "I'm serious," she insisted. "I want to make you comfortable."

"Candles are no problem."

"I guess we can call 'no problem' a step in the right direction."

She came around the corner of the screen after he'd stopped expecting her and offered him a brown stoneware mug and a smile. She was still dressed—same long flared skirt, same soft blouse, all in cream—and he wondered why. He reached for the mug, and water sheeted off his arm. She misinterpreted the question in his eyes. "Hot apple cider," she said.

"Thanks." He had to hand it to her. Her eyes never strayed from his face. "You really aren't going to join me?"

Her eyes seemed to tease him. "At some point in our relationship, you'll have to learn to take me at my word. I'm ready for you whenever you are, but I'm not rushing you out of the tub. Take your time."

"The water feels good, but it's not enough to make me stop thinking completely."

"It's going to take a major effort to make Wyatt Archer stop thinking, but I'm prepared for that." He chuckled. He should have figured she would be. "I know you're worried about John," she said. She couldn't see the smile slide from his face. She was lighting candles. He heard the scratch and smelled the sulfur, and he didn't want her lighting candles and talking about John at the same time. Maybe he did have some associations with candles from way back when.

"What do you want for him?" she asked.

He answered impatiently. "I want him to be okay."

"Then give him that thought now. *Be well, John.* And let go." He didn't like letting go. Somehow she knew that, and she added, "Just for now. Just for a little while."

"I wish I could take back some of the things I—"

"Let that go, too, Wyatt. You can't take any of it back. It happened." She appeared again with an offering of thick purple towels. "Later you'll talk with him about it. But not tonight."

She went away again, and he stayed, feeling safe in the water until it began to cool. She turned out the lamp, and more shadows flickered beyond the screen, where he knew she was waiting. The floral scent was pleasantly subtle. When he stood up in the water he could see over the top of the screen. She sat in the middle of the bed, legs in a lotus position, that wild mane haloing her serene face. It was vaguely disappointing that his movement didn't distract her from her thoughts. He wondered if his arousal would.

He wrapped one of the towels about his waist and dried himself with another. He felt sort of disarmed as he folded the screen and set it back against the wall. This was strictly her territory, and it was unlike any female territory he'd ever entered. Once again, the word *lair* came to mind. Neutral ground, like a motel, would have been much better with this woman. She seemed so self-assured as she waited for him, dressed in nothing but a damn towel, to come to her.

But what the hell . . .

"You turned the heat up," he observed.

"I stoked up the fire in both stoves, and of course—" she scooted off the bed and began rolling up her sleeves "—heat rises. A chill would ruin it for you."

He posed, arms akimbo, resting one knee on the edge of the bed. "I'm liable to work us into a pretty good sweat."

"You're not liable to do anything except relax. I'll do all the work."

"Listen, Lavender, the surest way to ruin it is for you to be setting all these ground rules. You don't strike me as the type who'd want to make love by some kind of—"

Her eyes were full of merriment as she surveyed him appreciatively. "I suppose that kind of arrogance is to be expected from a man with a body as beautiful as yours." She pointed to an arrangement of floor pillows covered with a royal purple satin sheet. "Lie down on your back, please."

"What the hell for? I'm not even..." *Interested* was the word, but he wasn't quite ready to say it. She was getting under his skin in at least a dozen different ways, and he was caught without his next move in mind. "I was, but I'm not now, thanks to your—"

"Just give me ten minutes, okay?" She knelt beside the pallet she'd prepared and patted the satin covering, entreating him with an invitation to pleasure in her eyes. "If after five minutes you want me to stop doing what I'm doing and do something else, I promise..." She offered a slow smile, and from where he stood, he could see just a hint of the curve of her breast. "I'll take all my clothes off and jump into bed with you. Deal?"

It was his turn to laugh. "You are the strangest—"

"I know. I'm weird." She patted the pillow again. "But the odds are in my favor, you see, because I'm a very good masseuse."

"I'm not a very good—" *She'd told him that before. He should have remembered.* "—subject for massage. They used to bring these guys in sometimes when I was competing—" He dropped to his knees on the pillows, obliging her even though he felt foolish and for some reason was telling her some of the reasons why. "I could never sit still for it, you know? Made me uncomfortable."

"*Five* minutes. Put yourself *willingly* into my hands for five minutes."

"'Course, they were always men. I didn't like the idea of letting a man—" He stretched out on his back. He would give her the five minutes, since he'd come this far.

"It makes no difference, Wyatt. It shouldn't, anyway." She surprised him by situating herself above his head as she went on talking. "By the time I'm through, you won't remember your own name, never mind your precious gender."

"You're going to massage my *head?*"

"And you're going to be quiet and go with the flow. My five minutes doesn't start until you're cooperating." She was stroking his hair, which seemed a natural thing for a woman to do. A comforting thing. No objections so far. Then she took a bottle of oil from a crock of hot water, and he thought he might take exception to that. But he watched her pour it into her slender hand, and he changed his mind.

What the hell was five minutes? In five minutes, he would put oil on his hands, too.

"Your head is what's causing most of your trouble, my friend. Once we drain this head of yours, the rest will be pure pleasure for you."

He closed his eyes and took that as a promise. Sooner or later, they would get to the good stuff.

She began stroking the middle of his forehead with her thumbs while she kneaded his temples with lightly oiled fingertips. Warm. Smooth. No threat in that. Draining was the proper word. He told himself he had nothing to lose but a jumble of "if-onlys" and a dull headache. Remarkably, she made short work of the headache. She manipulated his face and neck, even the top of his head, and it felt as if she were releasing a network of tiny knots, one by one. He had no idea how much time passed. A minute, maybe. Gradually there was more room inside his head for the distant plucking of strings, the soft scent of field flowers and the lingering sweet-tart flavor of apple cider.

She stroked his arms one at a time, rolling and pressing with such commanding skill that he stopped wondering whether she was impressed by his musculature. Ordinarily, when a woman touched his biceps, they flexed automatically. Lavender's hands smoothed that instinct away, but she knew it was there. He could sense her amusement. With all his tension melting, he didn't care. She moved his arm back and forth and made such a tingling marvel of his blood circulation that his arms seemed to float away from the rest of him.

How many minutes? Maybe he would give her one or two extras.

She worked the same magic on his hands, each in its turn, as she rotated them, then stroked every finger and kneaded his palms until they, too, tingled. He was soon past the point of keeping track of time. She stroked liquid warmth into his chest, and somewhere along the line he was liberated from anticipation. She sat above his head and smoothed oiled hands from his shoulders to his waist, drew her hands up his back and lifted him off the pillows, which gave him a sudden sense of expansion. Her strength surprised him, as did the deft way her small fingertips had of turning his thick, hard-muscled chest into something that quivered like gelatin.

He felt the towel go slack at his waist, and he made a vague wish for her to save that for later. But he didn't make a move. He didn't want to move.

"I won't uncover you," she said as she laid her hands on his abdomen. Her voice was soothing but distant. "I want to free the butterflies."

His face was too relaxed to form a smile, but he felt as if he were wearing one. "There isn't a nerve in my body."

"Good," she whispered. "This feels good to you, then."

"Terrific ... understatement ..."

She slid her hands toward each other, like two flatirons pressing the kinks out of his belly, awakening the life that flourished at the core of him with a call to sensuality that he'd never heard, not this way. He had no desire to act. Only to absorb. Merely to feel. With long, pressing strokes she stretched the feeling through his thighs and down his legs. In that instant his feeling suddenly had substance and elasticity. She placed her fingers behind his knee and her thumbs on the knee cap, and she revved up a stroke that released all the pressure an athlete harbored in his knees. He groaned with pleasure.

"Turn over now," she said.

For a moment he wasn't sure he could, nor did he want her to take her hands from him while he did. She knew that. She guided him to his stomach while she continued to reassure him with her touch. Even while the oil was replenished the contact between them was never broken.

Hand over hand she pulled the backs of his calves, then stroked and stroked and stroked his thighs. The towel fell away, and she rotated his taut buttocks under her palms. He had a sense of sexual gratification that had nothing to do with orgasm and everything to do with the woman who touched him.

"Lavender, talk to me," he muttered.

"Not now," she intoned softly. "Hear the music."

The tune was soft and bright, with violins and violas, but he wanted more of her.

"Your voice is music."

"I'm speaking to you through my hands, Wyatt." She knelt astride his thighs and kneaded his lower back until he groaned. "Your body listens well." He made a half-hearted start at answering. "Shhh," she admonished gently. "There's tension even in talking, Wyatt. I'm taking all that from you, and we're coming to the best part."

She pressed her hands firmly along either side of his spine. He began to breathe in rhythm with her strokes, letting his lungs fill as her hands slid to his waist, then gradually deflate as she pressed the air from his body with her upward strokes. Her breathing became one with his, lulling him. She kneaded his shoulders, then slipped her arms under his and clasped her hands behind his neck, again lifting him off the pillows like a sack of meal. He flirted with the notion that, for the first time in his life, he'd willingly succumbed to a full nelson with no desire to break away. Had she been a wrestler, she could have broken his neck with the illegal hold. But there was no tension. No contest. No thought of resisting as she stretched his body for total release.

She stroked his back, his legs, and finally manipulated his feet. His lowly feet received no less care than the rest of him, and by now that felt right. Good. Sublime. She went on stroking, stroking, stroking him softly now. Slightly now. Feather-touch lightly now. Fingertips touched toes as thoughts faded into dreams.

It was a shame that no one would know the comfort of her bed that night, but Lavender knew that this was no time to wake the man and move him to bed. She covered him with a cotton blanket, blew out the candles and slipped away quietly.

Touching him to soothe him had brought her more satisfaction than she had expected. Some of it had come from bringing her kind of serenity to new ground, but there was more. The new ground was Wyatt Archer, and she had enjoyed the experience right along with him. There was something especially rewarding about the way he'd given himself up to her. The passive role was unnatural for him, but for reasons of his own he had permitted her to touch him. She had made him forget all reason. But she, too, had been touched. She'd been touched when he'd confided in her earlier in the day. And she wanted to be touched more.

Ah, but they were not supposed to sleep together. Once a relationship became sexual, it was bound to change, and not necessarily for the better. She wanted his trust, and she knew she was trustworthy. But trusting him was another matter. He was a man, after all. He wanted respect, security, home and family. He'd said nothing of love.

She adjourned to the sofa, which was nearly as comfortable as a bed. She was so exhausted that she could have slept standing up. She laid her skirt and blouse over the backrest and curled up in her white satin slip under two lap robes and a ruana. Her hands recalled every contour of him, every hard muscle, every easy curve, and she drifted in the reverie of having him hold her through the night.

Sometime during the night the spell wore off and Wyatt woke, knowing instinctively that he was in a strange place. There was satin underneath him, and above there was starlight streaming right through the roof. He smelled flowers. Lavender. Her place, her loft and—he sat up slowly to have a look—her empty bed. He felt strangely bereft without her hands on him. She had touched him intimately, made him weightless and mindless, and then just left him there.

Wasn't it supposed to be the other way around?

He smiled in the darkness, thinking of the kind of reaction a question like that would bring from her. Some piece of vegetarian philosophy salted with a little feminine humor. The idea of tasting her flavor appealed to him, and he grabbed the loft rail, pulled himself to this feet and peered into the room below.

There she was, sleeping in a pool of starlight. Her hair cascaded over the edge of the sofa, and her face was luminescent. Apparently she'd meant it when she'd said

they weren't supposed to sleep together. Not even in the
same room with him on the floor. A few hours before,
when he'd been up to his chin in hot water and she'd been
waiting for him on the bed, he'd been predicting a different kind of arrangement.

He was learning, though. It was a mistake to try to an-
ticipate this woman. She hadn't seduced him. She had reduced him to his sensual essence and given him total ease.
Given the choice, he would still take sex, but he could go
back to sleep on the remnant of relaxation that was with
him still. But not on the floor. He crawled into her bed
and drifted on the comfortable sense that she was close by.

He had slept through her first morning visit to the loft
to gather a change of clothes, so the second time around
she brought him a cup of coffee. When she touched his
bare shoulder, he groaned and rolled to his back before he
opened his eyes to find her sitting next to him. He touched
her cheek with the back of his hand and offered the lazy
smile of a man remembering a night's pleasure.

"Did you sleep well?" she asked.

"Like a baby." He crooked his arm behind his head,
still smiling at her. "That was just plain apple cider you
gave me last night, right?"

"With cinnamon."

"With cinnamon. Well, that was some five-minute
massage that went along with it."

"It took us more than an hour."

He chuckled. "Around you, I must be back on Indian
time."

"Does that mean time isn't that important?"

"It means you forget—" He pulled his arm back out
for a look at his bare wrist. "Did I leave my watch beside
the bathtub?"

"If you did, it's still there." As if he'd been summoned, her mischievous black cat leaped up on the foot of the bed, claiming attention from both of them. "Unless Jasper got hold of it. Did you take his watch, kitty?"

Jasper sniffed Wyatt's blanket-covered toes, followed by Lavender's outstretched hand, but he found nothing of interest. He leaped again, this time to a bookshelf.

"I guess I don't need to know the time on Sunday morning," Wyatt decided as he propped himself up and accepted the coffee. "It is Sunday, isn't it?" Lavender nodded. "And I'm not keeping you from anything?"

"No."

"You know, you were amazing last night." The satisfied male look in his eyes made her laugh. "No, I mean it." She made a moue of disbelief, so that he had to laugh, too. "For once I really mean that. *You*..." and he stopped laughing "...were amazing."

"And you were very tired."

"I'm not now." He sipped his coffee, but he eyed her playfully over the rim of the cup.

"Good. I've made you an amazing breakfast, but you'll have to come downstairs. All I'm delivering to you in bed is coffee."

"That's a shame." She stood and waited expectantly. He grinned. "I don't have anything on, you know."

"What happened to your towel?" she teased.

"I forgot all about it, along with my name."

"And gender?" She picked up his jeans and tossed them on the foot of the bed.

"Damn near." He set the cup on the lamp table and tossed the covers aside as he rolled out of bed in one agile motion. He picked up his pants without so much as a backward glance to assess her reaction. Not until he was zipping them up, and then he caught her staring. "But not quite. And I don't think you really want me to."

"Of course not," she said lightly. "I'm sure it's just as wonderful to be a man as it is to be a woman, and I think the day is coming—"

"I think so, too." He closed in, still half smiling. He'd turned the tables unexpectedly. "What you did for me last night was great."

"It was my pleasure," she said honestly. He rested his hands on her shoulders, and she tried to remember why that look in a man's eyes was sure to complicate things. She'd known the reason once. Known it painfully well, but, foolish woman, she'd lost touch with it all of a sudden. And those mischievous little belly butterflies were back.

"Have you had a revised vision yet? I mean about what we're not supposed to do together."

She gave her head a quick shake. "Not yet."

"The prohibition is just against sleeping together, right? Kissing is okay."

"Kissing is—" She lifted her chin, and his lips came as a soft greeting, full of sunshine. They left her smiling. "Kissing is very nice."

"I'd like to pursue this." Another soft kiss defined *this*. When she opened her eyes, she saw no reason to doubt him. He touched the corner of her mouth with a forefinger and tipped his head to one side. "Maybe discover some more things that might be nice." He drew a deep breath and sighed. "But I'd like to use your phone first."

"I already called."

His hands slid away from her shoulders as he stepped back. "The hospital?"

She nodded. "And John's sister, when I couldn't get anything out of the hospital staff."

"What did Marla say?"

"John's holding his own physically." He waited, clearly sensing there was more. "They're moving him to the psych ward when they release him from intensive care."

Turning away, he planted his hands on his lean hips. "I was right, then."

"At this point everything is confidential."

"I need to talk to him." He glanced toward the bathtub and located his shirt draped over a chair.

"You can't. They won't let you see him now." On the ledge above the tub she saw the watch he'd asked about, and she got it for him. She knew full well that she ought to leave him now, let him get dressed and do whatever he was determined to do without getting herself more involved. Without offering any suggestions.

He took the watch from her hand, and she looked up, saw the concern in his eyes and couldn't resist. "I think what you could do is talk with the boys on the team. I'm sure they're going to think that John jumped."

"I *know* he jumped. I never should have—"

"Don't do that to yourself now. It won't help."

"This happens with too damn many Indian kids, Lavender." He buckled the watch without looking away from her face. "You read statistics, and it makes you sick."

"It's not just Indian kids." This was bound to be a mistake, but she was going to try anyway. "I want you to help me persuade the school to let me put together a suicide-intervention program. I've worked on them before, when I was a social worker out in California. Sometimes there's a copycat ripple. There's always talk, always speculation. All kinds of what-if's that need to be aired. And I know money is tight in the Glover school system. The guidance counselor is only part-time, right?"

"Yeah, she's teaching some English, too." He looked at her curiously. "You think this is going to become a big school issue?"

"I don't know. But I think I can help. I...I want to help." That wasn't exactly true. It was just that she couldn't *not* help. "If they'll let me."

Chapter 7

Lavender didn't get very far with her offer. School superintendent Harvey Borman didn't see how a suicide-intervention team could be necessary, since no suicide had been committed. None had even been attempted, as far as he knew. The boy had told his coach he fell, and that was good enough for Mr. Borman. He really didn't want to hear any more about suicide. As if on cue, the school secretary brought him a fistful of file folders. As he flipped through them, he spared Lavender a dismissal-time glance and thanked her for dropping by.

That should have been enough for Lavender, too. Off the hook. Offer tendered and refused. She'd burned out on counseling a long time ago. She was a weaver and a businesswoman now, and she no longer kidded herself into thinking that what she did would change the way of the world. Changing the look of it in a few of its well-kept corners was enough for her now. She had created her own world, where there were no federal monitors, no state regulations and no monthly reports detailing the most troublesome aspects of people's lives. The last thing she needed was to involve herself with social institutions again.

But there was something vicious afoot here, Lavender mused as she pulled the station wagon away from the curb in front of her red brick alma mater. She wasn't sure what it was, but she had one of those strange feelings going inside her again. John Tiger had been hurt. Teri Nordstrom had been hurt. This was a small community, and poison had a way of spreading quickly, especially among those who were too young to have built up any real defense against it.

If the school officials couldn't use her help, so be it. She had her job to do, and Wyatt would be able to talk with John's friends at school, maybe help them put whatever happened into perspective. For her part, after her meeting with Borman she went home to Jasper, who taught her by example that an independent soul never had to worry about rejection. She sorted through the reference materials she'd saved and set aside information she thought Wyatt might find useful if he chose to deal with the suicide issue rather than brood about it.

There. She'd done all she could do.

Teri was unusually quiet as she plied her shuttle across a blue-tone warp that Tuesday afternoon. Lavender would have preferred to be a sounding board for the girl, but she could serve as company, too. The clacking of the heddle frames was as soothing a sound as the background music Teri had chosen to put on the stereo. Sixties folk music. ''Blowin' in the Wind'' wasn't Teri's usual fare, but Lavender had music for every occasion, and that was probably where the answers were for Teri right now. Blowing in the wind, which was whipping hard at the cottonwood branches outside the window.

"Have you ever heard of anabolic steroids?"

The question surprised Lavender, then alarmed her, but she let neither reaction show. "Yes," she said, and went right on wrapping amber silk on a warp frame.

"What do they really do to people?"

"You mean, to healthy people who don't need them?"

Three seconds of heavily loaded silence passed. "Yeah. Healthy people."

"They say people get more muscular when they take steroids."

"Do they really work?"

"They can make women look like men, for whatever that might be worth. They can also make a mess of your reproductive system. Interfere with your menstrual cycle." Lavender knew damn well Teri wasn't talking about *fe*male people, but she was going to let Teri lead the way.

"What about personality? Do they make people act different?"

"I haven't had much experience with anyone using them, but I understand they can make people more aggressive." She switched to a lighter-hued linen thread, working over the frame methodically as her instincts for easing closer to the heart of the matter kicked in. "Do you know anyone who's on steroids?"

"I'm not sure."

"John?" Lavender asked carefully.

There was a pause. "He might be."

"Where would he get hold of..." Lavender caught the tip of her tongue between her teeth. Besides being too direct, it was a dumb question. The drugs were out there. Even in the middle of North Dakota, the damn stuff was out there.

"I'm not... I really don't know for sure. I was just wondering what they might to do a person because I..." Teri was tripping over her own tongue now, at once anxious to get her worries out and to make them seem less alarming. "Well, I heard things. I mean, I *over*heard something." She funneled her frustration into a clucking sound. "Don't tell anyone I said anything about this."

The girl wasn't looking for honesty now. She wanted a white lie. She wanted a way out, which Lavender couldn't guarantee. "I can't keep that kind of a secret, Teri. You know that. If you don't want to be involved, that's your choice, but I will have to—"

"I'm *not* involved." Teri's shuttle hand stilled. "And I can't say anything for sure. The doctors—they'd be able to tell, wouldn't they? Like, from tests they'd have to be doing anyway?"

"I would say so."

"So they'd know about it, and they'd help him." The girl laid the shuttle down and swiveled on the bench. She looked up at Lavender, her eyes plaintive. "They won't even let me see him."

"For now."

"His sister says they put him in the psych ward. They won't let him talk to anyone outside his family. She says he's getting better, but I want to see for myself."

"The hospital will protect his privacy, but in doing that they end up leaving some of us out in the cold." *Cold* was undoubtedly a good word for it from Teri's perspective. Her blue eyes were brimming with tears. Lavender set her work aside. "Especially you, and that's hard, because you care so much."

That was the signal to let the tears flow. "I don't think he tried to kill himself," Teri claimed as Lavender joined her on the bench. "He said he loved me."

"Whatever happened out there on that bridge, honey, it doesn't change that one iota," Lavender promised as she rubbed Teri's shoulders.

"I mailed a letter to him this morning, but I don't know if he'll get it. They might not give it to him."

"I think they will."

"When he said he loved me, I didn't say it back because, well..." The girl sniffed and shook her head and took a swipe at the tears with the back of her hand. "I didn't know for sure. I keep thinking maybe if I had said it then..."

"No, no, no." Lavender took a soft white hankie from her pants pocket and pressed it into Teri's hand. "Teri, you couldn't have changed anything. No way. Really. You told him how you felt about him when you went looking for help for him. You saved his life."

Ah, yes. Teri needed to hear that she'd done something right. Lavender saw the light of that hope shining through the tears. She patted Teri's knee. "He knows that. He knows his life is precious to you."

"Maybe he's too confused. I know he must be terribly confused. I told him in my letter how I felt." Lavender nodded, and Teri went on. "That this is all brand-new for me. And wonderful and scary, because I've never been in love before, and I'm pretty old-fashioned." She smiled a little, her lips made shaky by all the highs and lows she harbored inside her pretty young head. "Of course, he knows that."

"And appreciates it because it's so—" Lavender gave the girl an affectionate squeeze "—so Teri."

"In my letter, I told him how much I miss him and that he has to try to take care of himself and get better so they'll let me see him."

Already Lavender could see herself pleading Teri's case to the boy's doctor.

"About the steroids, Teri..." *Don't be an alarmist. She'll jump away like a cottontail.* "They can sometimes be dangerous. We do need to tell someone."

"I, um..." She blotted furiously at her damp face and tossed her blond curls, as if to brush away what she knew. "I just couldn't say anything for sure. It would be just like hearsay, and I don't want to cause trouble over something I only heard." Avoiding her friend's eyes, she added quietly, "Please don't ask me to, Lavender."

Wyatt Archer had been lucky to move into a little town such as Glover and get a nice duplex right off the bat. The most a single teacher could usually hope to find was a second-floor room with a bath in some widow's house. Then Lavender remembered, as she swished through the accumulation of cottonwood leaves in the front yard, that last year's wrestling coach had lived there, too. He'd had a wife and a small child. Two years with the Glover school system, two lackluster wrestling seasons, and off he went. So the duplex was part of the package, hmm? All for the love of the sport.

She'd given a lot of thought to broaching the subject of wrestlers possibly being on drugs, and she was prepared for the same kind of deaf ear she'd gotten from Borman. A coach didn't want to hear the word *drugs* any more than a superintendent wanted to hear *suicide*. It was bad luck to think it, much less actually say it. But she had to believe Wyatt was the good kind of coach. The kind who cared more about teaching than winning. She had to believe it because...well, partly because he was on her mind so damn much lately.

"Hey. Lavender." Wyatt held the door open wide. "Come on in."

His warm smile gave her a measure of confidence. He didn't mind having Lavender Holland's car parked outside his place at eight o'clock at night. He knew as well as she did that here in town people would notice. And she hadn't called. Okay, so it was sort of a test. She'd told herself it wouldn't bother her if he turned out to be less than hospitable when he found her standing on his doorstep, but she knew what a crock that was. He looked terrific in gray sweats and white tube socks, and she would have been crushed if he hadn't wanted her there.

"This is nice," she said, although she hadn't noticed anything but the hole in the toe of one of his socks. She tossed her white ruana off her shoulders, and he took it from her and laid it over the back of the sofa.

"It's dull, compared to your place, but what the hell. I'm not here that much."

Then her place was not so dull? She smiled and stepped away to assess this dullness he lived in. Indeed, the place had its masculine touches, mainly in the relentless use of black, white and tan. As far as she could see there was only one wall decoration. It was a professionally framed Remington print—an action-filled western panorama. Men against steers. The textures in the living room were all smooth, the lines all straight, and there was a motorized treadmill where a dining table should have been.

Lavender stared pointedly at the machine. "Why don't you just go for a walk, or a jog, or something?"

"I do. But when I can't, I use that."

"I suppose you have barbells in the bedroom."

"Nah. Not enough room in there for a good set. I use the free weights at school." He flicked a switch to show off the way his exercise toy hummed along in a choice of speeds. Then he shut it off, gave her a look and a shrug. "'Course, I have dumbbells in the bedroom."

She laughed. "Only you could manage a perfectly deadpan expression and make a remark like that *almost* work."

"Almost?" There was nothing dull about the way the light shimmered in his dark eyes when he smiled at her. "Would you like to see my dumbbells? C'mon, I'll show you."

"I'd go for etchings, but not dumbbells. Sorry."

"That's okay. They're not dressed for company." He ignored her groan. "Want to try my coffee? It's not as good as yours, but it's not as bad as some."

"Boy, I'm really rating the credit tonight. What's the deal?"

"I like to give credit where it's due," he said as he started for the kitchen.

"I really want to talk." He stopped and waited. She could tell by the way he rubbed the back of his neck that this day had already been long enough and he would rather just relax. But she added, "Seriously."

"Okay." He lifted his hand toward the sofa. "Let's talk."

"Have you seen John?" she asked, making no move to make herself comfortable first.

"I went up last night after practice. They wouldn't let me in to see him, but the doctor asked me whether we had any kind of a drug problem in school here. So I'm a little..."

Lavender took a deep breath and let it out slowly. "What kind of drugs is he looking for?"

"He named off a bunch of them, but I—" He shook his head and waved the notion away. "I'm thinking he was just fishing. John's new here. Where would he get—"

"They can get it, Wyatt. You know that as well as I do. If they want it, they can get it. Did the doctor mention steroids?"

"Sure, along with..." His hands went to his hips, his eyes hardening. "So you think, just because he's an athlete, he's gotta be using steroids. What happened to your open mind, Lavender? You got a few stereotypes you'd like to hang on to in spite of all this—"

"No, I don't." They stared each other down. He didn't want to hear any of this. She didn't want to tell him any more. There were two sides to the equation, and neither one wanted to supply the critical factor. But some kind of a machine had kicked into high gear, and they both knew everything was about to add up.

Lavender sat down. The sofa's vinyl cushions sighed, as if someone were letting the air out of a tire. "Teri was doing some fishing, too," she said. "This afternoon. She was asking about anabolic steroids and what effect they had on people."

"Did she say John was using them?"

"She said he might be." She looked up, saw his reservations and folded her arms beneath her breasts. "She's sixteen years old, Wyatt. She's not about to come right out and tell on anyone. But she's also scared not to."

"Oh, geez. I can't believe..." He let the denial drift away as he took the seat beside her. "Where would they get hold of stuff like that? I mean, you go to a city, you can always find some doctor who's willing to sell a prescription to make an extra buck, but not here."

"Bismarck's a city."

"Oh, come on. Bismarck might as well be five hundred miles away, especially for John. How would he...?" With a sigh, he slouched dejectedly, gripping his knees and searching the ceiling for some kind of special dispensation. It wasn't there.

"My God. That kid's been beefing up like . . . like . . ." He pillowed his head on the top of the backrest and recalled the way he'd praised the boy for it. He turned to look up at Lavender. His eyes were bleak. "Why didn't I see it?"

"Have you had much experience with steroids?"

The question made him stiffen. "I've never used them. I've known guys who did."

"And?"

He stared quietly at the lamp on the corner table. "Guy I knew had a fatal heart attack after he'd been using steroids heavily for three or four years. He was twenty-six."

"And that's what caused it?"

"Caused his blood pressure to skyrocket. You can have kidney problems, liver problems, tumors. . . ."

"Steroids can also make the user more aggressive," she suggested.

"Sometimes." He straightened in his seat. "But John wasn't . . ."

"He's shown some temper lately, according to Teri. Sort of exploded and walked away. She said he never really hurt her, but Friday night his behavior was—"

"Off the wall. It fits." Passing a hand over his face, Wyatt gave in to the truth. He knew it had to be the truth, and he wanted to puke. "Oh, God, it all fits. Attempted suicide fits, too."

"And you know that if one's using, there are bound to be others."

"Probably. He had to get the stuff from somebody." He pulled her ruana down from the backrest and deposited it in her lap. Then he dragged his tennis shoes out from under the coffee table.

"What are you doing?"

"We're going to see Marla," he said as he slipped the hole in his sock beneath the tongue of his shoe.

"But, Wyatt, she won't want to—"

"Once we're sure about what's going on here, I'll get the rest of them tested. The school board'll back me on this or they'll be looking for a new coach." With a vengeance he whipped the long white shoelace into a bow. "And then I'm going to find out who's behind all this. It sure as hell isn't John Tiger."

School-board president Karl Brinker, part-time rural mail carrier and owner of the Brinker Burger Drive-In, called an emergency board meeting on short notice. Short enough, Harvey Borman hoped, that the word wouldn't get around and attract the whole town to the meeting. He'd called the wrestlers' parents himself, and Archer was bringing the Indian boy's family along. Tiger's mother had been bused in from Miles City.

Borman didn't want this turning into a dog-and-pony show, complete with press, outraged citizens and one poor old Indian lady shedding tears for her son. He wanted the whole mess to be resolved quickly and quietly. If he was lucky, the Indian kid would turn out to be the only one using this drug, nobody would be too shocked, and the rest of the team would remain intact. No skin off Glover's nose. The boy wasn't really one of theirs, anyway. He'd been an import, just like the coach. Indians made damn good athletes, and Archer had already proved to be a humdinger of a coach, but they had their drawbacks. Just wait and see, Borman had told Marv Clark when they'd been looking for a coach last spring.

And now, here it was. A drug problem at Glover High.

Borman fancied himself a diplomat. A peacekeeper. A smooth talker. That was how he'd kept his job for eighteen years. He always made sure he had himself covered, and he'd already contacted the school board's attorney for advice. He would come out of this like Teflon, without breaking any activities-association rules, without offending any parents, without any adverse effects sticking to *his* back. Brinker and Archer had set themselves up to take the heat, which was as it should be. Harvey Borman planned on retiring right there in Glover, North Dakota.

He stationed himself at Brinker's right elbow. Seven board members filled the rest of the chairs around the meeting table that had been set up in the high school band room. Plenty of room for the public to attend the meeting if they *wanted* to. There were no closed board meetings in Glover. Sheriff Ron Christian was just seating himself in the back row of the folding chairs the janitor had hastily set up. Christian's boy was on the team. There were two empty chairs next to his. Beyond those, the two Indian women sat, mother and daughter, both looking dour. Coach Archer had parleyed with them earlier, and they'd agreed to cooperate. Archer took a seat in the front row. He was going to do most of the talking about the sticky issues.

Dr. Werner had agreed to come, and he was sitting next to Archer. Werner was the only doctor in Glover, one of the last of a dying breed of small-town general practitioners. He'd treated most of the kids' sore throats and set their broken bones. He was getting old, but he was still sharp as a tack. Glover was lucky to have him. He knew all about these steroids. Borman felt good about having an expert on board. His bases were covered, as always.

Marge Nordstrom was there with that boyfriend of hers. He was another import. Glover didn't need his kind, either—greasy guy with a big motorcycle—but Marge had lived in Glover all her life and exhausted all the local possibilities. And her dad had run the grain elevator for many years. Everyone liked ol' Ike Tinker. So Marge was…well, Marge was Marge.

Borman smiled and greeted people as they arrived. He continued to take count, and when he was satisfied with the showing of team members' parents, he nodded to Brinker, who called the meeting to order.

"We've asked you parents to come here tonight because we think we may have a serious problem with the boys on our wrestling team," Brinker expounded. "I and Harvey had a meeting with Mr. Archer here, and we think, after hearing him out, it might be best to go along with what Mr. Archer proposes. Now, he's going to explain it all, and we've asked Dr. Werner to be here, too, so he can answer your questions. I know you're gonna have a whole truckload of questions, because I sure did." He gave Wyatt a friendly nod. "Okay, Wyatt. You've got the floor."

Wyatt stood and faced the small group, most of whom sat with arms folded and eyes that warned, *You'd better not try to say you've got trouble with my kid.* He'd seen that look a hundred times. He took a deep breath and started out by recalling that one of the boys had been seriously injured in a fall from a train bridge on Friday night. He glanced at the two Indian women, who sat at the back of the room, faces expressionless.

Everyone else waited for him to tell them what this had to do with *their* boys. He explained that urine samples taken after John Tiger's fall showed evidence that the boy had been using anabolic steroids. It was too soon to discuss this with John, whose condition was stable but still critical, but his family had agreed to let Wyatt bring the matter before the board so that the rest of the team members might be tested for drugs.

"We want to know who gave my boy that stuff," the old Indian woman challenged.

Wyatt looked down at the floor. He'd asked her not to say anything. *Just be there. Let me do the talking, because we don't want them to get on the defensive right away.* He should have known she'd pipe up with something about "my boy."

She reminded him of his grandmother.

"But first we want to make sure our team is drug-free." He surveyed the room, trying to get a sense of any change in the crowd's mood. Again his eyes fell on the old woman. John's mother. A full-blood, like his grandmother. She was there for her boy.

He turned toward Borman and Brinker and took up where he'd left off, his tone crisp and polished. "This is a growing problem throughout the country. As a coach, I'm constantly warning the kids not to use any kind of drugs unless they're prescribed for a medical condition. But I guess I've been looking for alcohol and cigarettes more than something like this. This took me by surprise."

"I don't know much about this steroid business," one of the board members said. "Except about that track runner who got himself kicked out of the Olympics for taking them."

"This ain't exactly the Olympics," someone in the audience muttered.

Wyatt glanced toward the back row. The old woman was watching him. She was a grandma, he reminded himself. She had the right. Her wishes were to be respected above those of anyone else in the room. He had always believed that, even though he'd managed to avoid paying due respect publicly. Now, suddenly, he saw things as they were. She was an elder. She had no time for defenses and denials, so she got right to the point. And she expected him to hear her concerns.

"You're right," he said. "It isn't the Olympics. It's high school wrestling, and one of our boys is in the hospital." He looked at Grandma's parched lips, not her eyes, and spoke softly. "I let him down. I'm sorry."

The old woman nodded once.

"Tell us why you think the other boys might be taking this stuff," Brinker said.

Wyatt explained that some athletes were using anabolic steroids to promote an increase in stamina and muscle mass, but that both the athletic and medical communities were officially opposed to using the drugs for this purpose. He explained that evidence linked the drugs to life-threatening physical and mental side effects.

"This has been going on for a long time, but it's getting worse with kids lately," he explained.

"In New York or Los Angeles, maybe, but *Glover?*" Kirby Streeter's father challenged. "Come on."

"I said it couldn't happen here, too." Wyatt paused, then shook his head. "I was wrong. Anabolic steroids can be deadly. I've seen the effects, and I'm telling you, there's more at stake here than a wrestling season. There's John Tiger," he said quietly, turning to the back row again. "And John's a fine boy. He works hard, plays hard. He's loyal to his team and to his friends."

Wyatt stood hip-shot, tucked his thumbs in his belt and took a deep breath. It was time for the bombshell.

"So I want every member of my team to report to Dr. Werner's office first thing in the morning, where they'll all be tested. No exceptions."

Almost as one, the people sat up and looked at their neighbors. *Can he do this? Should we go along with it?*

He answered before they voiced the questions. "I can't force anybody to have himself tested. That's against the law. But I *will* bench anyone who refuses."

Bernie Sandland, who was twice the size of his heavyweight son, raised a forefinger tentatively, as though he were back in the classroom. "What if a kid tests positive?"

"Then he's off the team, of course. But that would be the least of his problems, Mr. Sandland."

Sandland nodded and sat back in his chair.

"If we refuse, and you bench my kid, I can sue," Streeter claimed.

Wyatt remained unruffled. "You sure can."

"The school board could fire you and hire someone else to finish out the season."

"And then *I* could sue. We could get a bunch of suits and countersuits going here, if that's the way you want to spend your time and money. Meanwhile, your kids might just be injecting themselves with poison. Or popping pills, or both. A lot of people use both to get the full effect." Wyatt swept his tweed sports coat back and shoved his hands in the pockets of his slacks. "Look, I don't know where the drugs came from, but this is a team. And guys on a team tend to share things.

"The other thing is..." He paused. He wasn't sure how far he wanted to go with this, but he decided he would lay it all on the table. "I'm a tough coach. That's why you hired me. That's how I put together a winning program. But some of these guys... I may have given them the wrong idea. I may have pushed too hard." He looked at John's mother again. "I know I pushed John too hard. I did the unforgivable. I mocked him."

"In front of the others?" the old woman asked.

"No," Wyatt said, as though he stood alone before her. "It was after the other boys had gone."

"You didn't tell them to use any drugs, did you?" Sandland asked.

"No, I didn't."

"Well, then, it's not your—"

"That Tiger kid is new in town. He probably brought the stuff with him," Streeter said.

Wyatt glared at the man in the orange hunter's cap. "I'm new in town, too."

"Yeah, and you're both—"

"What's it gonna be, folks?" Brinker demanded, cutting off a debate that was bound to get ugly. "Are we gonna do something about this, or let it get worse?"

"I, for one, want my son tested," Ron Christian said quietly.

Wyatt was relieved to see a nodding of several heads.

"So, what all does that involve, Dr. Werner?" Ron's wife asked.

During the discussion that followed, parents questioned Dr. Werner about the use and abuse of anabolic steroids. The consensus was that the boys needed to be tested, "just to be on the safe side." The school board voted to support Wyatt's decision.

After the meeting was adjourned, the crowd buzzed as coats were buttoned and car keys were sought. Who would have thought it? Not in Glover. Probably nothing to get excited about, but you couldn't be too careful with this kind of thing.

Wyatt tried to get to the back of the room before Marla and her mother slipped away, but they were too quick for him. His first thought was to follow. He owed them more than a public apology. He owed them reassurance. But he was distracted by a startling declaration.

"I know exactly where those drugs came from." Several heads turned. Marge Nordstrom waited until she had the attention she wanted. "Lavender Holland. Who else?"

"What makes you think that?" Sheriff Christian asked.

"She uses drugs herself." Christian waved the notion away as he put on his Scotch cap. "Well, you *know* she does. Have you ever been inside that schoolhouse of hers? She's got drugs hanging from the rafters, all dried in little bunches and ready to use. She's a hippie throwback, that woman."

Wyatt stood back from the crowd and watched for reactions. He thought about the little bunches of herbs and the pleasant scent that pervaded the schoolhouse. Marge was a biddy. Surely nobody believed her nonsense.

"Didn't she have a party for the kids a few weeks ago?" Marge demanded as she straightened the collar on her red jacket. "She might have given out some drugs then."

"I broke up that party myself," Wyatt said. Now they were all looking at him. He shrugged. "There was nothing going on there."

"So why break it up?" Marge challenged. She glanced at Starky for approval.

"We had a meet the next day. I don't think we need to turn this into a witch-hunt, Mrs. Nordstrom."

Something in the look Starky was giving her seemed to goad Marge on. "Well, why not? If we've got a witch living just outside our town, and she's selling drugs to kids—"

"Selling?" Streeter was getting into this now. "You think she might be selling drugs?"

"Oh, for God's sake," Wyatt mumbled. His gut was churning as he watched all the ears perk up.

"I think she practices some weird religion. They say she's got some kind of stone altar all set up...."

Wyatt could have set them straight if they were willing to listen. He could have told them about the dried herbs Lavender used in her vegetable soup and the circle of stones she supposed might be a relic of some kind. But he told himself it was no use, even as he decided that one year in Glover would be enough for him. He was going to get through this crisis and then mind his own business until he could get the hell out of here. Anyone who put any stock in Marge Nordstrom's notions was as empty-headed as she was. No point in wasting his breath on arguments, and no point in keeping their company.

But a twinge of guilt nagged at him. He'd put up too little defense on Lavender's behalf. Sure, he'd felt a strong urge to hit somebody for a minute there, but who? Wyatt Archer didn't go around hitting people. He was such a hell of a good citizen.

But why hadn't he come up with something more convincing than "I don't think we need to turn this into a witch-hunt" in answer to Marge's accusations? What had stopped him from turning on the woman and saying, *You should talk, lady?*

Better judgment, right? Keep the damage down to a minimum.

As he headed home, despite the school board's vote of support, Wyatt wasn't very proud of the showing he'd made this night.

Chapter 8

The first excuse he came up with when he took a right turn instead of a left was that it was only 9:00 p.m. and he was pretty keyed up, so maybe he would just drive around for a little while. Maybe he would head west, toward the river, kind of put his thoughts in order before he put them to bed. Maybe he'd just drive by Lavender's place and see if the lights were on. He thought about that herbal tea she'd mentioned once. She'd claimed it made a person sleepy. It wouldn't hurt to stop for a cup of whatever she might have brewing.

Poor choice of words, he thought as he touched the brake to give a foolhardy badger time to scurry across the road. *Brewing* conjured up cauldrons and potions and Marge Nordstrom's stupid accusations. He decided not to mention any of that nonsense to Lavender. Not that it would bother her, considering the source, but she just didn't need to hear it.

He'd made a lot of assumptions about her, too, at first, but he'd had the good sense to keep most of them to himself. He still wondered about her sometimes. Just how free thinking was she? Clearly she appreciated all things in their natural states. That had to include the mind, too. He hadn't asked her what she thought about drugs, and he knew it was foolish to jump to conclusions about Lavender. Once you got to know her, you forgot all about her more unusual notions.

He smiled to himself as he topped the rise, knowing in the next instant he would see the schoolhouse. You *almost* forgot, he amended. She surely wasn't like anyone else in this podunk town, and that was something he valued more each day, as her uniqueness seemed less and less strange, more and more attractive.

He pulled off the highway, homing in on the light above the Coyote's Call Creek sign. The words and the light, like the moon-and-star mailbox at the foot of the driveway, struck him lately as welcoming signs, just for him. The light in the side window told him that she was there and that he could go inside and smell the apples and the bunches of dried herbs and the wood burning in the stove.

He was getting too damned sentimental. As he shut the car door he reminded himself that apples were just apples, and wood smoke made soot.

He stopped in his tracks when she came to the window. Something tightened in his chest as he watched her lean close to the glass, like a woman looking for her man to come home. She was wearing a long, straight shift, and her silhouette reminded him of a shaft of wheat. The image he'd created long ago of the perfect home and the perfect woman waiting had lost its focus since Lavender had first welcomed him into her schoolhouse.

He knocked on the door and walked in without waiting for an invitation.

"Lavender? It's just me."

"Just you?" She came into the studio laughing, her arms outstretched. "It's not *just* you. It's *you.*"

"I know it's late," he muttered as he received the hug she offered as a greeting.

"It's not that late. I've been waiting," she told him softly in his ear.

"For me?"

"At least for a call from you." She took his hand and led him past the shelves that housed her rows of thread and into her cozy den. The electric blower on the wood-stove hummed in the far corner. "Did the meeting go all right?"

"The meeting." He wasn't sure. He'd spoken up for John, and he felt good about that. He'd gotten what he wanted, but he had a strange sense of foreboding now that he held her hand or she held his. She turned, waiting for him to put together an answer, but the thing he remembered now was the way her name had come up unexpectedly. Her smile was so pretty, and the urge to protect her waxed suddenly stronger. "Yeah, it went fine. They agreed. Either the boys test clean or they don't wrestle."

"And the testing will be done . . . ?"

"First thing in the morning." She squeezed his hand before letting go. A sign of approval? Sympathy? He wasn't sure. But she took cups from the cupboard and a blue enamel coffeepot off the stove, and he nodded *his* approval as he hung his topcoat on a hook. "You read my mind."

He took a turn around the table, surveying the array of pencil sketches she'd obviously just been working on. Front views, back views, coats, suits, dresses. The sketches were artistic in their own right, but he knew they were only a prelude to what would eventually come from her looms.

He draped his sports coat over the back of a chair and took a seat, then noticed the small crock on the table. "What are you eating?" he wondered.

"Pumpkin seeds."

"Oh." He grimaced. "Pumpkin seeds?"

"Toasted." She set the coffee down and plucked a seed from the bowl, feeding it to him as she sat down. "Aren't they delicious?" He chewed, chuckled, but offered no judgment. "Well, then how about some leftover spinach pasta?" she asked.

"I could get fat the way you're always trying to feed me, except that it's usually something like spinach and seeds. Don't you ever feel like cheating on this vegetarian diet of yours?"

"Once in a while. I do use eggs and cheese, sometimes fish, when I'm feel rebellious."

"Sounds daring." He popped two more seeds into his mouth. They were better than spinach. "What have you got against meat?"

"It's just a personal preference for..." She looked at him for a moment, and he sensed an assessment in progress. He waited. She wrapped her hands around her coffee cup, studied it, then spoke quietly. "I used to have a lot of problems with my menstrual cycle. I had recurring polyps. They drove me crazy with D & Cs, and finally I had surgery. You probably think it's silly—most people do—but I decided to make some changes for the sake of my health." He expected a deep sigh, but she looked up smiling. "As I started to say, it's a personal preference, not something I promote as a cause. I believe I'm much healthier now, living—" she gestured, indicating the crock of seeds " —the way I do."

"If you believe it, then it's true." By way of approval, he helped himself to four seeds this time.

"Is that what *you* believe?"

"Absolutely." But there was more to this, and he wasn't quite sure why, but he wanted the whole story. "So, after this surgery, can you still have . . . ?"

"After a partial hysterectomy, I can't have children."

"That's too bad." She had said it matter-of-factly, and he replied in a tone matching hers. But it wasn't that simple. *No children, no children.* There was a hollow echo inside his head and a feeling in his gut that this knowledge affected him, too.

He didn't know much about "women's problems." The women he'd grown up around had kept those things to themselves, and the men expected to be told when to stay away. It had always been that way. But this was Lavender, and suddenly he wasn't satisfied to shrug off her mysteries. The idea that she was "strange" didn't cut it anymore. More and more he found himself wondering what she thought and how she felt.

"Is that why your marriage broke up?" Her sharp look surprised him, and he tried to wave his question away. "I'm sorry. That's none of my business." He didn't even know why he'd asked. He didn't even like thinking about other men in her life, particularly her ex-husband.

"It wasn't quite that simple, but it was part of the reason. I know Phil wanted children of his own. And he was not . . . from the time I was diagnosed . . . particularly empathetic with my condition."

None of this came as a bid for Wyatt's sympathy. He felt it, though, watching her keep that stiff upper lip. Like it or not, he found himself envisioning this Phil. Pointed head. Thin lips. No neck.

Lavender smiled suddenly, as though she saw the image in his mind. But she explained. "The more important part was that I'm a strange lady by Phil's standards. I think I intrigued him at first, and I know I thought he needed me. Once we were married, I guess the novelty wore off and I just plain embarrassed him."

Wyatt felt his stomach tighten. Who did this no-necked Phil Thin Lips think he was, anyway?

Yeah, but who did this stiff-necked Wyatt Half-breed think he was?

Wyatt shook his head. "I thought everything was pretty laid-back in California."

"You haven't met Phil. Still, he was the normal one. I guess I'm just not supposed to be married."

"Not to me, anyway." She gave him a quizzical look. "Well, since we're not supposed to sleep together. Eliminates a lot of suspense when you just know these things right off the bat."

She nodded, laughing. "It does, doesn't it? We can just be relaxed with each other."

"No cat-and-mouse games."

"Right."

"You're the only woman I've been seeing." She greeted his claim with silence. No more laughing. "You know that, don't you?" he asked quietly.

"Since when?"

"Since I moved here. Since quite a while before that, even. But since we're not supposed to sleep together, I'm not sure why I keep coming back." It wasn't altogether true. He had sense enough to realize that he enjoyed her company. But he wanted more of her now. Much, much more.

"Deep down, I think you like my cooking." The light in her eyes teased him, and she pushed the crock closer to him. "Deep, deep down, you're not a meat-and-potatoes man."

"I've never met an Indian who didn't like meat. Certainly not a Sioux. We'd waste away and die." He wasn't surprised to hear himself offer a comeback such as that. He'd been thinking about the grandmas and the old "woman thing" taboos. And now the notion that his eating habits might have something to do with his background sprang forth full blown. He even elaborated. "In fact, we've done just that many times over the years."

She leaned forward with interest. "Do you teach much Native American history?"

"Just what's in the textbook. I have to follow the curriculum the way it's laid out." He wasn't sure that was true. He'd never pressed it.

"That's usually pretty skimpy, isn't it?"

"It usually says there were people here when Columbus came, and he thought they were Indians." He slid down a little, bracing his back squarely against the back of the chair as he stretched his legs beneath the table. "It goes downhill from there. Seems like, if I talk about what really happened, I'm looking for sympathy or handouts—the kind of stuff that makes people stop trying. Like tonight at that meeting. Marla and her mother—John's mother—they sat in the back of the room, where people expect Indians to sit. But, you know, they were willing to have us tell people that John was taking steroids. Nobody had to know that. They want us to get to the bottom of all this, so they said we could tell people what happened to John. And I know those people were sitting there thinking, 'Damned Indians are always making trouble.'"

"These people don't know anything about Indians, even though they live just across the river," Lavender said.

"They don't want to know anything. They want me to coach the wrestling team and teach by the book."

"But you're the teacher," she urged. "You can teach American history from the Native American viewpoint, and these people need to—"

"I don't know any more than you do." He gave a one-shouldered shrug. "The tipis and the buffalo are all gone, and I've studied the books the white men wrote."

"You know what your grandmother told you." He stared at her, offering no confirmation. "I'm sure she told you stories."

"A few." Family business. He shouldn't have asked about her marriage. That was family business, too, and it had gotten them both going on this kind of stuff. "Who's really interested, Lavender? I like history. But it's *history*."

"I'm interested."

He could believe that. He could also use it to his advantage. Smiling, he leaned across the corner of the table, getting closer, which was where he wanted to be. Much closer.

"Maybe that's why I'm here. Because you're interested." He touched the sleeve of her shift, running his fingertips back and forth over the loose weave. "And you're fascinating."

"I'm eccentric." She tipped her head to one side, and her hair brushed his fingers. "Is that fascinating?"

"Mmm-hmm. So what do you think? Is that why I keep coming back? Tell me what your intuition says."

"Tonight," she began, and he thought, yes, tonight, and almost missed the rest. "You're worried about this drug testing. You didn't want to go home and—"

He shook his head slowly as his eyes held hers. "Whatever happens, happens. I didn't even think about it. I just drove over here, just..." He took her shoulders in his hands as he stood, guiding her to follow suit. Her eyes spoke of willingness and wariness. He eased her closer. "I wanted to see you. Be with you."

"Maybe you need another of my—"

"I need another kiss." And he took it, even as he gave her the warmth of his own mouth and the tentative probing of his tongue. "It's like a massage in a way," he whispered against her lips. "This kiss of yours."

He watched her lips, parted and made moist by his. "These kisses are half yours," she said.

"Was the massage half mine, too?"

"I can do that for you now if you—"

"I know you can." But he needed more than that. "Another time, Lavender. Not tonight." She glanced away, and he felt as though she had taken herself from him. He touched her cheek to draw her back. "Where did you get a name like Lavender?"

"My mother..."

"It's everywhere, you know." He slid his fingers down her neck and touched the cloth that covered her shoulder. "This color. Your color. I see it around more than I used to."

"And you think of me?"

She had wondered, certainly. He came to see her when he needed someone to talk to. That was fine. That was what friends were for. But when he wasn't with her, was there room for her in his thoughts amid the strategies, programs and plans? Did he remember the color of her eyes and the sound of her voice as vividly as she remembered his?

"I think of you often."

His guileless answer made her smile.

"We don't have to sleep together," he said as he put his arms around her. "We could just make love together."

Her eyes widened. *If you say, I know you want it, too, I'll send you right out that door.*

But he said, "I want to make love to you, Lavender. Why does that scare you?"

She closed her eyes, cherishing his concern. "It scares every woman. Especially the first time."

"I don't want to scare you. I want to touch you." He slid his hands down her back slowly, then up again with firmer pressure. "The way you touched me. That was a first for me."

"I know." His touch was disarming. She rested her forehead against his chin and told herself there were no more firsts for either of them. She could not afford to forget that. "But that had nothing to do with making love."

"Yes it did," he averred softly, still stroking her back. "For me, it did. Never been much for massage. I like to do most of the touching. But I trusted you." He wanted to do more than touch.

"I didn't threaten you, Wyatt."

"That all depends on how you look at it. You got under my skin, and that threatens every man." The admission seemed so unguarded that she tipped her head back, hoping to see into his heart through his eyes. "Trust me now," he said. "It's my turn."

She wanted to trust him, because it was so good to feel his arms around her, and when he nodded toward the spiral steps, she responded with a tentative nod of her own. She went up first, and he followed. He filled the tub and lit the candles, and she watched him undress. Gloriously naked, he was totally unself-conscious. But then, he had a right to be, she thought. He was physically flawless.

"I want you in the water with me this time," he said, and he lifted her arms over her head.

"Don't be shocked."

"About what?" He whisked her shift over her head and tossed it into a chair. "The lack of underclothes beneath your nightdress?"

"It *is* a nightdress."

"And it covered you. Now it's gone." He brushed her hair back from her shoulders, then slid his hands as though he were outlining her neck, shoulders, the full length of her arms. "I've thought about how I could do for you what you did for me."

"It's not the same, Wyatt. If you think it's all the same, then—"

"I know it's not the same. It's never the same. I haven't been the same since..." He dipped his head, kissed her neck and told her, "I want to make love to you. And I *can* give you pleasure."

"Just looking at you is a pleasure," she said. She closed her eyes as his hands slipped beneath her breasts, lifting them. "Touching you—"

"I'm touching you."

He was indeed. Warm hands stroked her, and her breasts tingled, her nipples tightening in response.

"I'm prepared to protect you, too," he said.

"Protect us both?"

"Yes. Just makes me all the more trustworthy, doesn't it?" He smiled. "You had no reason to be prepared, because we weren't supposed to sleep together. But I did, because I'm supposed to make love to you."

They bathed together, soaping one another with lemon-scented lather, slip-sliding hands over smooth hips and sleek backs. Their eyes glistened with anticipation as belly floated against belly, coddling his arousal between them. Moist kisses ended in deep, soft groans. There was an unspoken agreement to prolong the ache that throbbed deeply, deliciously, down inside.

Unspoken, too, was the signal that brought them out of the water, hearts beating wildly as they dried each other and went to her bed with warm, damp, electrified skin. Kisses and caresses kept them warm and damp.

It was so much easier for her to touch than to allow herself to be touched this way. He made her want, and then he made her wait, still wanting. He touched, not to relax, but to incite, and her body rose to meet his entreaty. To Lavender, it was a wondrous, frightening thing. He pampered her desire, coaxing it out of hiding, bathing it with his tongue and polishing it to an exquisite luster. The bright light deep in her belly intensified, not because she willed it, but because he stoked it with his hands and spoke softly of his own growing need.

"I want to be here," he whispered as he slid his fingers into the nest between her thighs and teased and titillated to make her ready.

His fingers had their own specialty, just as hers did. His was more wonderful. His must not stop. His must not leave her now, not leave her now, not . . .

He rose above her, kissing her cheek, tonguing the porch of her ear. "Take me, Lavender. Please let me . . ."

Oh, so much more wonderful! He eased his way inside her, his antidote for her sweet ache. So much better, so much, yes, deeper, very much . . .

"...fill you up," he whispered, steadying her hips with his hands while he drew back, sliding through her like a bolt of silk. "I want to... fill this part of you with..."

"Wyatt," she gasped, soaring. "Fill me with Wyatt."

He held her close and said nothing for a long time. He could see stars through the skylight. A hundred of them, maybe. How many more were invisible, just in that small patch of sky? The possibilities intrigued him. Remarkably, he was filled with a youthful sense of wonder.

Lavender stirred in his arms and sighed against his skin.

"This was something new," he said.

"You said it was never the same."

"And I thought I knew what I meant." He'd thought he'd known how it would be with her. He tilted his head to see her upturned face, the innocence in her crystal eyes. "You're not the last of the red hot liberals after all."

She sighed. "Don't put a label on me, Wyatt. Not you. Please."

"It's not a label." He had to be as careful with her now as he had been moments ago. Her feelings were as fragile as her flesh. "I guess what I mean is, you're always a surprise."

"You asked me to trust you, and I did."

"Why?"

"Because I..."

He waited to hear *wanted to*. He wanted to hear *needed to*.

But she said, "Because you understood that it was a matter of trust. Maybe we should call it trustmaking instead of lovemaking."

His chuckle was throaty and deep. "You come up with some wild notions, lady."

"Unless it's just recreational, and then there are all kinds of words we can use."

He gathered her closer, brushing his lips against the smooth plane of her forehead. "Sex doesn't make for good recreation. I figured that out when I was about nineteen."

"You matured quickly, then."

"Yeah, well…even though I had it figured out…" He couldn't bring himself to accept that credit. There were all kinds of honesty in him now and no memories of other faces or other times. "Like I said, this is different." He rubbed a swatch of her hair against his neck, relishing the silky wildness of it. "This is good."

She brushed her knuckles over his muscular chest and spoke tentatively. "I know people talk about me, and I know they speculate. Glover is a very—"

He joined her in reciting "—small town," and they laughed together.

"Not only small, but isolated," Lavender said. "My mother had a time of it here, even though she tried to make the best of it. My father met her when he was in the army. She had a mind of her own, and she encouraged us to grow up the same way."

And you turned out just fine, he thought as he learned the shape of her ear by touch. "Brothers? Sisters?"

"One of each. One in Minneapolis, the other in Denver."

"Why did you come back?"

"This is a safe place, for one thing. And it's always bothered me that they…kept her on the outside. My mother," she explained. "I don't know why she wanted to be one of them anyway. But she did try."

She was exploring as she reminisced, and he wondered whether she would have preferred a hairy chest to his smooth one.

"My dad had a birthday party for her once. I think she was forty, but—" She smiled to herself, remembering. "She was ageless. About three people showed up. People had said they thought they could come. They'd try. They'd see."

He slid his hand between them and found her breast. Soft and round, no bones to support it. She could have his hand for support, he thought wistfully even as he tried to imagine this "ageless" mother, the woman who had nurtured the woman whose breast lay so sweetly in his palm. And he wondered where all this wistfulness he was feeling had come from.

She wondered whether her breast seemed puny to him.

But she told him the rest of her story. "We had a farm about three miles from here, but this is poor farmland, and my dad wasn't much of a farmer. Anyway, I decided I could live anywhere after I left Phil, and it's safe and quiet here. The air is clean. The water isn't polluted. My parents are here, in spirit, anyway."

"And you've given some of these women jobs."

"Oh, Connie Seiffert and Sherry Braun, yes. And, of course, Teri. They all do beautiful work. Sherry was my friend in school, even though her brother and I hated each other." She rested her chin on his chest and looked up at him. "He tried to get fresh with me when we were in sixth grade."

"Did he?" He smoothed her hair behind her ear and imagined some dumb kid accosting a younger Lavender. "Is he still around? Maybe he and I should have a little talk."

She smiled, and he went back to stroking the side of her breast.

She closed her eyes. "That feels good."

"The first time I saw you, I thought you looked touchable. Your dress, your hair, the look in your eyes, made you seem approachable. But you'd rather touch than be touched."

"Not tonight. You handle me so well." She feathered an appreciative kiss over his flat nipple. "With such care." Another kiss, and the nipple came erect. "Which is very good for trustmaking. And maybe there's some kind of loving in that."

"Some kind of loving," he echoed, shivering a little. "You make me feel..." *Lusty, for one thing.* "You make me feel lots of things, but since you mention it, I think maybe safe is one. Safe in your home. Safe in your arms."

"Now *that's* a funny thing for *you* to say."

"I know." But he wasn't laughing. "I'm not even sure why I said it, except that..."

"You're always on guard."

"In some ways, yeah. People expect me to be whatever they think an Indian is supposed to be, which usually isn't much. Like, when I interviewed for this job—well, it was sort of an interview. Marv Clark set it up with Harvey Borman at a restaurant. When I didn't order a drink, Clark made a big deal about how I never drank much when we were in school together, as though he had to reassure the superintendent that I wasn't a drunk. And I was told at least a dozen times that Glover was a small town and that everybody knows what everybody else is doing." He chuckled. "Like I don't know about small towns, right?"

"Why did you take this job?"

"They care about wrestling here. I care about wrestling. You look for a place where you think you'll get support. Maybe a team that's been in the cellar, but you think there's a good chance you can turn it around. That way..." He was drawing slow, lazy circles on her back with the heel of his hand. "You make a name for yourself."

"You already have a name."

"Some people build—" He shifted her in his arms, suddenly anxious to talk about himself, to tell her who he was. "I don't know, houses. Businesses. I build wrestlers. Wrestling is just one-on-one. No balls, no bats, no baskets. You build a man from the inside out, and you show him how he can face his opponent without any help from anyone."

"We all have to do that from time to time," she reflected. "Without help from anyone."

"Damn right, we do." Candlelight flickered over the curves of her face, and her eyes were windows open to a place to put his cherished secrets. "Eventually I want to coach at the college level and maybe beyond."

"Beyond?" Did that mean *professional?* "Not Saturday night TV bouts?"

He laughed. "That's all theatrical. But maybe the Olympics. I want people to know I'm here. I'm not part of some 'vanishing race.' I'm tired of having to prove myself every step of the way. Every time somebody looks at me with his prejudices written all over his face."

"You worry too much about what people think."

"Easy for you to say."

"Because I'm white? Maybe. But I'm a misfit in this town, just like my mother was. They don't know quite what to make of me."

He eased her back against the pillows, smiling and stroking her hair. "Neither do I."

"You don't have to make anything of me," she said. She lifted one hand to his face to touch the line of his jaw, his chiseled cheekbone, his aquiline nose. "Let me be myself, and I'll return the favor. I'll be a safe place for you."

"And what can I be for you?"

"That's a good question." If she said he could make her whole she would scare him away. "You've done enough. I thought I might not ever...take that step again." She smiled and rubbed her thumb over his square chin. "Trust like that again."

He slid his hand between them and covered her belly. "Was there much pain with these problems you had?"

She blinked, and her lips parted, then closed again.

"I know it's a dumb question," he said. "There must have been. It's hard for a man to imagine. Such a small, soft belly with so much going on inside." She turned her cheek against the pillow. He kissed her other cheek, the one close to his lips, and whispered, "Don't."

"It happened a long time ago," she said. "There's no more pain."

He knew there was. He smoothed her hair back from her face. "You need to be loved, Lavender."

"Yes." *But I'm not the woman you want, and we both know that. So don't...* "We all do. But we attach different meanings to the word."

Looking down at her, he couldn't say more about what it might mean to him.

Looking up at him, she was afraid to explain what the word meant to her.

"It does get complicated," she said finally, and then she sighed.

"Let's keep it simple." He knew how hopeless a statement that was. Nothing this sweet was ever simple.

"Do you have feelings, Wyatt?"

"Yes."

"For me?"

More softly. "Yes."

"And reservations, too. When you leave this safe place, you'll be tied up in knots again. It won't be simple."

"I'll worry about that later. Right now..." He lowered his head to deliver a long, slow kiss, and his heart pounded crazily when she whimpered into his mouth. He braced himself on his elbows and took her face in his hands. "I'm not going to worry about that. I'd rather make some more trust. How would that be?"

She lifted her head away from the pillow and kissed him back. "That would be beautiful."

He laughed and rolled to his back, taking her with him. "Beautiful," he echoed.

"And fun," she said as she reached down to touch him and found him ready.

He handed her a foil packet. "Decorate me."

She giggled, feeling wonderfully devilish. "Bet you could take me for a ride."

Quick, deep laughter rang through the rafters.

She squared her shoulders, and they threaded their fingers together and braced their palms against each other. The strength in his arms thrilled her, made her feel powerful as she teased him against the insides of her thighs.

"I might buck with you," he warned.

"I won't fall off."

"Damn right, you won't. You'll be—" He supported her while she gingerly found her seat. "Ahhh...a ringer."

"Wrong sport."

"I still think . . . Oh, God, Lavender . . ." She was playing with him now, but not a game. There was no contest. "I think we're making love."

She knew it was true, at least for her. This time he gave over to the soaring first, and she, riding high on the wings of his passion, followed him quickly.

Later they went downstairs for a snack. She tossed the white fringed ruana over her head, and he pulled his jeans on. They agreed on fried-egg-and-alfalfa-sprout sandwiches. Wyatt admired the side view of her—a strip of milk white skin every time she lifted her arms. He fed Jasper bits of egg, even though Lavender asked him not to. She arranged a pile of her colorful homespun-covered pillows near the woodstove and beckoned him to join her there.

They sipped herbal tea and stroked Jasper each time he passed their way. They stretched out on the pillows and stroked each other and made the human equivalent of purring sounds. So much satisfaction. Baskets of dried herbs scented the room. Spiky lavender, sprigs of thyme, silver-green wild sage and gold heads of yarrow in such profusion that the scent of wood smoke was secondary. White moonlight flooded the room through the tall, French-paned windows and brightened the bleached pine floor around them. They made love slowly this time. Silently, almost reverently, basking in the heat of the fire and then cooling in the autumn moonlight.

They did not sleep together. There was too little time to touch and talk before he would have to leave. And he would not sleep then, either.

His first overture toward taking his leave got them as far as the sofa. Later he retrieved the rest of his clothes from the loft, came down and sat beside her to put them on.

As he pulled the second brown sock over his ankle, he gave voice to the frustration they'd held at bay for a time. The subject they'd pushed to the back of their brains. "Why would they get into steroids?" he asked rhetorically. "They're just kids."

"They're young men, Wyatt. Nothing can touch you when you're that age. You know that." She handed him his shirt and watched him shrug into it. "And John was new. He had to prove himself. He may have been looking for too much too quickly. Maybe he was trying to prove some of the same things you feel the need to prove."

"He didn't do it for me." He stomped his foot into his boot. "And he didn't get the idea from me, either."

"Did you discuss steroids?"

"I said no drugs, period. I said it clearly and often." With a sigh he slid down, slouching dejectedly as he began buttoning his shirt. "How many will turn up positive? How many of these kids have I lost, Lavender?"

"Are they lost if they can't be on the team? Does that make them—" she pulled the billowy ruana close about her "—throwaways?"

"Only as far as this season is concerned. They're done for this season."

"In that case, do they go into mothballs?"

It was clear to him that her insight had reached a dead end, at least on this subject. "It's pretty tough for an athlete to set aside a whole season."

"There should be coaches for that, too, then."

He hiked an eyebrow, checking to see whether she was serious.

She was. "When the going gets tough, a kid needs somebody to coach him through it. Somebody strong.

Somebody who's been there." She laid her hand on his arm. "You've made mistakes, haven't you? And you're that much stronger for having learned from them."

"Have you ever used drugs?" It was almost an idle question.

"Oh, I dabbled in grass years ago, but meditation works better for me." She tipped her head inquisitively. "You?"

"No." It was no big deal to her, and that bothered him. "You wouldn't want to venture a guess as to where that stuff might have come from?"

"No, I wouldn't." She waited for him to look up, but he didn't. He flipped open his pants and stuffed his shirt inside, all the while avoiding her eyes. Her stomach tightened. "Was there any discussion of the possibilities at the board meeting?"

"Some wild guesses."

"Was I one of them?"

He rubbed his hands up and then down over his thighs, stalling.

"I was, wasn't I? Of course." She wrapped her arms around herself and pulled her bare feet under her wrap. "And you've been here with me most of the night, holding me and kissing me, touching me so sweetly that I thought I might burst, and all the while you've been wondering—"

"That question was the furthest thing from my mind."

"Until now." Heated anger and chilling disappointment both assaulted her at once. She worked to maintain an even tone of voice. "If you had learned anything about me, you would have known the answer. And they didn't ask, did they? They just said, 'It was probably Lavender.'"

She knew them well, except that they hadn't even said *probably*. And there was nothing he could say in his own behalf, because he'd done little to defend her. She'd said he was a strong man, but she'd given him too much credit.

"You'd better go," she said quietly. "It'll be light soon."

Chapter 9

Wyatt watched the silver key ring spin around his fore-finger, the fat collection of keys chinking as they twirled. Another wait in another damn clinic lobby. He'd done enough time this way as a kid. Endless hours in the Indian Health Clinic lobby, waiting, watching for somebody to come down the hall. Sometimes it was his mother and maybe a new baby, but most of the time it was his grandma. It was either sit in the lobby and make paper airplanes out of the fliers in the big wire rack or wait in the car. When he'd gotten old enough to drive, he'd chosen the car.

It was his experience that when they finally got around to you, doctors usually came up with bad news, and he had a queasy feeling about the results of the tests he'd herded the boys in for that morning. Some of them had joked about lining up to pee in a cup, and he'd laughed and said, yeah, they'd need to watch their aim. He'd also noticed which ones weren't laughing. Mostly the seniors.

Mark Christian's eyes reminded him of a cornered animal's, and there was a fine sheen of sweat on Kirby Streeter's face. Good kids, but they were *seniors*. Infallible and immortal for one fleeting school year. Just looking at them when they'd filed into the doctor's office had made Wyatt feel a little sick. Who in God's name had put this idea into their heads?

Not Lavender. He'd hurt her with the suggestion that she might know more than she'd already told him. Everything he knew about her added up to a natural high, and if he hadn't stuck his foot in his mouth, she probably would have been waiting this out with him now. She cared about these kids as much as he did. Maybe more.

Maybe she cared about a lot of things more than he did, and maybe he shouldn't be messing with her mind, asking her to trust him. What he cared about most was where he was going. He would see these kids through this season, come hell or high water, and then he would move on. He had his goals.

But his thoughts kept slipping into a scented purple haze. He took little notice of the woman and child who took a chair across from him. He was sitting there waiting for the other shoe to drop, but to imagine being with her in that offbeat haven of hers was a balm. Lavender touching him, speaking softly in his ear, giving the kind of pleasure that lingered long after she was out of reach.

So who was messing with whose mind?

The school day had been a real bust. Between worrying about the test results—Whatever happens, happens, he'd said. What a crock!—and trying to figure out how to apologize to Lavender, he wasn't sure what he'd actually managed to cover in class.

The door to Dr. Werner's office opened. Wyatt straightened suddenly, as though he'd been caught dozing. The doctor gave him the nod. Feeling like the kid who knew he was going to get a shot, Wyatt pushed himself out of the chair.

The doctor's face showed the strain of running a one-man practice. He sat on the edge of his desk, his scalp shining through thin wisps of gray hair, his stiff fingers bending the yellow forms that were clipped inside a file folder.

It seemed to take him forever to look up. His eyes were basset-hound sad. He shook his head. "You know, it's funny. All these kids knew their parents had signed release forms giving you access to the results." He seemed to actually see Wyatt then, and he quickly added, "I'm sorry. Have a seat."

"I've *been* sitting," Wyatt said.

"It's been a long day, I'm sure." He looked at the file again. "Anyway, they came in here on the understanding that you would be told about the results."

"It was either that or forget wrestling." The man had a flair for the dramatic, Wyatt decided. He had him hanging on every word.

"Well, three of the reports indicate the presence of anabolic steroids in the system. You'd think they would have just said, yeah, I'm using the stuff."

"They probably hoped it wouldn't show up. Bigger men than these guys have deluded themselves the same way." Wyatt heaved a sigh and bounced his keys once in his hand. "So, who are they?"

"Streeter, Anderson and Christian."

"Christian." It was no surprise after what he'd seen that morning, but he was still disappointed. "This'll hit his dad pretty hard."

"Ron's got a good head on his shoulders. He and Mark will learn from this. Now, Streeter, I don't know." The doctor set the folder aside and folded his arms over his rumpled white jacket. "I'm going to recommend that physicals and drug evaluations be done immediately, and we'll have to send them to Bismarck for that. And then I'd say Ron Christian is gonna be looking for a drug connection here in Glover."

"How long do you think it's been going on?"

"I don't know. I didn't see any discoloration of the urine, no really bad acne, which you know can be a sign." He looked to Wyatt, who bobbed his head. "Some blood-pressure readings I didn't like, but I didn't see any advanced stages. Now, with the Tiger boy..." He drew a deep breath and pursed his lips consideringly. "It affects people differently."

"Did you pick up any other drugs?" Dr. Werner shook his head. "I didn't talk to them about steroids." Wyatt pocketed his keys and sank into the chair he'd been offered moments ago. "I guess I didn't think it was necessary. Not way the hell out here."

"Well, they managed to get hold of them way out here, and they probably liked the results they were getting."

"Oh, yeah. The stuff works." Wyatt stared at the fluorescent light overhead. "God, I hope this hasn't been going on long."

"I don't suppose you've used the stuff yourself somewhere along the way?" Wyatt's first response was a dark look. Werner shrugged. "We all make mistakes when we're young."

He'd had that coming. He'd asked Lavender the same thing. Did he think he was above suspicion? Above reproach?

"I've made my share," Wyatt admitted, "but that wasn't one of them."

"You don't think the Tiger boy..."

"No, I don't." The new kid in town. The unknown. *The Indian kid.* "I don't, but I intend to check it out."

He intended to clear him. John had enough problems.

"This puts some holes in your team," Werner said.

"We've got some jayvees we can bring up. It's not the first time I've had to bench good wrestlers. I just hope this town sticks by its team when the points get harder to come by."

"It's a hard-nosed town, Wyatt. People like a good hometown win on Friday night to kind of take the edge off the low beef and pork prices they get in the sale ring on Saturday afternoon." He shoved his hands in his jacket pockets as he came away from the desk to offer, unexpectedly, a handshake. "You hang tough with those boys. They think you've got moves up your sleeve nobody's ever seen before."

"I wish I did. The boys I have to bench..." The handshake stilled, and Dr. Werner looked at him, waiting. "I'll be there for them, too."

Within two days the town was abuzz with shock and speculation. The word was out that "the kids were on drugs," but nobody knew much about these anabolic steroids. Sounded something like the growth hormones some of them used on their calves. The comparison brought up the point that those nature freaks were in an uproar over using hormones on calves, which brought up the point that Lavender Holland was a nature freak, which brought up the *whole point*, which was Lavender Holland.

She didn't belong in Glover, North Dakota. Being born there had nothing to do with it. People like Lavender Holland weren't satisfied to live your average, everyday life. They had to do everything differently. Live in a schoolhouse. Eat weird food. *Probably* use drugs, wouldn't you think? It was a good thing there weren't too many people like Lavender Holland around, because everything, *everything*, was going to hell in a hand basket, as it was.

Well, Marge Nordstrom was probably right. Lavender Holland undoubtedly had something to do with all this.

Well, sure. She dealt with a lot of people in a lot of states, shipping packages all the time and getting stuff shipped in to her. You could hide a lot of pills and weeds in those shipments of yarn or fabric or fancy-priced clothing. She'd brought this whole drug thing back from California, along with her soybean curd and devil worship.

And there was sure some kind of voodoo foolishness going on out there. Marge Nordstrom had spread the word about the stone altar by Coyote's Call Creek. And she'd seen chicken feathers in the yard. She knew a chicken feather when she saw one. If Lavender didn't eat meat, why was she butchering chickens?

Glover had two grocery stores, and Lavender was never impressed with the produce at either one. She divided her business between them because she believed in supporting the local shopkeepers, but it always seemed to her that Margaret Bosch, the clerk at Best Foods, was keeping a mental list of everything she bought.

"Haven't seen you in the store for a while, Lavender," Margaret commented, as she examined the label on one of the cans Lavender had set on the counter. "Artichokes, huh? Pret-ty pricey. Been keeping busy?"

"Actually, I was in last week, but I don't think you were working that day, Margaret." Lavender had been glad to see that Sissy Sandland had found an after-school job there at the store. "Yes, things are pretty busy."

Margaret lifted her chin to look down her nose at another can. "You hear about the special school-board meeting?"

"Yes." Lavender lifted a sack of whole-wheat flour from her cart and smiled at Greta Borman, the superintendent's wife, who had just lined up behind her.

"Well, you were there when that boy tried to kill himself, weren't you, Lavender?" Greta asked.

"No. We found him—"

Faith Hague, who'd suddenly lost interest in selecting Red Rome apples, moved in behind Greta with her two cents. "Where do you suppose those boys got hold of those drugs? Somebody must have some out-of-state connections, wouldn't you say?"

Lavender wondered whether three was a gang. "I understand steroids aren't that hard to get if you know—"

"If you know the right people, I suppose," Faith said. She adjusted the collar on her quilted jacket. "Ellen Streeter is pretty damned upset, and she can't figure out who it is that Kirby knows."

When Coach Archer walked through the door, the conversation abruptly stopped, as though the women had been speaking of the devil.

But they hadn't been. They'd been speaking about who Kirby Streeter might have known, and Lavender was tired of all the innuendo. She spared Wyatt a glance, then turned on Faith Hague and demanded, "Why doesn't she ask Kirby?"

"Well, the kids are kinda tight-lipped right now. Like they're scared of something."

Considering himself included by all the pointed looks he was getting, Wyatt stepped up to the checkout counter. "There's nothing left to be scared of. The worst has happened." He exchanged a look with Lavender.

"How are you?" she asked. She fought to keep her heart from going out to him. The children—and really, they were still children—needed her sympathy now.

"Hangin' in there." And since he knew they would find out soon enough, he elaborated. "The worst, Mrs. Hague, is that one boy almost died and three others are being evaluated. Steroids can cause serious side effects, and we're going to be educating the kids about them. Educating parents about what to look for."

"So what does this stuff do to them?" Faith asked. She cut a sharp glance Lavender's way. "Get them high?"

"Basically, they were trying to beef up their muscle mass," Wyatt said. "Steroids aren't like—"

"We've never had any trouble like this before," Greta Borman claimed. "I don't know where our kids would get any drugs."

"I'm sure we'll find out." He shifted easily into a congenial mode, which absorbed the three women's attention immediately. "Meanwhile, I hope you'll come out Friday night and support the team. Some of the boys are going to be a little nervous about being moved up to..."

Lavender took the opportunity to exit with her sacks of groceries. Wyatt was surely doing the right thing, seeking good will for what was left of his team. But the wool of the black sheep weighed heavily on her back, and she needed out. She needed air. What she didn't need was these people's suspicions, even though she'd had a lot of practice ignoring them.

She turned the key in the lock on the tailgate of the station wagon and watched the power window slowly disappear. She hoped they got to the bottom of all this soon. Although she would be exonerated, there would be no apologies made to her. She knew better than to expect any. It would all blow over, and life in Glover would go on the way it always had, with that strange woman, that Lavender Holland, living on its outskirts.

At least once a month she told herself she ought to move. She ought to stop trying to force herself down their throats. Volunteering at the school, for heaven's sake. Offering employment. She could bring a million-dollar-a-year industry into this stagnating town, but she would still be Lavender Holland. They would never accept her as she was. That was all she had ever wanted. They didn't have to *love* her. Just accept her, the way they ought to have accepted her mother.

Wyatt Archer didn't know her, either. It had been a mistake to believe that he was the man who would say, *Yes,* Lavender, come to me just the way you are, because that's the way I want you. How could he say that and mean it, when he didn't even know who she was? He saw only the trappings. She was an eccentric, but she was a woman, and since he was new in town, she would do.

She lifted two grocery sacks through the window and set them in the back of the car. Of course, she'd known better on that score, too. They weren't supposed to sleep together. She'd gotten the message, and she'd ignored it. She deserved to pay the price in heartache, because she knew better than to share herself with a man who had not the slightest idea who she was.

"Lavender, wait."

She turned the key as she turned her head. Wyatt stood there with his hands in the pockets of his leather jacket, waiting for her to reply. Her heart did some kind of a double take inside her chest, then shifted into high gear. She thought about sparing herself, ignoring him, walking away, but her feet felt embedded in the pavement.

"It's closed," he said, and he lifted his chin to indicate the back window.

She felt the quick, hot bloom of a blush in her face as she turned back to the window and its motorized clicking. Too quickly, she turned the key again and jerked it out.

"We need to talk," he said quietly.

He was standing too close. His spicy scent and warm proximity made her feel dizzy, and she remembered that low voice whispering sweet words about trustmaking and asking her, as no one else ever had, about her feelings, about the pain. How had he made the leap from caring to suspicion? She stared over the top of her car at the bare branches of a cottonwood etched against the late autumn sky.

"They were doing plenty of talking in the store," she said. "Everybody is."

"I know. The kids are in trouble, and everybody's scared."

Hard to imagine on one count. She turned to him and searched his dark, inscrutable eyes. "Are you?"

"Yes."

"Whatever happens, happens, you said."

"I know." He skidded his boot heels against the pavement and he shifted his weight, suddenly looking uncomfortable. "How did that sound? Pretty callous?" He looked down at his feet, then into her eyes. "I waited for those test results with knots in my gut."

"I heard about the other boys. I'm sorry, Wyatt."

"No, *I'm* sorry. I'm sorry for suggesting..." He touched her arm. Through the soft, natural fabric of her handmade jacket she could feel the urgency in his firm grip. "For even asking you. It came out wrong."

"How was it supposed to come out?" she asked. "The women in the store were getting at the same thing. Do I do drugs? Do I have a pharmacy shelf somewhere in my strange little hideaway?''

"I know you better than that," he said.

Faith Hague and Greta Borman emerged from Best Foods together, Faith chattering over her shoulder as, arms full of groceries, she held the glass door open with her elbow. She waited for Greta, who was similarly burdened. The door swung shut behind them, and the chattering stopped as they took stock of the two standing behind the brown station wagon. The women glanced at one another, then back at Wyatt and Lavender. Greta offered a nod, Faith a tight-lipped smile. Then they muttered something to one another and went their separate ways.

"They think they know," Lavender said with a sigh. "The next rumor will be that we're in on this together."

"It makes more sense to suspect me," he said as he dropped his hand. "I'm the one who might have something to gain by getting those boys all muscled up. Some coaches might even—"

"Not you." No, she wouldn't hear of it, and if anyone suggested it, she would set them straight. "You didn't make any attempt to sweep this under the rug. You could have. Some coaches might have."

"You know me better than that," he said.

"Yes, I do."

They gave in to a long, rapt moment, looking at one another, willing away the passing pickup and the unseen customer who'd just left Best Foods and clip-clopped down the sidewalk. He felt like a very small man just then. She felt chilled, as though he'd gone his way already and taken some part of her with him.

He finally broke the silence. "I'm driving Teri up to Bismarck to see John tonight. It took a little weaseling, but I got us permission." He offered a one-cornered smile. "Wanna come?"

"No. John doesn't need a big crowd right now." She shook her head and gathered her loose-fitting jacket closely around her. *And I don't think you want people jumping to any more conclusions.*

"I think he'll tell me, sooner or later."

"I hope so." She took a step back into the street. "I have to go. I have to stop at Sherry's to pick up some finished work."

"I'll call you," he said.

And she wondered when.

John was a strong, strapping young man. He was the kind of kid Wyatt especially hated to see laid up. A kid like John needed to be working out in the gym. Seeing his leg suspended in a sling and his upper body immobilized in a cast made Wyatt wonder whether there was any justice anywhere.

"Hi, John. How's it goin'?"

"Pretty good." The boy brightened. The comic book he'd been reading fell to the floor as he tried to turn his body toward the sound of his coach's voice.

"Relax," Wyatt told him as he patted the boy's uncast foot. "You never liked looking up at me anyway."

"They say I'll be out of commission for a while. They put me in this part of the hospital because I guess I kinda flipped out."

Wyatt sat on the side of the bed, putting himself within John's view. For a moment, because it could not be dismissed with an easy remark, they paid quiet deference to that terrible fact.

"I've never done anything like that before," John said. The boy was ashamed to look at him.

"Your sister told us about the steroids, so we know why you flipped out."

"I told her she should tell you. You know, after the doctor told me how bad they are for you."

Wyatt nodded. "You know we tested the rest of the team."

"Yeah. She told me that, too."

"So we know who else was taking them."

"Good. That's good." John glanced through the slatted blinds that covered the single window in the small white room. "We wanted to be the best. The biggest. The strongest. Unbeatable, you know?"

"There's no quick way to get there, John. I tried to show you the right way, but I guess I didn't warn you about the wrong ways."

"You told us not to use diuretics. I didn't even know what diuretics were before that."

"How did you find out about steroids?" Wyatt shook off his own question. "Why am I asking that? You've got ears. You've got eyes." This was not the time, Wyatt reminded himself. The boy needed something from him. Something for himself. He touched the big foot again, covered by the bed sheet. "I want you to know, John, that you are one of the best natural athletes I've seen."

"I should've stayed natural," John said quietly.

"I should've seen what was happening. But 'should have' doesn't change anything for us. We've learned a lesson now, haven't we?" Those brown eyes were too full of sadness to leave room for anything like wisdom. Too much youth. Too much disappointment. Too damn much pain. "Both of us," Wyatt insisted anyway. "We've both learned. John, I need to know where you got the drugs."

John looked at Wyatt. The need to tell was there, but so was the fear. He glanced away. "We were only doin' 'em a couple of months."

"I knew a guy who died using them, John. They can turn your body into a time bomb. We've got Mark and Kirby and Donny in for drug evaluations." John blinked a few times, looking more scared. Wyatt patted his foot again. Just about every other part of him was bandaged. "You guys are gonna be fine. It's all over."

"You don't have much of a team left, do you?"

"We'll fill in. These things happen." He wasn't very good at this. He was probably saying all the wrong things, but he felt as though he was supposed to come up with some sort of wisdom. "Nobody's ever so good that he can't be replaced." Geez, that sounded awful. Wyatt shifted uncomfortably and tried again. "That goes for me, too. When I leave, I'll be replaced. You'll graduate, and there'll be a new senior class. That's the way it's supposed to be, which is good for all of us. When things get bad like this, you know they have to get better."

"You know how it really is?" John looked toward the window again, and his lower lip quivered. "Things get better for a little while, and then they get bad again."

"I've been there, too, John. The only person you can depend on is *you*. *You* make it better."

"I felt like I was two people, you know? I was me watching this crazy person, who was also me." The boy took a deep, steadying breath and released it slowly. "God, it was weird."

Wyatt's hands felt clammy. It hurt to see this broken boy and know how desperate he'd been. It would have felt good to fight somebody just then.

"You guys took some bad advice, John. I'd like to know who gave it to you."

John shook his head slightly. "How come the other guys didn't get like that? I mean, none of them tried to fly."

"Maybe they had some of the same feelings but didn't talk about them. Did you tell anyone what was going on with you?"

"We just kept talking about how pumped up we were gonna get. We could see it, you know? We'd compare."

Wyatt had read about placebos having a similar effect on athletes. If somebody told them a pill would make them win, they wanted to believe it. Who was the *somebody* this time? Teri was scared. John was scared. Who were they protecting? "Was it Ally who got you the stuff, John?"

"Did somebody tell you that?" Wyatt could almost see the next worry forming itself in the boy's head. "Teri didn't know. She didn't have anything to do with it."

"I know. But Ally did, didn't he?"

John sighed. "Yeah. Ally was getting us the steroids. I don't know where. But Teri wasn't in on it."

Teri had known enough to ask Lavender about the effects of the drugs, but Wyatt respected John's need to shield her. Sooner or later, it would all come out.

"She asked me once," John supplied, as if he'd read his coach's thoughts. "I told her it was like vitamins, and she believed me. So don't let anyone say that Teri—"

"Will you talk to the police, John?"

"You can talk to them." At that moment, if John could have run, he would have. But he couldn't, so he looked to Wyatt for help. "I don't wanna talk to them. It'll look like I turned Ally in. I don't do that to my friends. I don't do that to my girl's brother." He looked away. "Besides, Ally was trying to help us out. It just backfired on me, is all."

"As soon as you feel up to it, I'll bring you some schoolwork. We'll try to get you caught up." Wyatt picked up the comic book off the floor and tossed it on the bed table. "Don't wanna be wasting your time on this stuff."

"I don't think they'll keep me here very long. The doctor said they'll probably transfer me down to the Indian hospital. My mom's talking about moving back to the rez. I'll probably just take the GED test."

Wyatt heard the hopelessness in the boy's voice, and his next breath came hard. "Is that what you want?"

John closed his eyes. "I wanted to graduate." Wyatt felt a stab of real pain, which intensified as he listened to the recounting of John's dreams. "When I heard you were coming to Glover to coach and Marla said I could stay with them, I thought, *Now's my chance.* I wanted to be like the famous Wyatt Archer."

"You could be a better wrestler than I ever was."

With a bandaged hand, John managed a gesture of disgust. "Yeah, right."

"You'll heal. And you'll graduate from high school if you want to. College, too. You wanna coach? You wanna teach? You could be a better teacher than I am." Wyatt had gotten the answers he needed out of John, but at what price? His voice grew hoarse. "Right now, that wouldn't take much."

"You're a great—"

"Hey, I'm the one who's here to cheer you up." Wyatt cleared his throat as he stood up. "And I brought just the thing. Who would you rather be looking at than me?"

John gave a mirthless chuckle. "Teri, but I don't want her to see me like this."

"She wants to see you just like this. Alive and looking a whole lot better than you did the last time she saw you. You scared her pretty bad that night."

"She's the..." John swallowed, and Wyatt knew exactly how desperate the boy was to see his girl, no matter how low he felt "...the nicest girl I've ever known, Coach."

"Be nice back, okay?"

Teri was waiting outside for the coach's signal. She tiptoed into the room as Wyatt left and came to the foot of the bed. The situation seemed to call for gentle care and soft tones. All those bandages must have meant he was hurting, which made her hurt, too. She wanted him to see that she'd worn a dress, and she'd fixed her hair and her makeup just so. For him. He was looking at her, but he wasn't smiling.

"Hi," she offered shyly.

John held his hand out to her. She took a deep breath and hurried to him, reaching. But the bandage was there, and she bit her lip and touched it tentatively.

"It's okay," he said. "It won't hurt. Not if it's you holding it."

That brought tears, and her tears brought his. She cradled his injured hand in both of hers, touched her forehead to his thumb and wept.

When she got hold of herself, she sat up, tossed her blond hair back and touched the hearts he'd given her. "I'm wearing my earrings, see?"

"They're—" God, he couldn't even wipe his hot, stupid, wet face. She smiled, and with her slight hand she did it for him. He smiled back. "You look pretty," he whispered, his voice thick with tears.

"Does this hurt much?" she asked.

John shook his head.

"Hoss Sandland said to tell you hi."

He nodded.

"I miss you, John." She held his hand to her lips for a moment, then told him, "I really...I just want to hug you."

His laugh was shallow, but the joy was there. He wiggled his toes. "My right foot's up for grabs."

After he dropped Teri off, Wyatt paid a visit to Ron Christian. There were no preliminaries, except for the offer of a cup of coffee. Wyatt declined. Ron ushered him into his home office and closed the door.

"John said it was Ally," Wyatt reported.

"Ally denies it, and so far the other boys won't say." Ron folded his arms over his chest. "You know when they're underage I have to have parental consent to take any statements. Some of the parents are pretty indignant, once the kid says he doesn't know anything."

"What about Mark?"

"Mark won't even look at me, and I can't—" Ron shook his head and turned away. "I don't know what to say to him. I was sure he'd make All State this year. I don't know why in hell he'd do a thing like this."

Wyatt sighed. He studied the pictures on Ron's office wall. Family pictures. Young Ron and his bride cutting a triple-tier wedding cake. Mark and his little sister with Santa Claus. Mark and Ron with rifles and a pair of pheasants they'd bagged. He swallowed hard and turned to Ron. "Somebody persuaded them that this was no big deal. Sort of like a super vitamin. I can see Ally selling the idea to the other boys, but somebody else sold *him* on it."

"The selling part—" Archer was quiet for a moment. Clearly the idea sickened him because it had been happening in his town, with his boy, and he hadn't seen it. "These kids don't have a whole lot of money to throw around."

"They must have had some. And they must have decided this was worth the price."

"And the risk." After another long silence, Ron turned to Wyatt, who saw that the man had aged in a few short days. "You know, a thing like this happens, some people can't accept the fact that their kid got himself into a bind. They look for someone else to blame."

"If we can find out who the supplier is, they'll have their man," Wyatt said.

"I'll find him, sure." Ron shrugged. "Or her. But there's gonna be all kinds of bellyaching about this. Just don't take it personal. You're doing a good job. And as far as the drug testing goes, it was the right thing to do."

It was the only thing to do, Wyatt thought, but he'd been given credit for it twice now. He was determined to do a hell of a lot more. "I want Mark to keep working out with us. Soon as he's able to come back."

"You know, they have withdrawals from that stuff. Depression. The doctors warned us." Ron shook his head. "But there's no sign of any damage to the liver or—" His voice turned hoarse, and he shook his head again.

"I'm sorry, Ron," Wyatt offered, laying his hand on the smaller man's shoulder. "I do take this personally. But I'm not a father. I can't claim to know how it feels."

"Listen, it's none of my business, but if Lavender Holland is..." His gaze was surprisingly sympathetic. "Well, at the hospital, I got the impression you were friends. When I went over to Nordstroms' to talk to Ally, Marge kept insisting I ought to raid Lavender's place. Of course, I've got no reason to search Lavender's place, but her name keeps coming up. The kids like to go over there to visit her, and she is kinda different."

"I'd suspect Dr. Werner before I'd suspect Lavender."
Wyatt waited for the shock to register before adding,
"And I don't suspect Dr. Werner. But he has access."

"Now you're talking crazy. Doc Werner's out of the
question."

"So is Lavender." For so many reasons, and all of them
came down to trust. She was a woman to be trusted. The
thought made him smile. "It isn't in her. We've become
friends, and I know it isn't in her. She's about as health-
conscious as they come. You know that. You've known
her longer than I have."

"Well, off and on, though. She left to go to college out
in California. Got married out there. Her mom died, then
her dad. That's when she moved back, when he was sick.
She was divorced by then." He gave an offhanded gesture. "I don't know why she stayed. Now, I don't think
she had anything to do with it, either, but I do think this
town's too small for her. She sticks out like a sore thumb
here, pretty much the way her mom did."

Sore thumb was not an apt description of the lithe and
lovely lady who lingered in Wyatt's head. He'd kept
wishing she'd gone with him to see John. He seemed to be
wishing she were with him every spare moment lately.
Hell, no, she was nobody's sore anything.

He, on the other hand, stuck out in this town like a raisin in a bowl of Frosted Flakes. Not that that was anything new, but until recently he'd been working on
minimizing it. He'd had this long-range plan to find a
woman who blended in with the mainstream, marry her
and slip into Middle America beside her with all his
awards and credentials. But the woman on his mind was

not the "blending in" kind. She never would be. In a tan town situated on a tan prairie, she was Lavender.

"She's definitely noticeable," was the only claim Wyatt made.

Chapter 10

Filling four holes on the wrestling team wasn't easy. The last thing Wyatt wanted was an inexperienced boy getting hurt. Even after he'd given the nod to four boys whom he figured could hold their own, the holes still gaped, just like the four empty desks in the American government class. Those holes seemed to echo with all the words Wyatt wished he had said, the admonitions he wished he had given, the lessons he was beginning to think he ought to be teaching.

He'd told them they had to want to win so bad that there was no thought of anything else. But there *were* other things. There were winners, and there were also survivors. There were those who held their own. There was honor in that, too. There was his grandmother, who'd raised her own kids and helped to raise her grandchildren, and all of it through tough times. There was his cousin Sheldon—the one who'd pelted him in the head with a rock—who'd made it through alcohol treatment last year and gotten back together with his wife. And there was Roscoe, his uncle, who'd been driving a BIA school bus for over thirty years.

And there were four young kids who'd suddenly found themselves promoted from jayvee to varsity wrestlers. They were going to do their best, knowing they would be lucky to win a match once in a while. His words about winning would haunt him until the end of the season. Who the hell did he think he was, anyway?

Well, he would just have to come up with some new words.

"It wasn't like they were trying to get high," Marty Brinker complained in his teammates' defense. "They wanted us to go to State, is all. I don't see why they can't have another chance if they just don't take that stuff anymore."

"Because it's a rule, and you play by the rules or you don't play. Not on a sanctioned team, anyway." Wyatt was working on Marty's headgear in response to the boy's complaint that it was too tight. Complaining had become the order of the day.

"Yeah, but, geez. Nobody thought it was all that bad. Just a little extra muscle can make the difference, you said."

"And I told you to *work* for it, Marty. You do. You work hard." He handed the headgear back. "Here, try it now."

"Mark worked hard. So did Kirby and John."

"I know they did. One other thing I should have told you, told them, is that it's possible to go overboard. Winning isn't everything." The words came hard. He wasn't used to saying them.

"It's a lot better than losing," Marty said. He wasn't satisfied with the headgear, either.

"We'll see." Wyatt made another adjustment. "I predict we'll win some, and we'll lose some."

"Yeah, right. Before we lost the seniors—"

"They're not lost. Understand? They are not lost." Wyatt studied the boy for a moment, then offered the headgear once more. "Why did you decide not to use steroids? Did you think about it?"

"I don't know. Chicken, I guess."

"But you knew about it." Marty said nothing. He fitted the protective device over his ears. "Where did the drugs come from, Marty?" More silence.

It was the same kind of silence the sheriff had met with time after time. Everybody wanted to know who was behind this, but nobody wanted his own kid implicated. Consequently, once a kid claimed innocence and ignorance, the parents tended to fend off further questioning. "We went along with the tests. Now, if he says he doesn't know anything, he *doesn't know anything.*"

It's not my kid. Thank God. It's somebody else's.

Wyatt laid a hand on Marty's shoulder. "Tell you what. You made the right choice about the steroids, and I guess I don't expect you to tell on your friends. The important thing is to get help for the guys who need it, and to bring these new guys along the best we can. Am I right this time?"

Marty's reluctant nod was at least a start. Nobody was better at being tight-lipped than a teenager.

The one person who said nothing about the incident was Ally Nordstrom. Ally had suddenly lost interest in trying to make people laugh. He wasn't asking any questions, and he was quick to do whatever he was told. But Wyatt found it difficult to talk to the boy. His eyes were as vacant as those four empty chairs, and his whole face was shut tight, like a drawstring bag. Wyatt tried to imagine what was going on inside Ally's head. Sometimes he thought there might be a conscience at work, but he didn't doubt that fear and the wild hope that this would all go away were paramount for Ally right now. He was keeping a low profile.

In many ways Wyatt was doing the same thing. It had been days since he'd talked to Lavender. He had made love to her, then said the wrong thing, or at least said things in the wrong way. Either way, he should have known better. No matter how independent she professed to be, she was still a woman, vulnerable as hell at a time like that, looking for added meaning in every word. He'd promised to call, but he hadn't done it. She wanted more than an apology.

And he wanted people on the street to treat him the way they had when he'd first come to town. He didn't like the cool nods and the crisp hellos. And the stares. God, he hated it when people stared at him as if he'd just turned some exotic color. Like purple. Lavender.

Or like red.

Even Hausauer and Clark were keeping to themselves lately. The warning signal had sounded, and all the prairie dogs had taken to their holes. Some of them were trying to find a way to blame her for all this, and Wyatt was just going about his damn business. It was the smart thing for him to do if he wanted them to stop staring at him.

Real smart. He felt like a lowlife bastard.

She missed the Friday night home meet, and Wyatt missed seeing her in the stands. He kept looking for her, hoping she would show up late, maybe not for him, but for the boys. The bleachers were full, and the fans were supportive. But Lavender should have been there. She should have defied all the speculation and taken her place next to Teri Nordstrom. He was disappointed when she didn't assume the role he'd conjured for her. For some reason, he expected her courage to exceed his.

Glover lost, but only by eight points, and Wyatt was pleased with the way the team pulled together. Hoss Sandland had pinned his man in four seconds. Mike Braun, who had replaced Mark Christian, got an escape and two reversals before succumbing to a pin, and Mike was only an eighth-grader.

When the meet was over, Wyatt tried to keep Ally busy in the locker room until everyone else was gone, but it didn't work. Ally got his chores done quickly and said he needed to catch a ride with Hoss. Ally was afraid to be alone with him. He figured there was a triangle of tension—Ally, Teri and John—that would eventually crack wide open somewhere. Wyatt wanted to be handy when it did.

He locked the gym door, then tugged on it just to make sure. He'd been thinking about John, too, and how they would talk about the meet when he took John's makeup work to him the next day. Jock talk might cheer them both.

He wondered if Lavender would be receptive to a little jock talk, too, since she'd missed the meet. She would appreciate the fact that he was revising his approach, talking less about winning and more about enjoying the sport. Maybe if he let her take some of the credit—said something like, "I've thought a lot about what you said about..."

Sure, he could be a little humble. He could apologize again. He could tell her how Ally was acting and ask her advice about dealing with him. He could... He would be damn glad to lay eyes on her again, and maybe just have her touch his hand or his shoulder in a forgiving way. He hadn't meant to hurt her.

The night was cold and cloudy, heavy with the promise of snow. The first flakes fell as his car crested the hill above the schoolhouse. His heart rose with it, but quickly sank when he saw no light in the window. Her car was there. He wondered how she would greet him if he woke her up. He wished he'd thought to bring her something, like a quart of ice cream, so he could say he hated to let it melt. Frozen yogurt, he amended as he turned into the driveway. She would be a frozen yogurt person. Lemon. He remembered the lemony scent of her soap and the bath they'd shared.

He didn't notice the graffiti until he reached the front step. Red paint was slashed over black, and the sign now read, "Coyote's Bitch Creek." He scowled as more spray-painted messages suddenly hit him like neon flashes. "Meditate This—We Kill Drug Sellers." And vertically, near the corner of the building, there was, "Burn Witch Burn!"

There were other words. Wyatt tasted the bitterness of bile as he turned his face from them and mounted the steps. Glass fractured beneath his boot. He looked to the window. One jagged shard, standing like a glass tooth, was all that remained. The door stood ajar.

The studio was a shambles.

"Ho-ly...Lavender!" He stumbled over a chair. His pulse thudded in his ears as he picked it up and set it back on its rockers. "Where are you? Are you hurt?"

The room dividers were overturned. Spools of yarn were scattered like toppled dominoes.

"Lavender, it's me. Wyatt. Are you all right?"

He heard a rustling near the back door, which stood open.

"Lavender?"

She appeared as a dark shadow in the doorway.

"Thank God," he breathed as he stepped over a lamp and kicked a pillow aside. "I was afraid—"

Good God, she was holding a rifle. "Lavender? You wanna put that down, honey? I'm not gonna hurt you."

"I don't know...who did this." Her voice was small and tight. Her face was shrouded in shadows.

"You know it wasn't me," he said.

"I don't know...who would do this."

He moved toward her slowly, one hand outstretched. "Give me the gun, honey. You're okay now."

"Wyatt?" It was a test of the name itself. "Whose side are you on?"

The question stabbed him painfully, because it was utterly fair. Even so, he pleaded, "Trust me, Lavender. Give me the gun."

She didn't offer it, but neither did she resist his taking it from her. "Who would do this?" she asked with childlike bewilderment.

"Stupid people." He set the weapon aside and turned to her. "Only the worst kind of stupid, stupid..."

She let him take her in his arms, and he felt a warm rush of gratitude and relief. "Oh, God, I was afraid you were hurt. Were you here when this happened?"

A soft whimper escaped her throat, and her chest vibrated against his. "I was upstairs. I was in the bathtub. I didn't hear anyone drive up or anything. The power went off. Then they started breaking the windows, and there was shouting and pounding." Within the safety of his embrace she drew a tremulous breath and went on. "By the time I had some clothes on, they were inside smashing everything. I crawled around up there, collecting things to throw down on them if they came upstairs."

"Did you see any faces?" She shook her head. "Recognize any—"

"I was scared spitless." She pressed her face against his neck, and he drew her closer. "There were at least three, maybe more. I remembered Dad's old rifle was in a closet downstairs. I was thinking about sliding down the fire pole and—"

"It's a good thing you stayed put," he said.

"It was over before I could get my wits about me." He felt a shiver shoot through her body as her story poured from her. "A terrible storm, and then quiet. The phone didn't work. They slashed the tires on my car."

She wore the same shift she'd had on the night they'd made love. He rubbed his hands briskly up and down her back and imagined her pulling the long dress on over her wet body. He felt cold, too. Cold and angry.

"You're freezing, honey. Let's wrap you up a little better and get you out of here."

"I can't find Jasper. I was just looking for—" Dazed and distracted, she started to pull away.

"He'll come back."

"Maybe they—"

"No, Lavender. He's okay." He would not release her arm when he saw that her feet were bare. "He's a cat. Cats look out for themselves."

"What am I going to do without my—"

"There's glass all over the place," he said as he lifted her into his arms. He headed for the wrap he spotted hanging on a hook. "I'm going to look out for you now. I'm taking you home with me."

"I can't. I have to clean this mess up." Her voice quavered as she gestured helplessly. It was too dark to fully assess the damage, but she knew as well as he did that it was bad. "I think the looms are ruined. And all the..."

"We're going to call the police and your insurance company as soon as we get to a phone." More glass crunched beneath his boots. It felt good to have her arms around his neck now, hugging him. "Okay? They'll take care of this. I'm worried about you."

"Oh, Wyatt, they hate me. They meant to kill me."

"Or scare you." By the light of the window he saw blood dripping from her foot, and he suppressed a groan.

"Why? What have I done?"

"Honey, this business is about what someone else has done. They've picked you to pay for it." He set her down on the kitchen counter.

"Why me?"

"Because you're not like them." He opened a cupboard from which he'd once seen her take a box of matches. With a little groping, he found them. "I don't know. Maybe it was... You don't think it was kids, do you?"

"The kids wouldn't do this. They were men's voices, not kids'." He struck a match and reached for her foot. "It's just a cut," she said.

"It's bleeding pretty bad," he said, and he felt the pain in his own gut.

"It's okay. I'll get some towels."

"Stay put," he said, and she did. He found a stack of clean dish towels, a ruana and a coat, piled them all in her lap and picked her up again. "You need anything else? Anything that's irreplaceable?"

"Just my cat."

He put her in his car, turned the heater on and gave her foot a cursory examination, blotting away blood and finding no embedded glass. Then he left her to wrap her foot while he took a turn around the yard, calling for the cat. In spite of what he'd told Lavender, he fully expected to find a carcass, and he was trying to decide whether to tell her the truth tonight when he heard a mewling response above his head. Jasper had taken refuge in a tree.

Recovering the cat boosted Lavender's spirits, but they spoke little on the way back to Glover. The smattering of lights twinkling in the distance was not a welcome sight. The quiet streets were thinly frosted with new snow. There were lights in some of the windows. Other houses were dark. Lavender wondered where the inhabitants were. Where were the people who despised her so much that they would destroy her home?

The bundle Wyatt carried into his house contained both Lavender and her cat. He took them into the bathroom, where Jasper nosed around the soap dish, then sprinted for the door. Wyatt carefully treated Lavender's foot. When he was finished, he looked up, still holding her foot on his knee, and told her, "I wish I'd been there."

She smiled tentatively, touching his shoulder. He was wearing a soft blue cotton sweater with a white shirt underneath. His thick black hair brushed the collar. "If you had been there tonight, they would have picked a different time."

"I'll find out who it was," he promised. He knew he was probably sounding like a no-class act, but he couldn't think of a better way to reassure her. "I'll pick *my* time. They won't bother you again."

She touched his cheek with her forefinger, indulging herself in the feel of unbearded masculine skin. "I think we'd better turn this over to the sheriff. And I do have pretty good insurance."

Ron Christian appeared at Wyatt's door within ten minutes after they'd called him. His eyes were those of the battle weary. First John Tiger, then the drugs and his son, and now this. He accepted the offer of coffee, but drank little of it as he posed his questions and made his notes.

He would drive out tonight, check things out again in the morning.

"I need another deputy," Ron said with a sigh, as he flipped his notebook closed. "All I got's Buck Braun, and it takes him ten minutes just to heave himself out of the car."

The three of them looked at each other across the table, imagining big Buck, with the discolored caps on his two front teeth and his jeans always sagging in the butt. They managed to shake their heads and laugh a little. When the laughter faded, they just sat there, Ron tapping his finger on the notebook, Lavender with her arms crossed and wrapped tightly around her waist.

So unlike her, Wyatt thought. *Tied up in knots.*

"Yep," Ron said as he reached for his jacket. "This job's been a bitch lately. I don't think I'll run next time."

"Can you get some help outside the county?" Wyatt asked.

"I need something to go on. Maybe I'll find it out to Lavender's place."

After he left, Wyatt offered to make Lavender something to eat, but she declined. She sat there curled up in the corner of the couch, quietly hugging herself. Hell, if hugging was all she wanted, he wanted to be the one doing it, but she looked so small and fragile. He wished the vandals had torn up his place instead of hers. It wouldn't have been half the loss.

"Will you come into the bedroom with me?" he asked finally.

"I can just take the sofa," she said. "I'll be fine."

"The hell you'll take the sofa. *I'll* take the sofa."

Damn, he was barking at her. What was wrong with him? She looked up at him, wide-eyed. God, tears. He sat beside her and pulled her into his arms before the first one fell. "I'll take *you*," he said as he stroked her hair.

"Take me for what?"

He plunged his fingers into her hair and pressed her head to his chest. "I want to make love to you, Lavender. I want to hold you and make you believe that you're safe with me."

She wiped at her eyes furiously, because she did *not* want to cry. "When I was up there hiding behind the bed," she said, working hard to keep her voice steady, "I remembered you telling me you felt safe in my house."

"Because it felt like a home. More than this place, which is just a place to stay." He gathered her into his arms, holding her like a child. For a moment he thought she was going to push him away, but then she put her arms around his neck, the way she had before. He felt favored. Almost trusted. "We'll clean it up, Lavender. We'll fix the schoolhouse," he promised as he carried her back to the bedroom.

"Oh, Wyatt, are you going to try to fix me, too?" she asked, her voice a soft bird song in the darkened room.

"Do you feel like you need fixing?"

"I feel empty." She lifted her head and looked at him plaintively. "I feel as though I've been taken all apart... again."

"I don't have the king's horses or the king's men," he confessed. "But I'm going to love you. I want you to love me back."

She had no choice. The love was there. He set her in his bed and kissed her, and she could do nothing but offer herself to him in return for the slow, sweet, gentle way that he stroked her body, first over her clothes, then underneath them. He removed the barriers between them—her dress, his sweater. She unbuttoned his shirt while his lips brushed praises over her breasts. He suckled her, and she felt a wonderful wrenching deep in her belly, as though somehow her missing womb were sending the signal to nourish him. He groaned and struggled with his belt buckle, desperate to get it out of the way before he gave in to the need to press himself into her tender harbor.

"Help me, Lavender," he rasped hotly. "Find me and hold me and make me..."

She pushed his zipper down and slid her hands over his hips, easing his pants out of the way. His buttocks were rock-hard, but they were not the part of his body he wanted her to find. She knew where it was, and she knew how he strained against its demands. She caressed the hardness of him, the velvety softness of him, until he caught his breath and pleaded, "Take me home. Take me to that warm place, Lavender."

She brought him to the entrance and opened herself to receive the length of him, stretched taut. He found passage. One sure, sensational stroke brought him to the hearth and touched fire to the tinder there. He gave her his power, and she returned her magic. They belonged together.

He made her want to do her best work. It was so simple. Every sigh and every touch became a thread. So many textures. So many beautiful colors. His fingers laced through her hair. Her tongue entwined with his. They would find a way to become one. He, slipping over, she, sliding under. They knew the way. They whispered the way. Over, under, over, under. Deftly, they wove. Exquisitely, they became one.

Long afterward they lay with their arms and legs loosely bound, raveling a little like worn jeans. They touched each other, marveling at the silky places, the hard places, the bumps and the indentations.

It was good to have her in his bed.

It was good to be in his bed.

"You know I can't stay with you," she said with a sigh. "I'll have to go back."

"If you do, I'm going with you." He propped his head on his elbow and gave her his most serious expression, hoping she could see it for what it was in the shadows of the moonlit room. "You either get police protection, or you get me."

"I'd rather have you."

That pleased him thoroughly. He brushed her hair back from her forehead and ran his thumb from the bridge to the tip of her nose. "Tomorrow's Saturday. We're going up to Bismarck to hire somebody to replace the windows. We're going to buy you four new tires and new locks for the doors."

"We?"

"Sure. It's the kind of stuff you need a man to help you with, right? Carpenter and car business, you want a man's opinion." She laughed, and he lay back and pulled her into his arms. "And we're going to stop in and see John."

"How's he doing?"

"Coming along. When the psychiatrist releases him, they'll probably transfer him down to the Indian hospital."

"Why?"

"Because he's an Indian, and he doesn't have medical insurance, so that's how it works. They don't do major surgery down there, so they'll send him back to Bismarck if he needs another operation. If he's lucky."

"What do you mean, *if he's lucky?*"

"I don't have much use for...well, for reservation life, I guess. Health care is bad. Housing is bad. Education isn't much to brag about." He pulled the comforter up around her shoulders. "I'll make sure John gets what he needs."

"Can you do that?"

"I can make a helluva lot of noise when I want to." He hadn't done it since they'd refused cataract surgery for his grandmother because it wasn't a "life threatening" situation. He hated the whole damn bureaucratic mess the reservation was mired in, but he would wade back in if he had to. For John.

"Anyway, we'll get the schoolhouse secured with some good locks," he decided, feeling suddenly like he had all the answers.

"Which won't keep them out. I was burglarized four times when I lived in San Diego, but at least those people had a purpose. They took everything they could fence, including the rings I told Phil he could have back." She chuckled, recalling that one little ray of satisfaction. "So at least somebody got something out of that deal. This was malicious destruction. Pure hatred."

"Somebody had a point to make. We don't know exactly who it was or what the point was, but there are some things we do know." He hooked his arm behind his head and turned the situation over in his mind. Outside his window the falling snowflakes glistened in the moonlight. "We know Ally is a pawn, and we know they've got designs on making you a scapegoat."

"You can't think anyone's getting rich selling steroids in Glover," she said.

"That's what's weird. Four high school boys don't add up to much of a market."

"But they could be the beginning of one."

"Ally's somebody's errand boy."

"And he's scared," Lavender contributed.

"And the person who springs to mind, even though I haven't really seen much of the man..."

"We can't make the same kinds of assumptions...."

"I know." Wyatt thought for a moment as he watched the snowflakes fall. At this distance, they all looked identical. "Starky's kind of like us, isn't he? He doesn't fit into the picture very well."

"He probably fits in better than we do." Her hand stirred softly against his chest. "You can fit in if you want to, Wyatt. You've got your ticket."

"I've lost half my team."

"No, you haven't. You've kept the team intact. After all the dust has settled, these people will see that, and they'll respect you for it. So, if you decide to stay..."

"I'm going to get through this season. This school year." Sometimes he had to remind himself that there was a difference. "The school year doesn't end until May. Long after the state championships." And he wasn't living for the sport. If he had been, it was time to stop. "You know, I really do know something about Native American history. I like to read about it."

"But not discuss it?"

"I get these funny feelings about it. I read about the treaties and the early reservation period, the government policies, and I get...kind of crawly inside my skin. So I'd rather teach about ancient Greece, or, uh..." He craned his neck to take a peek at wild honey hair and a creamy white shoulder. "What are you, Dutch?"

"On my father's side. My mother was Bohemian."

"That's quite a match." He touched her breast, and she looked up to offer a languid smile. "You know what I did when I turned eighteen?" She shook her head. "I changed my name."

"Legally?"

"It's easy to change your name through tribal court. Only costs a couple bucks. And it's perfectly legal." She waited, didn't press, so he offered. "My name was Wyatt Uses Arrow. My mother's maiden name was Uses Arrow, and I was her... What do they call it? Love child?"

"Her son," Lavender said.

"My grandfather's name was also Wyatt Uses Arrow. I never knew him."

"Uses Arrow," she repeated. "Archer. It means the same."

"It doesn't sound the same." He tipped his head back and chuckled. "Who was I trying to kid, huh?"

"Well, it put you at the top alphabetically." Again he chuckled. She scooted up, the better to look into his eyes and offer her thoughts. "People often take new names when they come of age. We say, this is who I will be as an adult."

"It also says, this is what I believe about myself."

"This is how I hope the world will accept me." She reflected. "Some accept. Some don't."

"You don't let it bother you," he said.

"It does bother me. It bothered my mother. She was always trying to get things started. A community library. A children's theater group. She tried to get the church choir to sing folk music."

He touched the center of her lower lip and made her smile. "Busy lady."

"Yeah, but none of it ever worked out. So I've only been interested in getting a business started. Teaching some of the women a lucrative craft. My dad used to say that people didn't argue with success." She laid her head on his shoulder, her hand on his chest, and she sighed. "I wish he could see how successful my business is. Or *was*."

"*Is.* If they drive you out, you'll take your business elsewhere." And your name, he thought. The one you were born with. "You haven't let them change you."

"I let Phil change me, and that was a mistake. I tried to be terrific at everything I did. All things to all people. After a while I wasn't myself, and I wasn't what he wanted, either." He covered her hand with his. She continued softly. "It hurts when you try very hard, and you're never quite up to par. So I don't want..."

"Yes, you do. You do want." He moved his hand, following the path from her hand to her arm to the underside of her breast. "You've been trying hard again, Lavender."

"Only..." She moved her hand a little. It covered his heart now. "To be your friend."

"You love your friends, don't you?" With his thumb he traced a circle around her nipple, and it puckered for him. "Come on, tell me."

"Yes."

"Do you love all your friends *this* way?"

"No."

"Being a lover comes easier for me," he admitted.

"I know that."

"Which is why you were wise to make a friend of me first." He took her hand again and moved it from his heart past his belly to the heat between his legs. "I want, too," he whispered. "And it wasn't part of my plan. I want to be with you. I want your hands on me, yes, I want you to be my lover—"

"Oh, Wyatt..."

"Because you've taught me the way to be your friend."

Chapter 11

News traveled fast in Glover. Early the following day the word was out that Lavender Holland's schoolhouse had been vandalized. The extent of the damage was speculated upon at the grain elevator and enhanced at the grocery store. No one cared to put forth the name of a culprit, but Marge Nordstrom couldn't wait to share her insight with her daughter.

"It doesn't surprise me at all," Marge said as she slit open the net bag of oranges she'd just bought. "People around here aren't going to stand for drugs and devil worship, and Lavender just might as well know that."

Teri's head was swimming. Night riders in Glover? "I don't know where you're getting your information, Mom, but it's wrong. It's stupid, and it's wrong."

"You calling your mother stupid, girl?"

She hadn't heard Starky on the basement steps, but there he was, lurking on the landing. The man gave her the creeps, and he knew it. He enjoyed it. He worked at being creepy, being sneaky, appearing in doorways. She hated the way he went around with a cigarette perched over one ear. He was definitely her mom's worst pick yet.

"She's not stupid." Teri stared icily at the man. "What she's telling around about Lavender is stupid."

"I'll tell you what," Marge snapped. "You just might never get over there again. If she wasn't paying pretty good money for that weaving, you wouldn't for *sure.*"

"And I've given you half of every paycheck and bought my own school clothes with the rest, so I don't think you really want me to quit. Anyway, I'm old enough to make up my own mind." She really wanted to go over there now, if she could get the car somehow. "I can't believe anyone could just wreck the schoolhouse like that."

"There are satanic cults everywhere these days, and people are taking matters into their own hands. We just saw something about it on the news the other night." The oranges tumbled into the refrigerator drawer as Marge tried to draw Starky into the discussion. "Didn't we, Drake?"

He grunted and lit a cigarette.

"Right here in North Dakota," Marge went on. "In Bismarck. They found some stuff on the golf course—a bunch of rocks, like some kind of altar, with symbols painted all over them. Probably in blood." She bumped the refrigerator door closed with her hip. "Probably the same kind of thing Lavender's got out there by her place."

"There's an old Indian ruin by Coyote's Call Creek," Teri said, regretting the fact that she was repeating herself. "Lavender didn't put it there. It's *been* there for a very long time. And there aren't any symbols painted on those rocks. They're just—" She shook her head as she turned away. "I shouldn't tell you *anything.* You jump to all kinds of—"

"Somebody wrote a book about this stuff that's selling like hotcakes," Marge countered. "Right, Drake?" She glanced over for another grunt of support, but Starky had moved on. "Well, it was all in the news. The whole thing. It's here in North Dakota, and these drugs go hand in hand with all that. I've seen the marijuana hanging from her rafters out there. She grows it herself, and everybody knows it."

"Steroids are something else entirely, Mom, and what's hanging from Lavender's rafters is *not* marijuana. It's— oh, God, what's the use?" With Starky out of sight, Teri stepped closer and lowered her voice. "Ally was supplying the steroids, Mom. Haven't you figured that out?"

Starky appeared in the doorway again, his beady black eyes accosting Teri through a lazy drift of cigarette smoke.

Teri swallowed hard. Her next claim had to be a lie, because she knew. Deep down, she knew. But deep down and all over, she was scared. Her eyes skittered from Starky to the spindly Christmas cactus that was dying in the kitchen window. "I have no idea where he was getting them, but I know—"

The sting of her mother's hand on her cheek took her by surprise.

"Don't you ever, *ever*, say anything like that about your brother," Marge warned. "*Ever*. You could get him into a lot of trouble making accusations like that."

Teri's cheek felt like flashing red neon, and she wanted to fight back. But she couldn't. This woman was still her mother. Ally—the weasel—was still her brother. She backed into the dining room. Rage crowded in on her vision. Starky, standing in the other doorway at the opposite end of the kitchen, was watching her. Her mother, bracing her slapping hand on the kitchen sink, was watching her. She turned, almost expecting to be stopped by one of them as she headed for the front door.

Ally was standing in the shadows of the hallway to the back bedrooms. She knew he'd been listening. He looked scared.

Damn him, she'd protected him long enough.

"I hope you're satisfied," she spat as she snatched her jacket from the closet.

Ally rubbed his hand over his eyes, but he offered no comment. Teri had almost made a circle, and Starky was now visible again. He hadn't moved. He was like a canker at the center of the house. A silent, smoking threat. Ally felt it. Teri could see that now. But he told her with a look, an almost imperceptible gesture, that she should go quickly.

Oh, Ally, I don't want you to go to jail.

Get going, Teri. Get yourself out of their way.

The cold blast of air from the front door felt good. Fresh air was a relief. Teri didn't want her mother's car. She went to her Aunt Janine, who was usually willing to loan out her old beater when it was running. Luckily, it was having a good day. She vowed that as soon as she'd saved enough money she was going to buy herself a car, so she wouldn't have to ask her mother for anything. Not *anything.* One more year and she was leaving. One more year and she wouldn't have to come up with an excuse when she wanted to visit a friend in the hospital or help another friend clean up the mess some creeps had made of her house.

One more year and she wouldn't have to worry about her mother's poor taste in men.

Ron Christian's car was parked beside Lavender's. When Teri saw that all Lavender's tires were flat and all the windows in the house were smashed, she thought about how terrified Lavender must have been. The story was that Coach Archer had actually been the one who called the sheriff. Teri hoped that meant Lavender hadn't been stranded all night at the schoolhouse.

Sheriff Christian stood on the step, hands on his hips, and waited for Teri. "What an awful mess," she said as she neared the front door.

"Sure is."

She glanced at some of the words. They made her feel sick. "Who did it, do you think?"

"Might have been kids."

Teri shook her head and squinted into the sun. "Not Glover kids. They all like Lavender."

"Do you know where she might be?"

"She's not here?" She stopped in her snowy tracks and lifted one fuzzy mitten. "Her car—"

"Well, she was in town last night, but I couldn't locate her this morning. I been out here three times already, checking this out." He jogged down the steps. "I've gotta get back. You, uh..."

"I thought maybe I could help out somehow," Teri explained. He seemed hesitant, and she wondered whether he thought she'd come to steal something. "This is where I work. I came out here to help."

"If you see her—" He shook his head and walked away. "Never mind. I'll be talking to her."

"Sheriff, what will happen to—" He turned, his eyes questioning. *My family. My crazy mother, who's been babbling around about devil worship, and now here's the payoff. To Ally. What will happen to Ally?*

"Happen to what?" the sheriff coaxed.

"To...to Lavender. Where will she...go?"

Squint-eyed, he surveyed the building. "This ain't too bad. She'll get 'er fixed up inside a week. You let me know if you hear any rumors, okay? Rumors caused this mess. Rumors'll probably lead me to the guilty party."

Teri nodded. There were things she wanted to tell him, but they were wedged in her throat.

A blue pickup slowed near the mailbox. Sheriff Christian stood beside his car and watched the vehicle make the turn. Teri was glad to see Sherry Braun behind the wheel. The friendly face of another weaver. Even in broad daylight it would have felt creepy to be there alone in the middle of piles of broken glass and spray-painted threats.

Sherry whapped the pickup door shut and greeted them both. "Buck went to work this morning over at the elevator," she reported to the sheriff, "but I'm sure if you need him to help you do something about all this..."

"Right now I need to talk to Lavender," Ron said.

"I thought I'd come out and see what I could do to help, but—" Sherry took a swipe at the straight blond hair that had escaped the rubber band at the base of her neck. She looked over the outside of the house. "This looks like an awful mess."

Ron tapped his fingers on the hood of his car. He, too, was looking at it as though he were at a loss. "There's still a lot of nice stuff in there that could get stolen or wrecked with the windows out like this."

"Lavender's not here," Teri explained to the older woman.

"I wouldn't want to be, either." Sherry shoved her hands into the pockets of her fleece-lined denim jacket and took a few steps closer. "Makes you sick."

"I've gotta be goin'," Ron said as he opened his car door. "I'll come around again later today."

The two blondes witnessed his retreat, then turned, almost in unison, back to the problem at hand. It seemed almost too big to tackle.

Sherry peered through a broken-out window, stepped back and made a little *tsk* sound. "It looks awful, doesn't it?"

"Lately my mom's been telling around that Lavender is like a witch or something. I suppose that's why somebody did this."

"People have always thought Lavender was strange," Sherry said. "Buck's never liked her much, either, but she's sure done a lot for me since she moved back. I guess I haven't spoken up when I should have."

"Neither have I."

"We have to start, don't we? Otherwise, we'll be out of a job." Sherry held the door open and kicked at some glass with the pointed, scuffed toe of her boot while she waited for Teri to join her. "And we'll lose a good friend. Actually, I think this whole town will lose a good friend."

Teri ventured into what had once been a cozy studio. Her favorite place to be. Both looms were overturned, and there were fabric and yarn and furniture scattered everywhere. Inside the oversize mittens, her hands became fists. "This town doesn't deserve Lavender."

"Maybe not." Sherry knelt beside the loom that Teri always used. "I wonder if we can fix this ourselves."

"I guess we know as much about it as anyone." Sherry looked up and smiled. It was confidence shared. Teri asked, "Do you think we can get that awful language off the building? I'd hate for her to see that again."

"I know what you mean."

Wyatt drove Lavender all over Bismarck that morning. The insurance agent said he had already spoken with the sheriff and sent an adjuster to look at the damage. The contractor who had remodeled the schoolhouse promised to send a man out immediately and to have the windows replaced within a week. After they'd filled the back of Wyatt's Toyota with new locks and tires, they stopped at the hospital to visit John.

John didn't need to hear about anyone else's troubles, and seeing him immobilized in the bed, his dark eyes stricken like those of a young stag trapped in the snow, made Lavender forget hers. She let Wyatt do most of the talking. John wanted to hear about school and wrestling.

"The team made a pretty good showing last night. You should have seen Hoss psyching his man out with killer looks." Wyatt laughed convincingly. "Poor kid practically walked out on the mat and said, 'Pin me.'"

John obliged his coach with a strained smile. "You replaced all of us okay?"

"You guys'll be missed, John," Wyatt assured him, his smile fading.

The boy nodded and glanced out the window. He spoke of a future they'd both known would come. "They're sending me down to the Indian hospital. Back to the rez."

"When?" Wyatt asked.

"As soon as the shrink releases me. They say I'll probably be in the hospital for another month because of—" he lifted his hand "—all this mess I made. I guess I'll be having that other operation. I don't know when."

"This doesn't mean you can't finish school," Wyatt assured him. "It just might take a little longer."

"You won't be that far away," Lavender put in.

"Yeah, I will." There was a faraway look in his eyes. He turned his face toward the open door and looked longingly at the empty space. "From Teri, I will."

"Just across the river."

"Yeah," he said hopelessly. "Just a short swim." He looked at Wyatt. "Like that song. 'Running Bear.'"

"Ooo-ga, oo-ga, oo-ga," Wyatt teased, tapping out a drumbeat on the bed table. Lavender laughed, and John managed another wispy smile.

"I might get crazy enough to try it."

"The river'll be frozen pretty soon," Lavender reminded him. "We'll put Teri on a snowmobile."

"No, you won't." The fun was short-lived. John looked from one face to the other, hoping they understood how scared he was. "I don't want Teri taking any chances. I don't want Teri gettin' in any trouble, or..."

"Teri's doing just fine." The boy's concern tugged at Lavender's heart. She touched his hand. "But she misses you."

"What are your mom's plans?" Wyatt asked.

"She's pretty old, you know." John thought he had to explain why she wasn't there anymore. She'd come for a few days, but then she'd had to take what transportation and lodging were offered. She had as little control over those things as John had. "She had me kinda late. I think she'd rather stay where she is, with her sister. And I won't be doin' much for a while, anyway."

"You have an older brother?" John shrugged, and Wyatt knew that meant the brother was around. Somewhere. "Don't worry about it, John. We'll get you well, and we'll work the rest of it out."

"Marla's been up to see me," John said softly. "But it's real hard for her."

"I know," Wyatt said. He also knew how alone John felt. "It'll be okay, son. You're gonna be okay."

"I wanted to go to college next year. I already had a couple of letters from coaches who were interested in me." The long, deep sigh of discouragement denied hope. "I really screwed it all up, didn't I?"

"It's going to be harder," Wyatt allowed. "It's going to take more time."

"But it's not going to be the end of the world," Lavender said.

Wyatt looked at her, remembered the present condition of her home and studio, and lifted the corner of his mouth in a slow-dawning smile. She was sunshine. "It's not the 'End of the Trail,' either."

"You really believe that?" John asked.

"We can be a little flexible, can't we?" Easy for *him* to say, Wyatt realized, and he caught the knowing smile Lavender returned. "If things don't work out the way we planned, maybe we're supposed to do something else," he added for Lavender's benefit.

"You mean, like, maybe we're *fated* to do something else?" she asked. The light danced in her eyes.

It pleased him to give her something to chuckle about. "Maybe we're supposed to try it a different way. Sometimes we can make fate change its mind."

"What sign did you say you were born under?"

Wyatt rolled his eyes, but he answered, "Leo."

"Figures." She took her denim bag off her shoulder, sat down in a chair and plunked the bag on her knees as though she were embarking on a project. She dug around in the bottomless bag as she spoke.

"This big lion is absolutely right, John. Right now you'll just have to work hard to get yourself all healed up. Are they feeding you a lot of animal fat? Don't let them load you up on animal fat." She came up with a Ball jar. "I've brought some of my special trail mix." She held the jar up in front of John's face, but in response to Wyatt's chuckle, she added, "Not *end*-of-the-trail, just trail mix."

"I think I've had this stuff before," John said. "I like it. It's great."

"Next time I'll have Teri deliver it."

"I'd like that. Tell her..." He took the jar and rested it on his stomach. "Just tell her I miss her."

They spoke little as they drove south, heading for Coyote's Call Creek. Neither of them wanted to talk about the schoolhouse. They would face it when they got there. But when they crossed the little bridge north of the house, they saw that they wouldn't be facing it alone.

The windows were covered with sheets of plastic. A cleanup crew had gathered, and under Sherry Braun's supervision the glass had been cleaned up first. Teri's friends, Beth and Heidi, were salvaging spools of yarn. Hoss Sandland and Mike Braun were setting up the partitions that had been knocked down. Sherry reported that the insurance adjuster and the sheriff had made their inspections, and that two other men had come to take out some of the window frames.

"Oh, and the R.E.C. truck was here," she added, referring to the rural electric company.

"Wow." Lavender looked at Wyatt, then at Teri, then back to Sherry. Her jaw dropped, but she couldn't think of anything other than another, "Wow."

"I don't know who did this," Sherry said, "but it's just not fair. I've heard some of the talk, and it's not fair at all."

Lavender heard only about half of what Sherry said. People were helping her. People were actually helping *her*.

"You guys, this is so nice of you, but..." She noticed Ally with a can of spray paint, and she scowled. Then the flowers registered. Big, bold flowers on the side of her house. "What's he doing?"

Teri grabbed her by the arm and pulled her closer to the house and to her normally errant brother. "Well, for right now we're just sort of decorating over the stupid stuff they wrote. You know, until we can do a proper paint job."

"Oh, no, it's wonderful," Lavender marveled. It was like discovering something beautiful growing in a crack in the cement. "I think I'll keep it. You're pretty artistic, Ally."

"I've used a spray can once or twice." His sheepish grin faded. "But I didn't have nothing to do with messing up your house, Lavender. I swear."

She thought about the boy in the hospital bed and then this one, his chin tucked into his collar for warmth, clutching a can of spray paint. "Good." Just a small break, she thought. That was all either of them would need. She laid a gloved hand on Ally's shoulder. "I was pretty sure it wasn't kids. I heard men's voices."

"You didn't hear anything like—" Ally glanced away, then back again "—female voices, did you?"

"No, Ally. I didn't."

"'Course, that doesn't mean . . ." He gave his head a quick shake, keeping his chin anchored in his puffy parka. "Nah, she wouldn't. She's been saying stuff, but I don't think she'd ever . . ."

"I don't think so, either."

He smiled a little, then took notice of Wyatt, who was pulling tires out of the back of his car. "Coach, I gotta talk to you about something."

"Sure, Ally."

"But it's private."

Lavender linked one arm through Teri's. The girl looked up at her, and they shared silent consolation for what was all around them and what was coming. They both knew what the talk would be about. The men would be thinking they were shouldering this burden like lone rangers, sparing the women.

Lavender turned and linked her other arm through Sherry's. The three were weavers together, women together, now friends together. True colors, Lavender thought, made the best fabric. "Let's go see if we can scare up something to feed this crew."

Ally ambled over to the Toyota as Wyatt eyed the stack of tires and wondered whether he was going to have to drive into town to get jack stands. Ally leaned against Wyatt's car and waited, watching the highway. One look at him, and it wasn't too hard to guess that the time had finally come. Wyatt closed the trunk of the car and joined Ally. For a time they watched the highway together.

"I'm going to have to block that car up to get the rims off," Wyatt said finally. "Got any ideas?"

"I got a problem."

Wyatt heard the gravel in the boy's throat. "I'm listening, Ally."

"I gave 'em the 'roids, Coach."

"Gave?" Wyatt asked softly. He spotted a coyote on the hill across the highway, and that was what he watched. He didn't have to look at Ally to know there were tears coming.

"Well, at first they were free." Ally cleared his throat. "Later we had to start charging something for them. Not that much. I thought it was going to be—"

"Who's *we*, Ally?"

"He'll kill me if I tell," Ally said, his voice painfully thick. "I really think he would kill me."

Now Wyatt looked. He searched the boy's tear-filled face, moved his collar aside and lifted his chin. The purple bruise on Ally's jaw might have been intended as a warning. Or maybe there were more. Ally clenched his teeth and turned his face away.

"If you're mixed up with a dealer, he might kill you whether you tell or not. This is no joke, Ally."

"We weren't dealing any real drugs. At least, I wasn't. Just 'roids. Just to kind of give the team a boost, you know?"

It was a *he*. Wyatt wanted to be right on the first guess. He chose the obvious. "Was it Starky?"

Ally drew a long, unsteady breath. "He said it wasn't the 'roids that made John go off the deep end. But then, after the other guys got caught, too, everybody started talking about high blood pressure, kidneys, liver, all the trouble they can cause." Ally was trying hard to stem the tears, but they were the least of his shame now. "I didn't know, Coach. I thought I was helping out."

"You knew you had to keep it a secret. That should have been a clue." *Save the lecture.* He laid his hand on Ally's shoulder and repeated, "Was it Starky?"

"He's got lots of connections, I guess."

"Starky?" Wyatt wanted confirmation.

"Yeah. Starky." Ally wiped his face on his jacket sleeve. "My mom's had other boyfriends. At first Starky treated me better than most of them ever did. But now I'm scared. I know he's got—" he glanced at the defaced building "—a sewer full of friends."

"They're probably not the kind of friends he can count on if he makes a mistake." Wyatt lifted his face to catch the cool breeze and slid his arm around the boy's shoulders. "Which I think he has."

They were not a man's shoulders yet, and even if they had been, they would have shuddered as the real world closed in. "They're gonna put me in jail, aren't they?"

"I don't know what'll happen, Ally. I do know you're gonna have to be straight with the sheriff this time. Tell him what you did. Tell him everything you know about Starky."

"Oh, geez, I can't face Christian again." Ally drew one long, shuddering breath and tipped his head back, then dropped his chin to his chest again. Shame clung to him. "He's Mark's dad, and Mark..."

"Mark's going to be fine. So are the others." He hoped it was true. "I'll go with you, Ally."

"You will?"

Wyatt squeezed the boy's shoulders. "I owe you a favor."

"What for?"

"That ad you put in the paper, remember?"

"You owe me a *favor* for that?" Ally sniffled, then took the risk of looking up. "You mean, it turned out okay?"

"Better than okay."

Lavender appeared on the doorstep, as if on cue. Wyatt smiled, and then he realized that his thoughts, sweet as they were, had not summoned her. It was the approach of Ron Christian's car. He and Ally had been too engrossed to notice.

Ally stepped away. "I'll do it, but not now. Not here, I mean." The look in the boy's eyes pleaded. "Okay?"

Wyatt nodded as Lavender tactfully gave them a wide berth on her way to greet the sheriff.

Ron got out of his car, took two steps toward her and stopped. Her smile melted away when she saw the look in his eyes. "Lavender, I'm going to have to take you in for questioning," he said.

She wrapped the front of her coat around her, lapping one side over the other. "I told you everything I could, Ron. I really didn't see—"

"It has to do with a box I found when I searched the premises this morning."

Wyatt stepped in, taking his place beside Lavender. "What kind of box?"

"It wasn't the box itself," Ron said. "It was what was inside. I had to take it over to Doc Werner to verify it, but I found a box of pills. Anabolic steroids."

The three stood there for a moment, puffing misty breath clouds, while the two words they were most sick of hearing reverberated in the air. One curious face, then two, appeared at the schoolhouse door, but they faded back again.

A few steps away, Ally was pulling himself together. But he'd caught wind of the bombshell.

"That's ridiculous," Wyatt bellowed, waving a hand toward the house. "Look at this place, Ron. A bunch of crazies were here last night, and this woman was terrorized. If you found any kind of drugs, you know damn well how they got here."

Ron wasn't anxious to tangle with anyone, but especially not Wyatt Archer. "I'd rather discuss this with you down at the courthouse," he told Lavender.

Wyatt took a wider stance. "She doesn't have to discuss anything without—"

"It's all right, Wyatt," Lavender said quietly.

"The hell it is."

She laid a hand on his arm, a gesture meant to calm him. It didn't. All he could see was the man who had come to take her *for questioning,* which was a crock.

"It's a setup. All this talk about satanism, and then he comes over to investigate a crime against you and comes up with..." He took her by the shoulders, setting her out of everyone's reach but his own, and he told the sheriff, "You're not taking her anywhere."

"He's just doing his job," Lavender said. With a look, Wyatt offered to stand his ground, to be her shield, but she shook her head and stepped away. "He has to ask his questions."

Wyatt was furious, but she was determined to handle this her way. "Do you know a good lawyer?" he asked her.

"I won't need one. I don't even keep aspirin in the house. Whatever Ron found wasn't mine." She smiled. "But you know that." He nodded dumbly. He wanted to fight this thing, and she was smiling, taking his hand and squeezing it as though his *knowing* would somehow help her. "Thank you," she said. And then she was gone.

A wild alarm buzzed inside Wyatt's head as he watched Christian's car pull out onto the highway. He turned when

when he heard the front door open again. Out stepped Sherry Braun and her boy, Mike. Then came Teri, Ally's loyal sister. And there stood Ally, wide-eyed and mute. What Wyatt knew about Lavender didn't mean a damn thing. It was what *they* knew that counted. What in hell were these people thinking? Whose side were they on?

He nearly ripped the door off his car getting it open, but before he got in, Ally finally moved. Wyatt gripped the top of the car door and waited as the boy edged closer. Ally was thinking. Wyatt could almost hear the gears grinding inside that unpredictable head.

"What are you going to do now, Ally?" he asked, boring a hole through the boy with his eyes. "Let the lady fry?"

"I didn't plant those 'roids, Coach," Ally said quickly. He swallowed, his adolescent Adam's apple bobbing like a yo-yo. "I didn't have anything to do with what went on last night."

"Who did?"

"I don't know. All I did was make a few deliveries."

"You have to tell the sheriff that. Otherwise it all comes down on Lavender." Wyatt stepped out from behind the car door and spoke carefully, as if coaxing a bird back to its cage. "I'm going to the courthouse. Do you want to ride along?"

Ally nodded, and his renewed tears came as a shower of relief. Wyatt took the boy back under his arm and thanked God the bird had not taken flight. "I know you're scared, son. I don't blame you. It's scary business."

Teri skipped down the steps and trotted over. "What's wrong? Where's Lavender going?"

"She has to talk to the sheriff again," Wyatt said.

Ally used his smeared sleeve to wipe his face again. "I'm gonna talk to the sheriff, too."

His sister stared at him for a moment. Sympathetic tears welled in her eyes as she nodded.

"I don't know where Mom fits into all this," Ally said. "I don't know if she knew about it. I don't know what's gonna happen. I just know it was a stupid thing I did, putting those guys onto steroids."

"Do you want me to go with you?" Teri offered.

"I want you to stay as far away from me and Starky and this whole damn mess—"

Ignoring him, she headed for the back seat of Wyatt's car. "I'm going with my brother, Mr. Archer."

They stormed the courthouse, the three together, gaining admittance by using the buzzer, since the building was closed on Saturday. Ron Christian hesitated to let them in, but Ally had the magic words.

"I'm the one who supplied the steroids, Mr. Christian."

With a sigh of relief, Ron stepped back and held the door for them. "Lavender's in the office," he said. They followed him down the dark hallway.

They all gathered in the sparsely furnished room. Wyatt refused a chair, preferring, instead, to stand behind Lavender's.

"Okay, Ally," Ron said. "What about the drugs?"

"I got 'em from Drake Starky."

"Wait a minute." It wasn't every day that Ron Christian made a drug bust. He wanted to make sure he went by the book. "If you're admitting to something, we've got to call your mother. You're not eighteen yet, right?"

"But she'll tell Starky. And he'll get rid of—"

The boy was nervous. He glanced at his sister, then his coach. He needed all the support he could get.

"Get rid of what, Ally?" Ron prodded.

"I don't know what he's got besides the 'roids. He's always bringing in more auto parts. You know, plugs and filters and stuff. A few times he's had me drop boxes off or pick some up, and I don't know what's inside.'' He ran two fingers over the edge of the desk, avoiding their eyes, fearing their judgment. ''I kinda don't think it's spark plugs.''

Ron's laugh surprised everyone.

''I'd say he unloaded some of his stash out on Lavender's last night. Oil filters.'' He opened a desk drawer and produced a red, white and blue box. ''Starky's brand of steroids, right?''

''It sure is,'' Ally said, smiling for the first time in what seemed like forever.

Ron turned to Wyatt. ''Can you handle being deputy for a day?''

''Where's Buck?''

''He'll be in charge of protective custody. That's you three.'' He picked up the phone and punched the first number. ''I hope Judge Schneider is home. There are a couple of good prints on the box. I need a warrant. I want to locate some more of these 'oil filters' in Starky's backyard.''

Chapter 12

The snow blanket's icy crust glistened in the noonday sun. It was a bright, cold and windless day. Smoke signals rose from the schoolhouse chimneys in two straight lines, telling Wyatt she was waiting for him. She'd called him and said that she was baking, but it was the sight of that smoke rising above the lonely expanse of ice that made him tingle with anticipation.

She must have seen the newspaper, he thought. He imagined it spread out on the kitchen table, and he tried to picture the look on her face. God, he hoped she was pleased.

He turned in at the moon-and-stars mailbox and parked his car beneath a bouquet of spray-painted black-eyed Susans. The house had windows again. He figured he would have to give it several coats of paint come spring. The mailbox he could handle, but not the birds and flowers on the side of the house. If she agreed to his plan, they would have to go back to a simpler color scheme. He wouldn't get rid of "Coyote's Call Creek," though. That much had to be restored.

He knocked before he stuck his head in the door and called her name. Jasper jumped down from a shelf. Wyatt hunkered down to greet the cat, but his offer of empty fingers was rejected. Jasper scampered away, and Lavender appeared.

Wyatt stood, closing the door at his back. He thought about burying his face in that beautiful, wild, honey-colored hair. But he would wait. He had to tend to first things first. Like flattery.

"Smells great." Flattery, then food. He handed her his jacket. "You still have apples from your trees?"

"Of course. I dried some, just for pies." She gave him a quick kiss and a sweet smile. "Just for you."

"Is Teri around?" He'd had to remember to ask that question lately. He wasn't used to greeting a woman with, "Where are the kids?" but he'd learned the hard way that it made a difference.

"She went up to Bismarck to see John."

"In that case, this—" The second kiss was longer and deeper. Tastier, too. Apples and cinnamon lingered on her lips. "—is just for you."

"Mmm. Nice." She nibbled at his lips in return, and they chased one another's tongues, his seeking nutmeg and hers looking for fun. "Hungry?" she asked.

"Damn right."

She gave him a winsome smile, and he felt a quick, hard ache as he watched her cross the floor toward the stove. It hadn't been easy for them lately, what with all the commotion of Starky's arrest, Ally's probationary placement—first with Wyatt and later with his Aunt Janine—and John's convalescence. Putting the pieces back together seemed to revolve around the two of them. Strangely, he'd had no urge to pull back from any of it.

Maybe because Lavender was there all along, offering more support than anyone had a right to expect from her.

"I was up there last night," Wyatt said as he took a seat at the table. "His surgery went well. With some therapy and a little luck, the doctor says he won't even limp."

"Teri's moving back home with her mother soon."

He heard the tinge of regret in her voice. "She'll be all right," he promised.

"I know." Lavender brought the whole pie to the table, along with plates and forks. She set it all down, sat down herself and studied it, as though she expected the pie to do something on its own. Then she sighed. "It's not the best relationship, because poor Teri is more like the mother, and Marge is..." She shrugged. "Well, Marge is Marge. I'm sure she really didn't know what was going on."

"They never charged her with anything," he recalled. She had been a suspect for a while, because the cache of drugs had been kept in her house. But Starky had finally admitted that she had nothing to do with his business. Probably the one decent thing he'd done in his life.

"Have you had time to get used to having someone else around the house all the time?" he wondered as casually as he could manage.

"I'm a loner, but I kind of like having company."

"I kind of don't like not being able to just—" he raised an expressive brow "—come here and be with you."

She made no comment. She missed that, too, but she also knew he was looking for another job. He'd done well with what wrestling team he'd had left, but he had his plans. She knew all about his plans, even though, lately, he hadn't spoken of them very much.

He watched her dish out the pie. "We haven't had much chance to talk," he said. "It's my fault. I've been pretty wrapped up in—"

"It's nobody's fault."

It came out more abruptly than she'd intended, but it wasn't exactly as though he was the only one who'd been busy. The holidays had evaporated. She didn't know what had happened to Thanksgiving. After the first flurry of arrests and court appearances they'd worked every angle they could come up with to keep Ally and Teri from being placed in a group home. The fact that Starky had blown the whistle on three other dealers was of less importance to them than the welfare of those kids. They'd had Christmas Eve together, but they'd taken Teri down to see John on Christmas Day.

"Don't you want us to talk?" he asked.

She eyed him for a moment. It wasn't supposed to be this way, she thought. Even if they hadn't made love, it wouldn't have been too much easier, but maybe a little. She tossed her hair back from her shoulders, hoping he wouldn't see how easily he got to her with just a little kissing. Friends didn't have this problem, which was why they had not been supposed to become lovers.

"Not especially," she said lightly. "I want you to enjoy your pie."

"That's easy." He put his fork to work. "Have you seen the paper?"

"Which one?" she asked. "I get two every other day, remember? And what with all the excitement, they've been piling up. I haven't gotten to the pile yet."

"Could you get to it, please?"

"Why?" His mischievous smile piqued her curiosity, and she brought her stack of unread newspapers to the table. She picked one at random.

Glover Drug Bust Leads To More Arrests

"Well, that's from last week," Wyatt said. "That one

we know firsthand." Drake Starky and three of his out-of-town cohorts were awaiting trial. Wyatt's one-day career as a deputy sheriff had almost been fun. It had felt like Christmas when he and Ron Christian had discovered the pharmaceutical storeroom in Marge Nordstrom's basement.

Lavender pulled out the sports section.

Glover Grapplers Third In Region

"That we know, too," she said and smiled. "We know the coach did a wonderful job, and it didn't matter who took first or second."

"Everybody loves an underdog." Wyatt swallowed a mouthful of pie before he added, "'Course, the goal was to take the team to State, and I didn't make my goal."

"That was your *original* goal. You revised that."

"Yeah, that's right. I revised it." He paused, studying her. "I revised a couple others, too. I had an interview in Bismarck, up at the University of Mary."

Her eyes widened. "For wrestling coach?"

His slow smile stunned her. Bismarck? He'd never mentioned applying in Bismarck. It was a small school. They didn't have the kind of program he'd been aiming for.

"It'll be a job and a half. They're trying to get their program off the ground. But you know what?" There was a touch of boyish excitement in the telling that tugged at Lavender's heartstrings. "They want me to teach Native American studies. They like the idea of hiring a Native American to teach Native American studies. How do you like that?"

She slid into the chair across from him, her heartbeat tripping into a higher gear. "Are *you* all right with that?"

"My master's is in physical education, but I've got the basic qualifications, and I can take more courses." She looked surprised. He smiled, thinking, surprises? She ain't seen *nothin'* yet. "Yeah, I'm all right with that. They're not interested in me just because I'm an Indian or just because I've won a few trophies. They asked for a résumé. And I've got a pretty damn good background. Starting from day one."

"I'm glad you won't be going too far away."

Her smile was warm, her eyes soft and he couldn't stand this anymore. He dropped his fork and pushed his chair back. "Where's today's paper? There's something in it I want you to see."

Now they were both on their feet and sorting through papers, with Wyatt shaking his head. "Nothing ever works out the way I plan it."

Lavender found the right one. She laughed as she spread the paper on the kitchen table, just the way he'd imagined. It was a real game now, the kind she loved to play. He stood behind her and slipped his arms around her waist.

"Oh, here it is." She pointed to a full-page advertisement and looked up at him, her blue eyes twinkling. "This big clearance sale at Dayton's. You didn't want me to miss that."

Playfully, he bit her shoulder. "Will you turn right to the classified section, please?"

"Classifieds?" She turned one page at a time. "Are you selling your treadmill or something?"

Finally, there it was. He slammed his hand down on the page to keep her from turning it, and he pointed to the "Find-a-Friend" box. He'd worked too damn hard on this to let it go unnoticed.

Lavender read it aloud.

"Wanted: a Scorpio willing to take a chance on a
Leo. A yin for a hard-headed yang. A vegetarian wife
for a meat-eating Jack Sprat. A pair of magic hands
for a muscled body bound in knots. A free spirit for
a needy heart. I've decided to get a life. Willing to
negotiate the necessary compromises, all but one.
Lavender. I love Lavender. Lavender is my best color,
my favorite fragrance, the light of my life. I want...."

She'd taken each sentence more slowly than the last.
Each phrase came dearer, each successive word a little
softer, until she ran out of voice. She turned to him and
found his lips parted, as though he'd been reading along.
Her heart pounded as she searched the depths of his eyes
for some indication that this was, indeed, Wyatt Archer.

"'... Lavender all around me, forever,'" he finished
from memory.

"That's beautiful," she said, a little breathless.

"It's about as poetic as I know how to get."

"It's very poetic." Astonished, she tucked her head
beneath his chin and hugged him close. "Wyatt..." She
closed her eyes for a moment. She could hear his heart
beating the same way hers was. Ramming speed. It was so
hard to believe. She looked up at him again. "I know I'm
not what you had in mind."

"My mind was too small to imagine you." He lifted his
hand to her face to touch her smooth cheek. "I imagine
you now, though. A thousand times a day or more."

"We're so different."

"I know." He chuckled, and the light danced in his
eyes. "Isn't it great?"

"It would be if... if there were any way we could..."

"There are all kinds of ways. I found a piece of land on Apple Creek near Bismarck. This house would look good there."

"You'd move it?"

"I love it. Of course I'd move it." He sat back in his chair and pulled her down on his lap as he told her all the things he'd been thinking lately. He couldn't help himself. He had it all planned out. "Your shop is up there. The women who weave for you here can go right on weaving, and the hell with the rest of them. You don't need to be here. You don't need their acceptance."

"Do you?"

He shook his head slowly. "I just need your acceptance." With a jerk of his chin he indicated the newspaper. "To my proposal."

Then came the hard part. The part that made her stomach ache. "What about children?"

"I know lots of places where we can get some. This is no holds barred, lady. I can counter any objections you might have except one." His expression became serious. "If you say you don't love me, then I'm all out of moves."

"That's the only argument I can't honestly use." It was her turn to touch his cheek. "Because I do love you."

"Then I win the match." He stood, still holding her, and did a little victory spin that got them both laughing. "It's gonna be a hell of a match, Lavender."

"That's for sure."

"Especially if..." he grinned and cast a glance at the spiral stairs "...you should ever get the feeling that we're supposed to sleep together."

"Oh, yes..." She tipped her head back and let her honey hair flow.

"Yes, what?"

"I'm beginning to get a brand new feeling."

"And...?"

"That we should sleep together regularly." Feeling giddy, she lifted her head, nibbled his ear and whispered, "After we get married."

"Oh, nice little reversal, there." He set her down. Hearts full, they stood there smiling into one another's eyes. He chuckled. "I think I just got pinned."

* * * * *

The spirit of motherhood is the spirit of love—and how better to capture that special feeling than in our short story collection...

Curtiss Ann Matlock
Carole Halston
Linda Shaw

to
Mother
with
Love
'92

Three glorious new stories that embody the very essence of family and romance are contained in this heartfelt tribute to Mother. Share in the joy by joining us and three of your favorite Silhouette authors for this celebration of motherhood and romance.

Available at your favorite retail outlet in May.

Silhouette Books®

FREE GIFT OFFER

To receive your free gift, send us the specified number of proofs-of-purchase from any specially marked Free Gift Offer Harlequin or Silhouette book with the Free Gift Certificate properly completed, plus a check or money order (do not send cash) to cover postage and handling payable to Harlequin/Silhouette Free Gift Promotion Offer. We will send you the specified gift.

FREE GIFT CERTIFICATE

ITEM	A. GOLD TONE EARRINGS	B. GOLD TONE BRACELET	C. GOLD TONE NECKLACE
# of proofs-of-purchase required	3	6	9
Postage and Handling	$1.75	$2.25	$2.75
Check one	☐	☐	☐

Name: _____

Address: _____

City: _____ State: _____ Zip Code: _____

Mail this certificate, specified number of proofs-of-purchase and a check or money order for postage and handling to: HARLEQUIN/SILHOUETTE FREE GIFT OFFER 1992, P.O. Box 9057, Buffalo, NY 14269-9057. Requests must be received by July 31, 1992.

PLUS—Every time you submit a completed certificate with the correct number of proofs-of-purchase, you are automatically entered in our MILLION DOLLAR SWEEPSTAKES! No purchase or obligation necessary to enter. See below for alternate means of entry and how to obtain complete sweepstakes rules.

MILLION DOLLAR SWEEPSTAKES
NO PURCHASE OR OBLIGATION NECESSARY TO ENTER

To enter, hand-print (mechanical reproductions are not acceptable) your name and address on a 3″×5″ card and mail to Million Dollar Sweepstakes 6097, c/o either P.O. Box 9056, Buffalo, NY 14269-9056 or P.O. Box 621, Fort Erie, Ontario L2A 5X3. Limit: one entry per envelope. Entries must be sent via 1st-class mail. For eligibility, entries must be received no later than March 31, 1994. No liability is assumed for printing errors, lost, late or misdirected entries.

Sweepstakes is open to persons 18 years of age or older. All applicable laws and regulations apply. Sweepstakes offer void wherever prohibited by law. Prizewinners will be determined no later than May 1994. Chances of winning are determined by the number of entries distributed and received. For a copy of the Official Rules governing this sweepstakes offer, send a self-addressed, stamped envelope (WA residents need not affix return postage) to: Million Dollar Sweepstakes Rules, P.O. Box 4733, Blair, NE 68009.

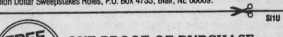

SI1U

ONE PROOF-OF-PURCHASE

To collect your fabulous FREE GIFT you must include the necessary FREE GIFT proofs-of-purchase with a properly completed offer certificate.

(See center insert for details)